DAUGHTER OF FOXES

Fictive Kin book one

DAUGHTER of FOXES

Nico Silver

WHITE RAVEN PRESS

Third Edition, 2024.
ISBN: 978-1-998212-14-9
This book was originally published as *Vixen* by Nic Silver, and then as *Daughter of Foxes* by Nicole Silver.

White Raven Press
North Cowichan, British Columbia, Canada

Cover design and digital alterations by Nik Sylvan
Model stock © Neo-Stock via www.neostock.com
Animal stock © 12qwerty via Dreamstime.com
Background stock (road and moon) © Dary423 via Dreamstime.com
Background stock (city) © Songquan Deng via Dreamstime.com
Fur brushes © witherlings via DeviantArt.com
Fog brushes © Krist A via brusheezy.com
Title typefaces: Eva Antiqua Heavy by Spiece Graphics, and Snell Roundhand by Linotype

Content warning: This book contains material that is not suitable for all audiences. It is recommended for readers 18+. Some content that may be triggering for readers includes explicit sex, violence, and sexual violence.

for H.I.F.
because of the fox women

Chapter One

ALL I WANT is to sit in the darkest corner of the bar, sip my drink, and people-watch. I have a double of twelve-year-old Scotch on the table in front of me. No soda. No ice. Neat.

Every now and then I lift it to my lips and sip. Feel the heat fill my mouth, seep between my teeth, and slowly burn down my throat. I drink it slow because if I don't, I'll have another. And another. And in the morning there'll be a hangover. I don't get hangovers like other people. I get hangovers that literally make death seem like the better option. And that's *actually* literally, not hyperbolically literally, the way most people use it. I get a hangover, and death seems like a happy choice. So I do my damnedest not to get hangovers.

And I sip. If a waitress or a bartender gives me hell for taking up space, I buy coffee and say I'm waiting for a friend. But tonight they seem to sense I'm on edge and they leave me alone. And hell, a double of good single malt costs enough they damn well *should* leave me alone.

After the evening I've had, I'm liable to rip someone's head off. Not literally, but not far enough from it for comfort.

I sit alone and nurse my drink, and watch the people, and wonder if I was ever like them. Carefree, happy, normal. Human.

Someone bangs the door coming in and I turn to look. It's a boy –

okay, man, but half the time I still think of myself as a girl at twenty-six and he's got to be a year or two younger than me. He looks like he's had a rougher night than I have, but boy is he nice to gawk at. Dark hair falling in his eyes, nice build. He almost trips over a woman perched on a stool at a table near the door and turns to catch his balance and I get a nice view of his backside. It's a very fine ass, indeed.

Yeah, hi, I'm Su and I haven't had sex in way too long.

The woman on the stool glares at the cute boy and he bends over her for a moment and says, "You smell good."

And, dammit, just as my muscles are beginning to relax and I'm feeling better about how my evening went and those three words throw me right back into the feeling of crap.

I cut across the park on my way home, even though it can be a bad idea for a girl to be there after dark. Well, for *anyone* to be there after dark, really. But I'm not an ordinary girl.

I knew the vamp was tracking me from the moment I stepped in under the trees, but I wasn't too worried. Vampires are a little leery of being discovered to be more than folktale boogie monsters, so they tend not to attack people unless they're really sure the person won't be missed, or they're desperate, or stupid. And there aren't many stupid vamps. They don't last long. They get eaten by their own kind. And there are a lot easier – and safer – ways to get blood.

This one seemed too clever to be desperate, the way he was stalking me, but then I'm not exactly human. Whatever I am, it seems to be uncommonly attractive to vamps.

So when I hit the thickest part of the forest, I was prepared. He dropped out of a tree in front of me, and I met him with a kick in the crotch. Then I ran. Better to avoid a fight, if I could. Unfortunately, I couldn't. The kick slowed the vampire, but not enough. He was in front of me again before I got more than a few steps.

I moved into a fighting stance. He thought I was human, so I might be able to catch him off guard again. And somewhere, I couldn't remember where, or when, someone had taught me kung fu, and I was pretty good at it.

I blocked his first strike and got in a hit, but not enough to do any damage. This vamp was old, and canny, and *fast*. Before I could strike again, he had me pinned against a tree, one of my hands trapped behind my back. He held my other wrist in his right hand, ragged nails digging into my skin, and with his other hand he held my hair, yanking my head to the side until it hurt. My body he kept pinned with his own.

He pressed his nose into my neck and I twitched, anticipating a bite. Instead he inhaled deeply.

"You smell good," he said and licked my neck, tracing a straining tendon with his tongue. *He* smelled like dirt and unwashed male body. Most vamps keep up some semblance of hygiene to blend in better. Some are naturally fastidious, and a few are even vain. This one, it seemed, liked the smell of the grave.

I twisted my body to see how much he would let me move. Not much. The hand pinned behind me hurt, but I didn't really mind. It was right next to the silver-tipped stake I keep in a leather sheath strapped to my belt. If I have to be unusually attractive to vampires, at least I can carry protection. I flexed my wrist, scraping it against tree bark and the studs on my belt, but I could almost reach the stake.

The vamp inhaled again. "No, I am wrong. You smell *divine*."

If it had been a human threatening me, I'd have said something cheeky, but I'm not stupid. Not *that* stupid, anyway. Of course, if it had been a human, he'd still be rolling on the ground, clutching his pulped testicles.

"My progeny will *so* enjoy you," he said.

Great. A vampire papa, looking for a special snack for his offspring.

He pressed closer to me, and I gagged on the heavy smell of male armpit. He ground his pelvis against mine and I heard his breathing quicken. I have really good senses, so I could even feel his pulse speed up and faint warmth spread under his skin. I didn't need superhuman senses to feel him hardening against me.

Contrary to common belief and most folklore, vampires aren't actually dead. They die – sort of, I think – in the process of being made a vampire, but then they are reborn. They have a much slower metabolism after, but it doesn't stop. They breathe, their blood flows, their digestive juices gurgle away – they probably even fart – and their hearts beat. They even age. It just all happens much, much more slowly.

Except at two times, when their pulses pound just as much as a human's does: when they feed, and when they fuck. A lot of vamps like to do both at once.

This vampire licked my neck again and I finally couldn't keep my mouth shut any longer. "I thought you bloodsuckers got smart and stopped killing people. So, you know, you could keep pretending you don't exist."

He lifted his head from my neck and looked at my face – I think it was the first time he looked me in the eye the whole time. He frowned.

"You know we exist, and you are not afraid."

"Oh, I'm afraid," I said. And I was. But I was also pissed, and my temper had a tendency to override my other emotions. It gets me in trouble, and loses me lovers.

"Perhaps you are very stupid," the vamp said, pushing his hardness against me again. I guess stupidity wasn't a turn-off for him. "Or you are more than you seem, which will make you an even better meal for my son."

I bit back the urge to ask what sort of "more than I seemed" he thought I might be and concentrated on wriggling my pinned hand closer to my stake.

"My progeny will grow strong on your blood. He will grow so much stronger than cold blood could make him. So much more quickly. And he will make *me* stronger. And soon the Reborn won't have to hide in the shadows."

Great. A vampire with delusions of grandeur, who planned to make vamp children, feed them up, and eat them himself. Vampires are not above cannibalism. Not at all. Vamp blood makes them stronger, satiates them faster. And, I'm told, tastes better.

"Now shut your pretty mouth and spread your legs. I haven't had a good fuck in ages."

Neither had I, but I sure as hell wasn't going to do it with *him*. He let go of my hair to yank my skirt up around my waist, which let me relax my upper body into a more natural position. And he had to lean his body away from mine to get himself out of his pants. That was all I needed to get the stake in my hand and my hand from behind my back.

I wasn't fast enough for a clean kill, not quite, but I was desperate enough not to get eaten or violated by a vamp to jam the stake in far enough to hurt him, to make him stumble back, his incongruously pale member flopping out of his pants. And I was mad enough to execute a perfect spinning kick and drive the stake the rest of the way into his chest to impale his heart. My skirt being hiked up actually helped – it wasn't in my way at all.

For a moment, the vamp stared at me, blood leaking from the corner of his mouth, penis slowly deflating like an old party balloon. Then he seemed to crumple up, to fold in on himself. He collapsed.

I tugged my skirt back down into place and bent over the vamp to retrieve my stake. His blood was already congealing in thick, stringy clots. Death seems to speed some processes up for vamps, as if their physiology is suddenly trying to make up for lost time. His face was looking older, too, and in an hour or so he'd be as bloated as if his corpse had been a week in the heat. Unfortunately, the pop culture lore about vampires disintegrating into dust when staked is as true as the lore about them being dead. Which is to say, not true at all. Sunlight, though – sunlight *will* burn a vamp, even a dead vamp. So as soon as I made sure he was good and dead, I grabbed him by the lapels of his coat and dragged him up a short, steep hill to a spot I liked to sit on nice days. It was a shame to soil a good sitting-and-thinking spot, but it was away from any likely foot traffic, and it was open to the morning sun.

Come sunrise, the vamp's flesh – and any identifying clothing along with it – would burn to ash and even his bones would not survive. There would be only enough fragments to puzzle a forensic specialist, should anyone come across it before those fragments succumbed to the weather and returned to dirt.

Before I left, I rifled his pockets. Two hundred in cash, a handful of change, and a credit card. I looked longingly at the plastic, but eventually put it back. That was far more trouble than it was worth. I pocketed the cash.

He had no jewelry but a nice brass pocketwatch with an attractive interlace design and gears visible through cutouts in the face. That, I kept. It might identify him to the right people (or for me, the wrong people), but I liked it, and I could sell it later if I needed some money. Who could say I didn't find it in the park, dropped by its unlucky owner?

I looked down at the dead vamp. He looked smaller, and not so dangerous at all, now. That wasn't the first time I'd killed a vamp, though I hoped – even as I knew it was unlikely – that it would be the last. The last time I'd staked a bloodsucker I'd almost died first.

Lucky for me, just getting bit by a vamp wasn't enough to make you one, so even if I *had* died, I wouldn't have been re-born. There was some arcane ritual for that – how much was symbolic and how much was real magic, I had no idea. Though vampires rarely kill these days (or rarely kill anyone noticeable), and attack the unwary only now and then, something about me seems to attract them. They seem to know I'm not quite human, but they don't seem to know what I *am* any more than I do.

Looking at the dead vampire, I was suddenly overwhelmed with anger. I kicked him in the face as hard as I could with my right steel-toed boot and felt it cave in like an overripe watermelon. I was quietly sick behind a bush, trying to puke and wipe brain off my boot at the same time.

"I need a drink," I said to the empty air. I was starting to shake, and it wasn't the growing autumn chill that was causing it. So instead of going home for a good, long sleep as I had intended when I first headed across the park, I turned my steps toward the nearest bar.

One Scotch – one *double* Scotch – and then I'd go home and sleep.

So I'm in the bar enjoying my Scotch and almost unclenched enough to climb into bed and dream, and a pretty boy has to walk in and remind me that I could very easily have been raped and eaten not an hour before.

Because the young man is a vamp – I can just smell the dirt and blood on him from where I sit, though it's almost overwhelmed by old fear and new confusion.

"Crap," I mumble into my drink. "What is this, Su's night of vampire fun?" It looks like the boy might cause trouble and then I might feel obliged to help. But then woman the boy tripped over tells him to fuck off and shoves him in the chest and he stumbles away from her to sit slumped on a stool at the bar.

He looks around, his blue eyes too bright – and how did I not notice *that* the moment he walked into the bar? He's just a baby vamp, I think. Hell, he looks practically newborn. There's still a trail of dried blood down the side of his neck where his parent vamp was sloppy. The way he smells of confusion, I'd guess he hasn't figured out what he is yet. He's so new, he might not even have begun to remember his previous life, his human life, yet. He certainly doesn't know how to act like a vampire, let alone a vampire blending in with humans.

I look around, wondering if his parent is already here and that's why he stumbled in. At the very least his maker should be looking after him. But if he's as new as I think he is, he should be kept safe in some mommy-or-daddy's lair until he learns a thing or two about how to survive.

A new vamp is not only a danger to humans, and therefore a threat to vampire hidden-ness – because they don't know any better than to attack whatever's closest when they're hungry and they don't have the control to stop feeding before their prey is dead – but a newborn is a danger to himself. Stumbling around without a clue about how to act or how to protect himself is going to draw the attention of other vamps.

The boy looks up as the bartender bends over to ask, "What can I get you?" For a moment he just stares, and then he smiles – a smile so sweet and innocent it has no place on a vampire's face.

"You smell *good*," the boy says.

The bartender scowls but then his attention is drawn away by a yahoo at the other end of the bar wanting a refill.

The boy looks around again. His eyes don't seem able to focus on anything.

"Jesus," I say into the last sip of my Scotch. He must have been born in the last day or two, he's so clueless. And then I catch his dirt scent, his blood scent, again, and I know why he's stumbling around with no parent. I killed Papa Vamp barely an hour ago.

"My progeny will enjoy you," the whiffy old vamp had said. So this is the progeny whose dinner he had intended I be.

The boy is unprotected because of me.

Not that I regret killing the old bloodsucker, mind. Not a bit. But this poor, beautiful infant was going to become lunch to fuel the strength of some older vamp, and he probably hadn't even had the chance to do anything nasty himself yet.

What I really ought to do is take him out in the alley and put him out of his misery before he learns that his kind are cannibals that prefer to eat their own for the rush, and because they're tastier.

The boy's gaze finally fixes on me and his mind seems to clear a little. Yeah, I'm Su, the vampire magnet. He smiles his angelic smile at me and I feel my resolve to not care vanish. He probably hadn't asked to be reborn as a vampire – vamps are rarely interested in anyone who *wants* to be one of them. And just because they feed on human blood doesn't make all vamps evil. I know a few who are pretty decent people. For criminals. Most of the people I know in this town are criminals, because I am one myself. Just a pickpocket, but it's not exactly an honest living.

So there I am, feeling sorry for a fucking vampire so soon after nearly becoming lunch for another one. Well, the same one, really, but it was the other one that was going to do the feeding *to*. Hell, now *I* was confused.

So maybe if this boy had been a decent human being, he might turn out to be a decent vampire, too. I sigh and drain the last drop of golden, burning nectar from my glass and stand up.

And yeah, I have to admit, hormones are probably a big part of it. Vamps aren't the only ones who like to get laid. Apparently whatever I am likes sex an awful lot, too (consensual sex, that is), because I looked at that pretty young man and the first thing I thought about was how to get him out of his clothes. Well, after getting rid of the dirt-and-blood smell.

"Fuck," I say, then I cross the bar and hook my arm into the vampire boy's. He smiles wider and I feel hot between the legs. He has killer cheekbones and crazy sexy lips.

"There you are," I say, and pull him off the stool and towards the door. "Looks like you've had a few already. I'd better get you home or you'll never make it to work tomorrow." I smile dazzlingly at the people nearest the door as I maneuver the boy through.

"I can't let him go anywhere alone," I say, and give a tinkling laugh of the sort I most loathe as I let the door fall shut behind us.

"You smell good," says the boy.

"I'm sure I do," I say. "But I am not your meal. We'll get you some takeout."

The boy smiles again and seems content to walk beside me for now.

One advantage of being a thief, not quite human, and a supernatural vampire magnet is that I know all the dealers in not-strictly-legal goods in town. And I know exactly who to talk to to score some black-market bloodbags in the middle of the night.

It will mean spending more of the old vamp's cash than I like – I'd rather have added that to my stash for next month's rent – but I guess it was money that should have been vampire boy's inheritance, in a way. Not that I intend to hand any of it over.

And if I'm going to help him, he needs blood and soon, and there's no way I'll feed him on my own blood. Even if I liked the idea of playing blood donor – and I don't – he's newborn and there's no way he'll have the self-control to stop sucking before he kills me.

So stolen medical supplies it is. Well, stolen by someone. I'm not stupid enough to steal from vamps (unless I've just killed them), or from those who steal to supply vamps.

I'll feed him, and teach him how to be a vampire, and hopefully keep him alive long enough to start to regain his memories and learn to fend for himself.

And since I don't keep a pet – dogs and cats get nervous around me and birds are even worse. Hell, even fish in a bowl just make me hungry when I look at them – the boy will give me something to talk to besides the spider that built a web in the corner of my living room window that doesn't close right.

He bumps his hip against mine as we walk and I can't stop myself from thinking, *And maybe once he's recovered from the newborn stupids, I can get laid.*

Chapter Two

I SHOULD MAYBE QUALIFY: I may have abnormally active sex hormones that make me want to climb into bed with every not-unattractive boy and girl I see, but I don't actually sleep around that much.

I might be less uptight if I did, but the thing is, I'm *picky*. I can't bring myself to actually sleep with anyone I don't like first, and finding out if I like someone takes time. And emotional intimacy. And I've been avoiding any sort of close contact ever since... well, since I woke up with no memory of who I am. Or what I am.

And there's a videogame cliché for you. *You wake up in a hotel room with no memory of how you got there or who you are. Follow the clues and find out.* Only I didn't wake up in a hotel room, I woke up on a park bench and there were no clues to follow. My first thought was thankfulness that I didn't die of hypothermia, and my second was that it must be the morning after Hallowe'en, judging by the candy wrappers and orange and black streamers all over the place.

Then I realized I had no memories. At least, not of myself. I knew where I was and how to function, I just couldn't remember my past. The wallet in my pocket gave me a name – Panya Su Fuchs – which told me I'm probably part Asian, Korean or Chinese or both, and part German, which is pretty much how I looked when I checked the little mirror I also found in my pocket.

The address on my driver's license turned out to be an old one, and the only other things in the wallet were a thick stack of twenties and an ATM card I didn't think I'd be able to use because I had no idea what the PIN would be. When I took the cash out to count it I found myself automatically turning each bill around to lie upright on top of the next – the way a cashier does before making a bank deposit – which told me someone else had probably put the money there. I'd have assumed the wallet was stolen, but the face in the driver's license photo matched the one in the little mirror.

So with only an address to go on, I set out into the city. And as I said, the address wasn't mine anymore, and the person I woke up far too early in the morning didn't know who I was or anything about the previous tenant of the apartment.

So I went back to the park bench. And that night was when I found out there are vampires and nearly died the first time. And yet, even bleeding and scared, it still didn't occur to me to go to the cops for help. By the time it did, I had learned that I heal unnaturally fast, that vampires are only one of the secret things that go bump in the night, and that I was very good at picking pockets and not getting caught. By then, staying alive seemed more important than finding out who I was. As it turns out, finding out who I am could be the *key* to staying alive.

The newborn vamp clings to my arm as we walk down the street and his confusion looks enough like drunkenness that no one bothers us, though a beat cop eyes us for a long time from across the street.

Luckily, we don't have far to go. I may practice my… craft, shall we say, in populated high-traffic areas, but I like to drink close to home (when I'm not drinking *at* home), just in case I break my own rules and have one too many. And home just happens to be in an industrial area that has the highest concentration of dubious businesses in the city. It's a good place to hide, really. Everyone there has incriminating secrets, so no one pries. It's also an area with a lot of non-human activity and maybe because of that, I have a lot less trouble with vampires than I do elsewhere in the city. I guess

I don't stand out as much.

So it's only a short walk from the bar to the market run by one of the not-so-evil vamps I know – and I use the word "know" here in the sense of "have seen around enough to recognize and be recognized and have some idea of the business practices of." Okay, and we've had a few actual conversations and even kissed once, but when he confessed how hungry I made him, I decided not to go any farther. He's the only person who even has an inkling that I'm not only not human, but completely clueless about what I am. I told him I'm researching non-humans, but I suspect he realized it was more than that that made me ask what he knew about creatures that attract vampires.

With baby vamp hanging onto me, it takes twice as long to get to Liam's as it should have, and when we arrive there are three guys hanging around the door who take entirely too much interest in the confused boy. I steer him inside – the place looks like any run-down corner store barely clinging to existence in an area mostly full of warehouses, except there's a little too much dust on the merchandise, and the hours posted on the door are dark hours only. No daylight service at Liam's Corner Market.

Liam himself, rusty-haired and blue-eyed, lounges behind the grimy counter. He straightens when he sees me, and smiles – a vampire smile is not entirely a comforting look, but I *think* he's being friendly – and I have to look way up at him, though I'm not especially short, even for a half-Asian girl.

"Su. What brings you here today?" he drawls, traces of an Irish accent still just noticeable in his voice. Then he looks at the boy on my arm and his whole demeanor changes. It's not like he moves, or even shifts expression or anything. He just goes still. Then he slips out from behind the counter and past me to the door. He pokes his head out, says something pitched higher than human hearing range – a handy vampire talent that makes it difficult even for me to tell what he's saying – and then locks the door.

"You shouldn't have a morsel like that out without rather more protection than you can provide," he says, turning around and leaning against the door.

"I know," I say. "But it's kind of my fault he doesn't have a protector to look after him."

"What have you been up to, Su, my girl?" He straightens and walks over to the newborn. The boy smiles his angelic smile.

"I'm hungry," the newborn says.

Liam bends his head to smell the boy's neck and I reach for my stake. He inhales deeply and speaks on the exhale. "God, it's been a long time since I tasted another Reborn."

Did I mention vamps call themselves "Reborn" (caps and all), and never, ever "vampires"? It's because they die, just for a moment, then when they're infected, the symbiont takes over and they're reborn.

Liam sounds hungry, almost sexual hungry. He inhales the smell of the boy's hair. "Jesus," he says.

The boy turns so he's nose-to-nose with Liam and sniffs. "You smell good," he says, then he looks at me and says, "I'm hungry."

"Didn't you even feed him?" says Liam. "Do you know how dangerous he is?"

"That's why I brought him here. It was either that or stake him in the alley behind the bar."

"That might have been kinder," Liam says. Then, "A hundred for a week's supply. If he can't take care of himself by then, I'll take him."

"You'll take him and do what?" I ask. "Eat him?"

"Drink him, actually," says Liam, then he looks the boy up and down and adds, "Well, maybe eat him first, then drink him, then drain the rest and sell his blood at a very nice profit."

I step closer and push Liam back a step or two. He laughs. We both know he's stronger. Mostly. Unless I can get Angry Su to take over, let that part of me that has kept me alive this far show her kung fu prowess. Except it's not like I'm really two people. More like I have these strengths that only kick in when my life is in danger, and which I can't access otherwise, no matter how hard I try or how scared I am.

"I'll give you the hundred," I say, "But I'm not going to carry a whole week's worth of bloodbags back to my place right now."

Liam shrugs and kisses the end of my nose. How I wish I could call on that life-saving kick-assery right then and wipe his condescending smile right off his face. I'm also glad I didn't sleep with him when I had the chance, because it's turned out he's kind of a dick. Useful, but not as likeable as I'd once thought.

"You can take a day or two's worth and get the rest later," he says.

"Let him have his fill now, too," I say. "Here."

Liam frowns. "This is a grocery store, not a restaurant. Do you eat the produce right in the store?"

"Yes," I say. "And sometimes I leave without paying, too." That's not really true. I may be a pickpocket, but I have a conscience. I only the pick the pockets of lawyers and people who drive expensive cars, and I never steal from small businesses. But Liam doesn't need to know that.

"Well, you'd better not steal from me, lassie," Liam says. "Or I'll find out why *you* smell so good, human girl." He puts extra emphasis on "human," maybe to remind me that he knows I might not be. "Come through to the back room. Newborns can be messy eaters."

The back room turns out to be tiled floor-to-ceiling in black and white ceramic, and it has a drain in the middle. There are a lot of chains and stainless-steel surfaces that I don't dare look at too closely. It smells like blood and bleach.

Liam takes a box out of a glass-fronted cooler and tosses me a bloodbag out of it. I hand it to the newborn who smiles at me and tries to bite it. His fangs slide off the thick plastic.

"Jesus," says Liam. He takes the bag from the boy and shows him how to use the bit where the IV tube is supposed to attach as a straw. The boy sucks, swallows, and makes a face.

"It's cold," he says.

"Get used to it," says Liam. Then to me, "If you have a microwave, you can heat it to body temperature. Just put it in a cup first – the bag will explode. And stir once in a while."

"I don't have a microwave," I say.

"Do you have a stove? A pot? Water?"

"I have a hot plate."

"Then heat the bag up in a pot of water, like milk for a baby."

"You expect me to know how to heat milk for a baby?" I ask.

"I thought all girls knew that stuff," he says.

"All *women* do not know that stuff," I say. "It's not genetic. And it's not the Dark Ages." I emphasize "women." Sure, I frequently call women "girls" and men "boys," but that doesn't mean I have to let other people belittle me. Then I look at Liam more closely. "How do *you* know how to heat milk for a baby?" I ask.

A fleeting look that might have been sorrow passes over his face, quickly replaced by the usual vampire stillness. "I'm old," he says. "You learn a lot when you live a long time." He turns suddenly away to busy himself with the cooler door.

"I'm sleepy," says the newborn. I look at him, and he does look like he might fall asleep standing there.

"How long is he going to be stupid?" I ask.

Liam shrugs and hands me a box of blood bags. "It's different for everyone. Some stay like that forever. Or for what little time they manage to stay alive. The damaged ones don't tend to last long."

"I hope this one remembers quickly," I say. "I don't fancy playing nursemaid for long."

Liam leans close to my ear and says, "Oh, I can smell exactly what you'd like to be playing at." His voice is low and sexy and utterly repulsive. But he's right. My body, at least, wants that pretty young man naked and hard and sweaty, even if my brain isn't interested in him in his current mental state.

"Fuck off," I say, and pull the box the rest of the way out of his grip. It's heavy but my anger is enough that I don't care.

"No, pretty Su," Liam says. "Fuck *on*." Then he steps away and grins, as if he had never said anything offensive and was just a guy I knew who'd helped me out. "You'd better get that child home before he falls asleep on the floor," he says. "Feed him again when he wakes up. If you're lucky, he'll have started to remember, and then you can fuck him and send him on his way."

"I doubt it will be that easy," I say. "Can I get you the cash when I come back for more bags?"

Liam nods. I want to kick his teeth in, or at least get very, very far away. When I said that vamps are more-or-less regular people, I guess I was thinking about the worst creeps the human species has produced. The nasty tendencies are harder to keep hidden, I suppose, when you find yourself stronger and faster and craving blood.

I nudge the newborn with my elbow on my way back to the front of the store. "Come on, pup," I say. "Let's get you to sleep." I almost say "bed," but I can practically feel Liam leering behind me.

The boy says, "Sleepy," and follows me out. The vamps are gone from the front of the store, though I wouldn't be surprised if they were watching from some alley. The way the boy is stumbling now, he'd make an easy target. But we make it to my place, and up the industrial elevator to the warehouse floor I turned into something resembling a loft. I even manage to steer him to the ratty couch before he falls over and begins to snore very softly.

Then I go and take a very cold shower. It doesn't help, though, so I close my eyes and stand under the frigid spray and run my hands over my breasts – I don't know if it's the cold water or lust that makes my nipples hard and I stifle a cry as my palms slide over them. Then I slip a hand between my legs where I'm swollen and hot and I rub until the pressure builds and builds and finally breaks. I stand under the water until I'm shivering and feel a little more sane. Then I take a deep breath, dry myself, and crawl into bed. I make sure to put enough obstacles between the couch and my bed that the newborn will wake me for sure if he gets up and tries to snack on me.

Chapter Three

HALFWAY THROUGH what's left of the night I wake to the sound of growling from the other side of the loft. I have really good night vision – my eyes even reflect green like a cat's – so I don't need to turn on a light to see what the baby vamp is up to. I turn on the light anyway, because whatever part of me is human finds it comforting.

The newborn is crouched on the back of my ratty sofa, pressed against the dirty glass of the big window. He's growling and biting at something on the other side of the glass. A spider, probably. They seem to like my windows. Maybe I attract flies the same way I attract vamps, though most bugs actually seem more inclined to ignore me.

"Hey," I say. "You can't eat that. I'll warm you up some B-positive."

He turns, and his fangs are fully extended. His eyes flare in the light of the lamp and I remember again why I sleep with a silver-pointed stake under my pillow. For a second I can't move. Fear trickles through my limbs, makes me tremble, and for a brief, unpleasant moment, I think I might piss myself.

I can handle vamps when they're passing for human. Hell, I even find them sexy, with that edge of danger that somehow makes men and women more appealing, no matter how much we might want it to be otherwise. But when they drop the pretense and let the symbiont show through, then vampires are pants-shitting scary. The fact that they still look a little human makes it worse.

And right now, the baby vamp I'd felt bad for was all vampire, and because his human memories hadn't recovered from bonding with the symbiont yet, he's acting only on the symbiont's instincts, filtered through the most primal human need to survive. All vampire and no memories is fucking *dangerous*.

I was stupid to have forgotten that.

The human part of me wants to flee but is frozen in fear, but the part of me that's not human – the part that gives me strength to save my own life time after time when the underbelly of the world, the secret dark-and-scary of every child's nightmare, throws its worst at me – that part of me stills the trembling. That part of me walks calmly over to the ancient, 50s-deco-blue fridge in the corner, takes out a bloodbag, and tosses it to the vamp.

He catches it, and for a long terrifying moment he just continues to stare at me. His jaw has unhinged in his hunger – vamps have jaws like a snake, or a shark, where the mandibles can unhinge and the maxillae, the upper jaws, are jointed so they can move, too. It seems excessive to me, since vamps mostly live on blood and rarely eat flesh. Raw, blood-dripping flesh.

Then he looks at the bloodbag in his hand and smiles, which pulls his jaws back into human alignment. As his head moves, the angle of light in his eyes shifts and the blue-orange reflection vanishes.

"Food," he says, and begins to suck. He scowls at the cold, but keeps drinking.

"In the fridge," I say, pointing.

"Mmm," he says.

I don't know if he understands, but at least he's done being scary for now. And I've had a much-needed reminder of the stupid danger I put myself in, all because I felt bad for killing Papa Vamp, and because I wanted to get laid. I'm not feeling quite so horny anymore.

There was a while there where I thought I might be some kind of vampire half-breed. I mean, vamps like the way I smell, and not just as food. I can see in almost complete darkness, and I have the cat-eye-reflecting thing, though mine don't glow blue-orange in incandescent light or purple in fluorescent. My canine teeth are longer than they should be – if I were human – and even my molars are more sharp-edged. That was when I met Liam, asking around about vamps to find out if I was one.

But no, I'm not a half-vampire. I learned that while a lot of the things the symbiont does for vamps makes them stronger, it also makes them sterile. It forces them to make more vamps by infecting them with the symbiont.

So no sexual repro for the Reborn. Sex and feeding speed up their slow-moving metabolisms, but don't make babies. And the symbiont acts like a parasite in other ways, too. Though it extends the lives of the infected by slowing down the aging process, it can also slow down the normal replacement of dead and dying cells. So a vamp that doesn't feed much, or have sex much, will slowly shrivel away, while still not exactly aging.

It's a weird balance, and I'm not sure how much of it I understand. Hell, I'm not sure how much Liam understood when he told me. But feeding slows the shriveling by allowing the body sufficient metabolic energy to regenerate. Or something like that. Very, very old vamps still tend to end up looking like Count Orlok and – Liam says – a few even become living mummies for years before they eventually just stop being alive.

Anyway, it means that vamps feed pretty often, and have sex as much as they can, to try to stave off the shriveling. Why that doesn't make them age faster, too, I have no idea.

I watch as the baby vamp suckles his bloodbag and I'm very, very glad that I'm not one, or even half one. A vampire. I'd rather never find out what I am than be a vamp.

He looks up at me and grins, and blood drips down his chin.

"Hi," he says.

"Do you remember your name yet?" I ask.

He cocks his head to one side and licks his chin with a disconcertingly long tongue. What's more disconcerting is how the trickle of blood makes me hungry. That was another reason I'd wondered if I was a vamp. But then, a lot of things make me hungry. Even bugs, sometimes, though I refuse to try eating one.

The vamp opens his mouth, then closes it again. He tips his head to the other side, then shakes it.

"No," he says finally. "The old one called me 'Child' and said I should call him 'Father'."

"Yeah," I say. "He made you. Rebirthed you, or whatever you call it."

"I am Reborn," he says. It's almost a question.

"Yes." I wonder if telling him I killed his vampire dad is a good idea. Probably best to wait until he has his memories back.

"He was cruel," the newborn says. "He made me do things."

I stare at him.

"He liked to bite me and lick the wounds." He shifts on the couch, climbs off the back of it and sits, almost human. He puts the empty bloodbag on the coffee table.

I nod at it. "You want another one?"

"Can I have it warm?" he asks.

I get another bag from the fridge and put it in a pot of water on my hot plate. Time to find out if all girls are good at caring for babies.

"He liked me to bite him, too."

I poke the bloodbag in the pot and studiously do not look at the vamp.

"He would tell me to do things, and I had to do them," he says. "Even if I didn't want to, my body would do them anyway."

"He was your father," I say. "You vamps – Reborn – you have to do what your parent says. You can't help it." I poked the blood again, willing it to heat faster.

"He didn't act like a father," he says. "My father, my human father, was nice. He made me hot dogs and took me to baseball games, and taught me how to make things out of wood."

I look over at him. He's starting to remember. So I'm looking right in his eyes when he says, "But Reborn Father made me suck on him. Pleasure him. He said it would keep him young until I was strong enough for him to feed off of." I'm maybe imagining it, but his eyes look moist. Can vampires cry?

"I'm sorry," I say. I feel sick.

"Is he dead? Reborn Father?"

I nod and look away.

"Why are you helping me? Did you rescue me from him? Why?"

He might have remembered a few things from his human life, but the newborn still has the mind of a child.

"I guess I did," I say. "But I didn't do it on purpose." I poke the blood again, and it feels warm, so I pull it out of the pot and toss it to the vamp. I don't want to get too close to him just now.

"I killed him," I say. "With a stake. He was going to rape me and then take me back to his lair and feed me to you."

"You didn't want to pleasure him," he says.

"No."

"Neither did I." He dips his head down to drink and I turn away to collect my robe and a blanket. There's no way I can spend the rest of the night in here. There are too many weird thoughts swirling in my head, and the cause of all of them is the newborn. And I can't get the sight of him, hungry and jaw gaping, all vamp, out of my head.

I leave him on the sofa with his snack and lock him into the loft, then head for the stairs to the roof. I often spend time up there, when walls — even the widely-spaced walls of the loft — become too close for me.

I curl up in my blanket in a spot sheltered from the wind and stare up at the stars. In the city, even on the outskirts here in the warehouse-industrial district, there are only a few stars visible, and even they waver uncertainly. But at least I can see them. I've thought about moving to the country, but it seems more likely I'll find out more about myself here where maybe there might be someone else like me, or somebody who remembers me. I curl tighter, and drift off to sleep.

I wake again to growling, but quiet, like whomever is making the sound is trying to suppress it. Did the newborn get out of the loft somehow and follow me?

I lay very still, and try to remember where I left my stakes. One's in its holster on the bathroom door handle. One's under my pillow. And the other? Where did I leave it? Ah. Under the couch cushions. I'll have to remember to stash one up here, too.

The growling moves closer, and I hear a foot scrape against the tarred roof.

"Where is she?" A low voice, farther off than the growling.

Then the sound of deep inhaling.

"Close." That's Growler. Then he adds, in the high-pitched vamp speech so I almost can't make it out, "Be quiet."

"She's just human," says a third voice, in vamp speech. "She won't wake."

Crap, I think. *Vamps, and me without a stake.*

Slowly, I extend my arm to feel around on the roof. There's a tired old tree nearby the warehouse that sometimes loses branches. Maybe one blew to a convenient location. But no. Whatever I am does not attract such extreme luck.

But my groping hand does find a chunk of something that feels like stone. A broken brick, maybe. There's a low brick wall all around the edge of the roof. It's better than nothing.

Growler's foot scuffs again, very close. He sniffs. For all their reflective eyes, vamps can't see without ambient light, and the moon has long since set. The only light is from distant streetlamps, and most of the roof is in deep shadow, anyway. That means I can see a lot better than they can.

Low-voice says, "I hear something over this way," and moves away.

"Yeah," says the third vamp. "I hear it, too."

Good, I think. *I can bash their heads in one at a time.*

Then Low-voice grunts, breaths a wheezing breath, and is quiet. Growler turns to see what happened and I take my chance. I explode from my blanket and am on Growler's back and bashing my brick on his head in an instant. He's not as fast as Papa Vamp had been, which is a good thing because even with surprise I couldn't out-speed that one.

I'm vaguely aware of more grunts and odd breathing coming from Low-voice's direction, but I'm too busy trying to bash in Growler's brains to pay any more attention than that required to tell me that no one else is too close.

And then someone else *is* too close. Another vamp appears in front of Growler just as he throws me off to land sprawled on the roof. To my astonishment, the new vamp thrusts a stake into Growler's chest and he collapses in a heap.

"Hi," says the new vamp. It's the newborn.

"Hi," I say, because I can't think of anything else to say.

"I don't like them," he says.

"Where are the other two?"

"Dead."

"Oh," I say. Then, "How did you get out? I thought I locked the door."

He shrugs. "The window was open. I just fit," he says. "And I wanted to tell you. But these ones got in the way. They wanted to hurt you. And me."

"They –"

"They were outside that store," he says. "I heard them say Reborns taste better than humans. I thought maybe they could make me do what they wanted, like Father could."

"They can't," I say.

"Not anymore," he says.

"Not before, either," I say. "But they should be stronger than you. You shouldn't have been able to kill them so easily." I crawl over to Growler. He's lying there with my favorite stake sticking out of his chest. I *do* recognize him from Liam's market.

I pull the stake out and wipe it on the vamp's shirt. I wonder if my other stakes are sticking out of the other vamps. I'll have to retrieve them before the sun burns the vamps to ash, or the stakes will burn, too. First, I rifle Growler's pockets. Some bills, some coins, some simple gold jewelry I can pawn.

"You steal from the dead?" the newborn asks.

"He's not going to need it anymore. And besides, he tried to kill me."

"True," says the newborn. He looks around. "It's quite dark."

"Yeah." I stand up from Growler's body and go looking for the others. The newborn follows, stumbling on every unevenness in the roof.

"You can see?" he asks. He sounds awed.

"Yeah," I say. "Just a tiny bit of light, and I can see. Not in color, though." I find one of the other vamps. Low-voice, I think. I turn out his pockets, too, and pull my stake from his chest.

"Should we bury them?" the newborn asks.

"The sun will take care of the bodies."

He helps me turn over the last vamp.

"If you can't see," I ask, "How did you move so fast?"

He shrugs. It seems to be his answer for everything.

"I just did," he says. "I don't know how."

I wonder. Maybe Papa had been feeding his offspring something stronger that humans to fatten him for the hypothetical slaughter. It made sense that an extra-strong newborn would make an extra-potent feast for an older vamp.

"Well, you should get inside before the sun comes up," I say.

"Father said it burns."

Then I remember something he said earlier. "You said you wanted to tell me something," I say.

"Oh yes," he says and claps his hands like a child. "I remembered my name. It's Evgeny. That's Russian, isn't it?"

"I suppose it is," I say. "Well, Evgeny. Nice to meet you, and thanks for saving me. I'm Su."

"Su." He takes my hand and shakes it. "Nice to meet you, too. Now we're even, I guess."

Now we're even.

Chapter Four

BACK IN THE LOFT, the newborn – Evgeny – looks around like he's looking for a place to hide. And he is, I guess, because it'll be light soon and he probably doesn't want to start the day by bursting into flames.

I look around, too, because this is the part of my plan – the part that shows it's not a plan at all – that I really didn't think through. Where do I put the boy during daylight hours? The only place I can think of right off is the elevator. It's nice and dark and doesn't come in window-range on any of the three floors of the building. Problem is, I'm not the only one who lives in this warehouse.

The hallway's a possibility, maybe. I could block the window at the end of it with the heavy curtain that's around my bed. I must've wanted a canopy bed as a child, or else watched a lot of movies about princesses, because one of the first decorative touches I made in this place was to acquire a huge bed and rig a curtain around it.

Or, I suppose, I can let Evgeny spend the day in my bed with the curtain drawn. I'm really going to have to get him fending for himself soon. Having a vampire roommate is bad enough, but giving up my *bed*…. True, half the time I don't even use the curtains, but it's still my bed. And as often as I have days when the loft feels too closed in, I have nights when it's not closed in *enough* and all I want is a cozy little nest to curl up in. And those days, even with a giant bed, I usually do sleep curled up, right in the center of it.

The sky is beginning to turn grey, and Evgeny shifts from foot to foot like a nervous kid. I sigh, and walk over to the bed and pull the curtain around it. It's dense, black, and heavily lined.

"You'll have to stay in here," I say. "It's the only place I have that's dark." I don't even have a closet he could hide in, just a couple of small wardrobes, and even the bathroom has a huge window since it wasn't actually built as a bathroom originally, and only had walls and plumbing added so the landlord could rent the place as a studio instead of storage space, which isn't exactly in demand these days.

"You'd give me your own bed?" he asks.

I shrug. "We don't have a lot of options," I say. "Anyway, eat something if you're hungry, and use the can, then settle in."

"I ate," he says. "On the roof."

How did I miss that? When did he have time?

Then he heads for the bathroom and I get myself a glass of apple juice, just to have something to keep me busy. Now that the vamp-attack adrenaline has worn off, I can feel a fatigue headache starting. I haven't exactly had a lot of sleep tonight.

When Evgeny comes out of the bathroom, his hair is damp around his face, and he looks fresher.

"I smell like the old one's lair," he says. "Like dirt and dead things."

"He smelled worse," I say.

He smiles at that. "You smell nice," he says.

"Are you sure you don't want some nice blood from a bag?" I say, and take a big sip of my juice.

He looks startled. "I don't want to *feed* on you," he says. He even sounds a little offended.

"Well, you're not going to fuck me, either," I say.

Again, the startled look. I guess he really doesn't know what other vamps are like, which makes sense, if Papa was just raising him for slaughter.

"I don't want to *fuck* you, either," he says. "Well, I do, but…". He looks confused. "Not while I smell like *him*," he says. "And if I were to ever… you know… with you, I wouldn't want to just fuck." He looks embarrassed. I think he's even blushing a little. He stares at the floor and speaks to his shoes. "I would make *love* to you," he says.

I almost laugh. He's so sweet and young just then that I can almost forget he's a symbiont-infected Reborn killer.

"Well, thank you," I say. "But if you got hungry enough, you might drain me before you even knew what you were doing."

"I would never," he says. "And anyway, I'm full. And sleepy."

I motion towards the bed and he takes his shoes off and climbs in, through the part in the curtain. I hear him moving around, getting comfortable. Then he's quiet. I finish my juice and collapse on the sofa. I line my three stakes up in a neat row on the coffee table and use a paper towel to clean off any remaining traces of vamp blood.

A few minutes later, Evgeny's voice comes from the curtained bed. "Su?"

"Yeah?"

"What if I have nightmares?"

Do vamps have nightmares?

"Uh," I say. "Wake yourself up. That's what I do." Another bit of folklore that's wrong – that vamps spend the day in a coma-like state. Really, they just sleep like anything else sleeps. They can have a bad day's sleep just like a human can have a bad night's sleep. I think they can even get insomnia.

He's quiet for a little longer, and I'm starting to drift off in the pool of early-morning sun that hits the sofa. I can relax, because no vamp can touch me in full sunlight. Just as I'm about to fall asleep he speaks again, and his voice is small, like a child's.

"Su?" Even with my super-acute hearing, I can barely hear him.

"Yeah?" I'm so tired I'm not even sure it comes out as a fully-formed word.

"Would you lie here with me? Just until I fall asleep?"

I try to keep the picture of him hungry, jaw unhinged, and eyes blazing, in the forefront of my mind. I've already made enough stupid mistakes with this boy. But there's something in his voice I can't resist – and it's not a vampire come-hither superpower. That only works on the stupid and the easily-suggestible, and even mostly asleep I'm not that. It's more like he's expressing a deep loneliness that I can feel echoing in me, even though I've never felt especially lonely before. I'm kind of a super-introvert and like the company of others only for short intervals at times of my own choosing. Other people are exhausting, which is probably another reason I haven't had sex in way too long.

"Please?" he says, and it's that what decides me. It's not even lust, just a need to feel another living creature close by. So I get up and cross the loft and climb into the bed. He's curled in the middle, the same way I sleep, and he smiles that unearthly smile when he sees me by the dim light that enters with me.

"Hi," he says, shyly.

"Hey," I say. I curl up next to him, back to back, our spines pressing together like two puppies in a basket.

"Thank you," he says. Then I feel him relax and his breathing deepens and he's asleep. I'm certain I'll never sleep, not curled next to a vamp who could wake up and kill me at any instant. Hell, he could probably drain me dry in his sleep. But I do fall asleep, and he's in my dreams. Not scary, not sexy, just sweet. I think I'm dreaming about his human life, or whatever my brain has made up his human life to be. It's nice, his life. He was a decent guy, with nice parents, a sister. No girlfriend, though he had a serious boyfriend for a few months, and there's a woman he fancies at the local coffee shop.

In my dream, he doesn't really like baseball, but his dad does, so he pretends to be interested so they have something to share. He goes to art college for a while, studies photography – ironic, kind of, since light and silver are two essential components of traditional photography and they're also two things he can't bear as a vampire.

Then Papa Vamp appears and takes Evgeny – in my dream – and turns him. And before Evgeny can remember his past, Papa Vamp feeds him his own family members, one by one.

When I wake up, my face is wet with tears and it takes me a moment to realize the body-wrenching sobs aren't mine. Next to me, Evgeny is crying. I roll over and look at him. He's still curled up, his face buried against the bedclothes, his arms curled over his head, every muscle tense.

I've never seen a man cry like that. Hell, I've never seen *anyone* cry like that.

"Hey," I say. Then I curl myself around him, put my arm over him, and murmur meaningless comforting words into the back of his neck.

When he worried about nightmares, I'd imagined horror dreams, not something that would make him sob as though his heart was breaking.

After a while, the sobs stop and he relaxes. He sniffs and I feel him scrub his face with both hands.

"Thank you," he whispers.

"Nightmare?" I ask.

He rolls over and lies nose-to-nose with me. I can smell toothpaste and absurdly wonder if he borrowed my toothbrush earlier.

"He made me drain them," he says. "My family."

I feel cold, suddenly, and only partly at the horrifying idea of being made to feed on your own closest kin. Those dreams I had – were they *his* dreams?

He seems to realize something's wrong because he stares at me. I don't think he can actually see me, though, it's so dark behind the curtains. But I can see him, and his concern for me is baffling. Even if he wasn't a vampire, he should be consumed with thoughts of himself, of his own pain. But the Evgeny in my dream was selfless. Could selflessness survive the takeover of the symbiont?

He touches my face. "What is it, Su?"

So I tell him. He listens quietly, then says, "Are you psychic?"

It sounds so silly I laugh. "I never was before," I say. "I've never dreamed anyone else's dream before, either, though I don't usually sleep anywhere near anyone else."

"How strange," he says.

"Yeah," I say.

We lie like that, noses touching, his hand on my face and my arm around his ribcage, for a long time. His eyes drift closed and I think he's fallen asleep, so I start to move away. I'm thinking about coffee, or a good strong pot of tea.

But his fingers tighten, gently, and he slides his hand into my hair, behind my neck. He's careful, like he's afraid of startling me. He opens his eyes again, and they glow softly.

"I wish I could see you," he says. "But it's too dark."

I try to make a joke. There's a sudden intensity in the atmosphere that's making me nervous, and I'm longing for the roof again. "That's okay," I say. "I'm not all that much to look at."

"Oh, you are," he says. And then he kisses me. It's just a soft little kiss, his lips brushing mine. Then he's still again, his hand burning hot against my face. He's aroused – I can smell it on him, and it overwhelms the remnants of dirt-and-grave the old vamp left on him.

He strokes my cheek, and touches my hair. "Why do you keep your hair all braided and coiled away?" he asks.

"Because it's long and it's always in my way." My hair *is* long. Like crazy long. If I didn't keep chopping it off, it'd be down to my feet in no time, like some half-Asian Rapunzel. As it is, it's down to my butt and due for another pruning.

"It must be glorious," he says. He touches the elastic that holds the braid in place, like he wants to let it free, but he doesn't. "I could brush it for you," he says.

It's such an unexpected comment that I don't know what to say. So I kiss him, a little harder than I mean to, and our front teeth bump together. He pulls away a bit and think I've made a mistake, but then he kisses me again and he's gentle, but strong, pushing against my lips to open them and sliding his tongue into my mouth.

I want to climb on top of him and tear my clothes off right then, but I do have *some* class. And some restraint. So I hold myself still and just enjoy the kiss. He seems to be concentrating on it, like kissing me just the right way is the most important thing in the world, and *damn* but it's too bad he's a vampire. I just don't think I can ever be fully comfortable so close to a vamp.

By the time our mouths part my skin is so flushed I feel like I might burst into flame like a Reborn in sunlight. He sighs and tilts his head so our foreheads touch.

"Now what?" I say softly.

For a moment he doesn't answer, then he says, "You don't trust me."

"I *can't* trust you," I say. And then, for reasons not really formed in my head yet, I tell him about being a vampire magnet. Hell, I tell him everything. Everything I know about myself, and everything I know about vamps.

He listens attentively, eyes closed as if trying to catch every sound that comes out of my mouth. When I'm done, a little frown crease forms between his eyebrows. Absurdly, I want to touch it with my fingertip.

"I want to help you," he says.

"I don't know what you can do," I say.

The frown-crease deepens and I kiss it without thinking. *Jesus*, I better not be falling for this boy. He smiles and I think, *Fuck it, who cares if I am?*

"If nothing else, I can help you think of things you might not have thought of." He pauses, then shakes his head sharply. His nose bumps mine. "Once this fog clears from my stupid brain," he adds.

So he's aware of his case of the stupids. That's probably a good sign.

"Okay," I say. "But I thought you said we were even."

He gets that startled look again and I just about toss caution aside and wrap my legs around his, but I restrain myself and lie still.

"I only meant you saved my life and I saved yours," he says. "I didn't actually mean to keep *score*."

That was exactly what I thought he did mean, and I'm stupidly happy that he didn't.

"And anyway," he says. "You just keep helping me, so I want to help you. And –" He stops. I feel him flush. A vamp that blushes.

"What?"

"I *like* you," he says.

Then I do wrap my legs around him, and pull him close enough to feel his hardness press against me through our jeans, and his chest muscles – lean and wiry, just the way I like 'em – press against my breasts. I kiss him and he slides his hand up my back, against my skin. I'm about ready to start shedding clothes when he pulls away, gently unwinding my limbs.

"Wait, Su," he says. I can tell he wants to, even if I hadn't felt his erection. I smell it on him like an intoxicating musk. And I know he can smell me, too.

"What's wrong?" I say. I pushed too hard, didn't I? Too soon. And I start thinking it's good he stopped, because I was about to make another big mistake, being so vulnerable with a vamp. But that's what I get for acting like a nun for so long. Hi, I'm Su, a sex-deprived nympho.

He traces my lips with his fingertips and it tickles. He shakes his head. "This is going to sound dumb," he says.

"Try me."

He presses his hand over his heart. "It's too new," he says. "This sorrow." And I remember suddenly the dream, his family. The old vamp fed him his own family, and I'm trying to get into his pants. I feel ashamed.

"I'm so sorry," I say. The urgency fades abruptly.

"It's okay," he says. "I want to. God, do I want to. But not yet."

I nod, then remember that he can't see me in the dark. "We'll wait," I say, but I'm thinking I just narrowly escaped another big mistake. "Of course we'll wait. Just let me know when you're ready." Because, mistake or no, I still want him.

"I will," he says. "Soon."

I sit up and crawl towards where I know the curtain will part.

"Su?"

"Yeah?"

"It *will* be soon."

"Okay," I say.

"*Very* soon."

And I'm maybe a little disappointed and a lot frustrated, and sad, and all sorts of other churning, confusing emotions, but I'm also peculiarly happy.

Fuck. I'd better not be falling for a *vampire*.

Chapter Five

T HE FIRST THING Evgeny says when he climbs through the bedcurtains is, "I need to go back to Reborn Father's lair."

I'm rummaging around in the fridge for something to eat and almost crack my head standing and turning because I didn't hear him get up.

"Geez," I say. "Don't sneak up on me."

He looks confused, because he's still standing next to the bed.

"You startled me," I say and he smiles. He walks across the room, deliberately stomping and bumping into things. "Is this better?" he says, grinning. With his fangs retracted, his smile is almost human — except you can kind of see where the fangs will be when they extend because there's a narrow gap between the other teeth. The rest of his teeth are just a little crooked in an attractive-imperfection sort of way and when his smile widens to a grin a dimple appears in his left cheek.

"Yes," I say. "Much better. At least for when I've got my head in the fridge." I put some leftover takeaway curry on the counter and get the water going on the hot plate. Not for the first time, I wish I had a microwave. It's not like they're even that expensive these days. It's just that whenever I have the cash in hand, I can always think of more important things to spend it on. Like rent or food. Or silver for stakes.

When I get a blood bag from the fridge, Evgeny takes it from me and plops it into the pot. "I can do it," he says. I don't argue. The sooner he can take care of himself, the sooner I can have my life back. And my bed. All to my lonesome.

I get a fork and lean against the counter, eating cold lamb vindaloo and watching Evgeny. Vamps tend towards expressionlessness unless they're going for a specific effect, though some of the older ones have almost managed to mimic the way humans show every thought on their faces so they can blend better. But it's like the symbiont missed installing that stillness in Evgeny, or maybe it's there but only when he wants it. Because he looks human, standing at my counter, poking the pot with a wooden spoon. His eyelids flicker and his lips twitch as if whatever he's thinking about amuses him. He turns and sees me watching and arches an eyebrow. I've always wished I could do that, but I've never learned.

"What?" he says.

"What did the old vamp – Reborn – feed you on?" I ask, because I'm wondering if his differences from other vamps have anything to do with the way the old bastard was feeding him up to be lunch.

"You mean besides my own family?" And now his face does go still. His whole body goes still, like he's a robot been shut down.

I can't believe I'm so unfeeling. "I'm sorry," I say and it sounds lame. "I didn't mean to remind you." I set my food aside, still hungry but no longer feeling like eating.

Then the stillness goes away and he's himself again. "It's okay," he says. Then he tilts his head the way he did last night when trying to remember his name. "I'm not sure," he says. "A lot them… a lot of them weren't human, I think, but he didn't tell me what they were. And he usually gave me the blood in a bottle, already drained out, unless he wanted to watch me kill something."

"So, not animals."

"Some of them smelled like animals," he says. "Or *he* did, when he brought me their blood." He flares his nostrils, like he can smell them now. "Like animals and humans at the same time."

I think about this.

"Wet dog," he says. "A few of them smelled like wet dog. But not quite dog."

"Werewolves, maybe," I say.

"Werewolves are real?" His eyes go wide. He's a vampire, and he's surprised that werewolves exist?

"Among other things," I say.

"Is everything real? All the stories?" And of course he wouldn't know. Tonight, he seems like a much older vamp, but he's still practically newborn, and Papa Vamp probably didn't tell him anything.

"A lot of them," I say. "But a lot of the folklore, and most of pop-culture, is wrong."

"Like vampires are dead?" he asks. "And hate garlic?" He doesn't seem to mind being called a vampire instead of Reborn. I guess Papa Vamp didn't teach him that, either.

"Like that," I say.

He fishes his breakfast out of the pot and starts to drink. After a few gulps, he says, "You smell a bit like that."

I stare at him while I go back over the conversation, trying to work out what he's talking about. Finally, I say, "I smell like a wet dog?"

He grins and a drop of blood escapes his lips. I'm suddenly hungry again and pick up my curry. He wipes his mouth with the back of his hand.

"Not really," he says. "But a little bit." I must have an insulted expression, because he adds, "I like the way you smell. Clean and warm." He blushes and changes the subject. "What are you eating?"

"Curry." I hold out the container and he sniffs.

"It smells good." He makes to take a piece out and looks at me.

"Go ahead," I say. "But Reborn don't really eat, besides blood."

"Your curry smells better." He fishes out a piece of lamb and pops it in his mouth. He chews and his eyes light up. "It's good," he says. "But very spicy." I just look at him. Maybe I should have warned him that it's vindaloo.

I guess there's no real reason vamps can't eat human food. They're still mostly human after all. Or kind of human, anyway. I've just never heard of them eating anything but blood once they're re-born. And they need blood to stave off the shriveling effect. I think. I'll have to ask Liam.

I think about what he said, about how I smell, while he finishes off his blood. Then we share the rest of the curry.

"I'm not a werewolf," I say. "Or a were-anything-else. I've never turned into an animal."

"Maybe you haven't…." He pauses, fishing for a word, I guess. "Matured."

I laugh. It's not the right word, but I know what he means. "Maybe," I say. "But the guy downstairs is a werewolf, and he's never said anything. And besides, they're pack animals, and I like to be alone."

He gets all serious at that. "I'm invading your home," he says.

"It's okay," I say. "I don't *hate* people. And you're not so bad."

"Well," he says. "That's why I need to go back to Father – to the old one's lair. To see if anything of mine is there. I must have a home somewhere. An address."

I nod. I know how he feels. "Can you find your way back there?"

"I think so," he says. Then, "Can I take a shower?"

So while he's in the bathroom, I get my favorite stake holstered and strapped to my belt, and as an afterthought, I add another one in my boot. It doesn't fit very well, but it's comforting.

He comes out of the bathroom shirtless, frowning at the t-shirt in his hands. "It smells," he says. He scowls at it, but I'm too busy looking at his chest. In the dream, he was such a nice, sweet boy, but in real life he's got a beautiful blackwork tattoo of a raven on the left side of his torso, wing wrapping across his chest and stomach, and both nipples are pierced with stainless-steel rings. Suddenly I'm way too hot between the legs and want to be outside, *right now.*

He sighs and pulls the shirt on, and then notices me staring and goes all shy again. "I like birds," he says. "I always wanted to fly." I fervently wish vamps could turn into bats, like in the movies, so he could have his desire.

"It's a beautiful piece," I say.

When he's ready, we head out into the night, aiming for the park. Our route takes us past Liam's and I gesture at the market. "We'll have to stop in on the way back and get you some more snacks."

"I'll pay you back," he says, and before I can even protest, he adds, "I want to repay you. I don't want to be a burden."

I shrug and we walk on. In the park he's more uncertain. He closes his eyes and inhales, like maybe he found his way out of there blind. And maybe he did. He wasn't in the best shape when I first spotted him in the bar. But also, of course, smell is connected to memory, so maybe he's trying to remember better. I follow him on a meandering tour of the park, and then when we get back to actual city streets he becomes more confident of his way until finally, for the last few blocks, he strides without hesitation and I have to trot to keep up. He's barely taller than me, but he sure can walk fast.

When he stops, we're outside a restaurant's back entrance. There's a cellar door in the concrete to one side of it that didn't get shut properly – there's even a garbage bag jammed in between the two halves of the door. Evgeny pokes the trash with his foot. "Here," he says. His confidence seems to have evaporated and he wraps his arms around himself and shivers.

I put my hand on his back and step closer, like he needs my warmth. "I really don't want to go in there," he says.

"He's gone," I say. "Staked and burned to ash in the morning sun."

"My family," he says. "Their bodies could be in there."

I slide my arm around him and squeeze. "You'll be able to bury them," I say.

He tilts his head so his cheek rests against my hair, then he nods sharply and steps forward to pull open one of the doors. It's steel and must be heavy, but he lifts it easily and lets it rest on the pile of trash next to the opening. It's dark down there.

He's about to go down, but I stop him. "Let me go first," I say. "I can see in the dark better than you. And my nose is better." He hesitates, so I solve the problem by sliding past him and starting down the rickety steps. Dim light filters in from the alley above and it's all I need to locate a breaker panel on one wall. There's a switch that looks well-used and it's in the "off" position, so I switch it on. One by one, a line of bare bulbs comes on, leading down a concrete-walled hallway. It's a dismal-looking place, and not surprisingly, it smells like damp. I breathe in deeper, though I don't really want to smell whatever's in the old vamp's lair.

The stairs creak and then Evgeny's standing at my shoulder. "Do you smell it?"

It's there, faintly, the dirt-and-grave I've come to associate with Evgeny's papa vamp.

"Yeah," I say. There's fear-smell too. And confusion. Some of it's Evgeny's. As we start down the hall he takes my hand. And here's something I really like about him: he doesn't try to pretend he's comforting me. He's the one who wants a friendly hand to hold, and he's not afraid to let me know it. That's way more gutsy, to my mind, than the usual guy bluster of oh-poor-girl-you-must-be-so-frightened that's really all about covering up their own fear. It's also way more sexy.

Not that I'm not apprehensive, mind. It's possible Papa Vamp shared this lair – some vamps like to assemble "families." Some like minions. Some just like to know they're not the only ones. He could also have other progeny he was fattening up, and by now they'll be hungry and raving.

The first room we come to is set up like a viewing room at a funeral parlor, compete with coffin and wilted flower arrangements. It seems Papa Vamp was a traditionalist. The dirt-and-grave smell is stronger here. There's old dried soil on the coffin, like it was dug up from a cemetery to serve as Papa's bed. Evgeny lifts the lid on the coffin to make sure there's no one taking a nap in there who might surprise us later. It's empty, of bodies at least, but there's a thick layer of dry earth in the bottom.

"He really *was* a traditionalist," I say. Evgeny gives me a questioning look, so I say, "How much do you want to bet that dirt is the native soil of wherever he came from?"

"Like in *Dracula*," he says.

One of the bits of folklore from *Dracula* that doesn't often make it into pop culture is that vampires can't leave their native soil, so when they travel, they have to take a box of dirt with them, to sleep in. It's not true, any more than a lot of the other lore is, but Liam says some of the older vamps follow it anyway. They say "tradition." I say "security blanket."

At the end of the hall there's a big room, where we find the old vamp's other progeny. What's left of them. It looks like Papa's been feeding on his own children for a while, because we find six corpses, shriveled and drained dry, still chained to the wall. Then there's an empty set of chains, half-torn from the wall and looking like they were wrenched open. I glance at Evgeny and he's staring at those chains and absently rubbing his wrists.

Surely he couldn't be *that* strong.

There's not a whole lot else there, in that room. A big industrial refrigerator has a few lonely-looking bloodbags in it and several wine bottles, probably also full of blood. They're labelled, so I start pulling them out and setting them on the scarred wooden table that runs in front of the wall of chained corpses.

"I should make sure they're dead," Evgeny says. They seem pretty completely deceased to me, but he's right; it's best to be absolutely certain when you're dealing with vamps.

I start reading wine-bottle labels. They're stick-on labels like you'd use for file folders, but look like they were written on with fountain pen in a dark brown ink. Expensive-looking ink. The writing is really old-fashioned and hard to read.

"Lycanthrope," I make out on one. Several others have the same label, so I arrange them together on the table.

"Looks like he was feeding you werewolf, all right," I say. "And kept some for himself."

Evgeny looks up from examining one of the vamp corpses – the grave smell comes from them, too, but it's not so much a rotting-flesh smell as a generally dank, musky sort of odor. Not a nice smell, but not as nausea-inducing as you'd expect from dead things.

"Mmm," he says. "These ones are definitely dead." He sounds thoughtful. Maybe he's wondering if he drained them himself, when Papa didn't bring back supper. I try not to think about that, and turn back to the bottles.

"*Síog*," says one. The word is familiar. Irish, I think, and for a moment I wonder how I know so much about languages. Was I a linguist, or just good with words? Then I remember my fairy tales, Irish folklore. *Síog* is one of the words for fairy folk.

"Fairies are real?" I say. Yeah, yeah, I shouldn't be surprised. After all, I was just marveling about a vamp surprised that werewolves are real. But the other thing is, in folklore "fairy" covers a huge range of beings. In fact, in Celtic myth, a creature that turns into a wolf and one that likes drinking blood would both probably be thought of as types of fairy folk. Or types of demon, which is really the same thing if you go back far enough.

Evgeny laughs. I think he's remembering the "werewolves are real?" incident, too. His laugh is strained, though. He gets up and heads for a door across the room. "I'll see what's in here," he says.

I nod absently and look closer at the bottle marked *"Síog."* There's another line of writing under it that I can't really make out. I move closer to one of the lightbulbs and bring the label up close to my face. It might say, "Jinny Greenteeth," which if I remember my folklore correctly, is a creature that hangs out in green-scummed ponds and drowns the unwary. I uncork the bottle and sniff. It even smells a little like pond scum. I re-cork the bottle and put it on the table.

The rest of the bottles are all marked *"Hexen."* That's "witch" in German, I think. So werewolves, Celtic fairies and German witches would all have a grudge against Papa Vamp. Interesting.

"Su?" Evgeny's voice is excited. He peers around the door. "Come and look at this."

The other room is small, kind of a big closet really, but it's got shelves and filing cabinets and cupboards on all the walls and a rickety metal desk in the middle.

Evgeny's opened a box on the desk and he's holding up a wallet. "My things," he says. "Some of them, at least." He opens the wallet and hands me the driver's license. "Evgeny Kostas Alexeyevich." Kostas? That doesn't sound Russian, but then a lot of Russian names derive from Greek, don't they? There's an address, too, and it's on a sticker on the back with a recent date to show it was updated not long ago. If the rent was kept up, Evgeny's probably still got an apartment.

"Your middle name's Greek," I say. Like it matters.

He frowns for a moment, then smiles and it lights up his face. "My mother is Greek." Then he closes up again. *"Was* Greek."

"I'm sorry." I put my hand on his arm and suddenly he's hugging me and crying again. It's so quick I almost lash out. I don't like thinking about how quickly he can move, how completely dangerous he is. But he's weeping quietly into my hair, so I can hardly be angry. Instead I kiss his cheekbone and murmur nice things to him until he relaxes.

"Sorry," he says. "Again."

"It's okay." I want to tease him, to call him "crybaby" and see if I can make him smile, but he might not find it funny and I don't want to make him feel worse instead. So I look around the room. On the shelves are all kinds of books – mostly folklore and myth and legend – some of them very old, and all of them with slips of paper with writing on them marking pages. I pull one off the shelf and flip it open. It's in German, in thick blackletter type, and I can only make out a few words, but among those words is "*hexen*."

I take down another book and it's on the mythical beasts of China, going by the pictures; the book is in Chinese. Did Papa Vamp know all these languages or did he get someone to translate? All his notes – written in that same luxe brown ink with a fountain pen – are in English with an oddly formal bent, like he learned to make letters in a stricter time.

"He was studying…" and here I stop because I don't know a word that encompasses all the different scary-things-that-go-bump-in-the-night. "Fairy" or "spirit" might come close, but really, most non-human-but-not-animal-either beings are as different from each other as each is different from humans that such a word is kind of a silly idea anyway, however useful it might be at a time like this.

"Us," says Evgeny. And he doesn't mean just vamps, but yeah, all us whatever-we-are that's not exactly human. *Others.*

He's found a coat in that box, and from the way it fits him perfectly, I'd guess it was his when Papa Vamp took him. It's long and black. Leather. And it looks good. *He* looks good. It's hard to believe such a tattooed, pierced, leather-coat-wearing man was such a sweet, kind human. He sure looks the sexy pop culture vampire stereotype now.

"Are you ready to go?"

He nods. "Whatever he did with my family, they're not here." Then he looks around. "Should we take some of these books?"

"I'd like to take them all," I say. "I think your papa was up to something, and I'd like to find out what. And maybe…." I don't want to put my hopes into words, in case I jinx them, so Evgeny does it for me.

"Maybe you'll find some hints about what you are?"

I just nod.

He turns and upends one of the cardboard boxes of stuff – the possessions of the old vamp's progeny, perhaps – and starts filling it with books. "I'll start with the ones that have titles in English," he says.

I dump out another box then on a whim I open a filing cabinet. Most of it looks like business information, like whatever Papa Vamp made his living on. So I turn to the desk. There's only one drawer, but in it are three old-fashioned-looking notebooks. I open one. It's his notes on his experiments with feeding his progeny different things. I toss those in my box. There's also a very nice fountain pen and a bottle of brown Montblanc ink. Those I stash in my pockets. And there's a cryptic note. A line on it catches my eye: "Soon we'll come out of the shadows." He said something like that to me when he was trying to kill me. I fold it up and jam it into my pocket, too, then I get back to packing books. I grab anything that looks Asian.

We can't carry them all, even with Evgeny's super-vampire strength, but we do get a lot of them. "I'll come back for more later," he tells me. I wish I had a car so we wouldn't ever have to come back here.

As we pass back through the big room, I look at the bottles on the table. "You want any of that?"

"I suppose I should," he says. "It'll save some money." He wedges one bottle in the top of his box.

"We'll have to come back for the rest."

"We can get it when we get the rest of the books."

We. In the space of a day, it's gone from *me and you* to *we.* It's nice, but it also makes me very, very nervous.

Chapter Six

EVERY NOW AND THEN I think I remember something from before… well, from before that autumn night when I woke up on the park bench not knowing who I was.

I'll be walking down the street maybe, and I see something and suddenly everything stops for a minute and I stare at whatever it is. A storefront, a person, maybe just the way the light from a streetlamp hits a puddle. And I try to figure out why it's familiar. It's like déjà vu – hell, maybe it is déjà vu – but it's the most intense sensation of familiarity. Like I know whatever it is I'm looking at, only I can't figure out how or why.

Then the world seems to start up again, and I'm left with the feeling that something's missing. And of course something is missing. My memory. But at least I'm not like a vampire, made a mindless beast of instinct without my memories. At least I'm still me. Though I really have no idea if I'm anything like I was before – how could I know? But I believe I'm still me, still Panya Su Fuchs.

And as we're walking back, laden with boxes of books, it happens. I stop and stare and almost drop my box.

"Su?" Evgeny turns and walks back. I'm staring in the window of a little Asian variety store, where there's a display of ceramic figures in the window, little Chinese and Japanese deities and mythological creatures. I'm not even sure what it is about the display that catches my eye.

He takes the box from me before I drop it. "What is it?"

I shake my head but before I can answer a woman comes out of the shop. She must've been cleaning or stocking shelves, because it's late enough the store should be closed. She starts talking to me in Chinese – Mandarin, I think, though I'm not sure because I have no idea what she's saying. It surprises me, that I don't catch a single word, and can't read any of the characters painted on the window, yet I know a little German and Irish Gaelic and who knows what else. I mean, one of my names is Chinese – the name I actually use – and I've obviously got some kind of Asian ancestry, so if I'm going to know a bunch of languages, why wouldn't I know Chinese? That question almost pulls me out of the mega-déjà-vu.

The woman is old and has a long white braid over one shoulder and she's wearing a Chinese quilted silk jacket with typical western old-lady slacks in beige. She's got black slippers with bright red dragons embroidered on them and I wonder if she got them out of her own store stock. Just for an instant, the déjà vu becomes nearly overwhelming, but then it's like I realize she's not part of whatever's causing it and it fades.

"I don't understand," I tell her. She frowns, then says something else in a language that sounds almost the same to my North American ears, but isn't. Cantonese? This time, there are words that I almost catch, but not quite. I shake my head, and she purses her lips. She speaks again, hesitantly, and I do understand a few words this time. "Luck," I think, and "honor." I wonder what dialect it is. Not one she knows well, judging by the way she keeps pausing.

"Luck?" I ask.

She switches to English. Her accent is perfectly North American, though she's careful choosing her words. "You," she says. "Are luck." She gestures to her store and the display in the window. "Great honor, to see you. But also you can bring sorrow. Much sorrow. I hope you will bring me luck."

"I don't understand," I say. "I'm not anyone special."

She smiles, revealing a row of immaculate, if age-yellowed, teeth. "Not someone, maybe," she says. "Some thing." Then she presses a ceramic figure into my hand. It's warm from her body heat.

"What am I?" I say. "Can you tell me?" I want to grab her thin shoulders and shake her, and I want to fall at her feet and beg.

She shakes her head, still smiling. "Luck and sorrow. Love and vengeance. Laughter and terror." Then she turns away. I want to follow, but at the last minute before the shop door shuts on her, she says, "I cannot tell you. If you were Chinese, maybe I could guess. My father was a wise man. But you…." She shrugs. "Chinese, Korean, maybe Japanese. Euro. Who knows how they mix?" Then the door closes. I take a step towards it, and it opens again. "You're unfinished," she says through the gap. "Still sleeping. And when you wake, you will choose between luck and sorrow. Choose well." Then the door closes and locks, and I stand there staring at an advertisement for canned eel and suddenly I want to eat fish.

"Su?" Evgeny is waiting on the sidewalk, next to the two boxes of books. "What did she mean, luck or sorrow?"

"I don't know what she meant about any of that."

"Maybe you can come back tomorrow. Maybe she'd at least tell you what she thought you were when she thought you were Chinese."

I nod, then remember the figurine she gave me. I open my hand. It's a white fox like the ones they have at shrines in Japan, though the black-on-gold sticker on the bottom says, "Made in China." I guess everyone gets their souvenirs from China.

"What is it?" Evgeny asks. "A dog?"

"A fox," I say. "An Inari fox."

"Inari." He sounds thoughtful. "The Japanese god of rice, right? Are you Japanese? Why would she give you a Japanese god if she thought you were Chinese?"

I shake my head. None of it makes any sense. I tell him my full name. Panya Su Fuchs. Korean, Chinese, German.

"Fuchs," he says. "That means fox." I guess vampire boy was interested in languages, too. And mythology. Maybe we have more in common than too-long canine teeth and missing memories.

I stare at the fox figurine. "She couldn't have known."

"Are you sure?" he says. "If you can't remember your past, how do you know she doesn't know you?"

"If she did, she wouldn't have tried to speak to me in Chinese."

"Well, then it's a clue," he says. "We'll look at it that way."

We again. But he's right. Maybe the old lady won't talk to me, but she did give me this figurine, and it certainly can't hurt to read up on Inari and foxes in Japanese mythology. Or in folklore in general, for that matter. I hope we grabbed the right books from the old vamp's lair.

After I managed not to die, that first time I got attacked by a vamp, that night I first learned vampires were more than just the latest fad in urban fantasy movies, I became obsessed with reading about non-humans. I learned that folklore is full of things that look human but aren't, or that used to be human, or that don't look human at all but can fool us into thinking they are. At first, I assumed that because vamps are real, everything else that goes bump in the night must be real, too.

I still don't know for sure all of what exists and what doesn't, I but I did learn that generally, the stuff that's the most fantastical is least likely to be real. But that doesn't mean, necessarily, that it's the most human-seeming that exists, while the most other doesn't. Actually, it sometimes seems the other way around. Wizards, for example, aren't real. Witches are, but they have limited abilities to manipulate perception and probability – they don't actually have magical powers. And you can't just become a witch. It's genetic and these days – at least according to Liam – largely dormant in the few families that still carry the right combination of genes. It makes it more tragic, I suppose, that Papa Vamp found one of the few remaining and drained her. Yes, her. Like color blindness is tied to the Y chromosome in humans, witchy-ness is only expressed with a double X. Which I guess means a trans man could be a witch, too. Unless it's not the chromosome but some other property of woman-ness, in which case, a trans woman could be a witch.

Anyway, I absorbed everything I could find out, almost getting myself killed a few times in the process. From Liam, I learned a lot about vamps, and he's the one who told me my downstairs neighbor was a werewolf. I just thought he spent a lot of time around dogs. The day I went to talk to him was one of the times I could have ended up corpsified, if he was a different sort of werewolf.

I knocked on his door with the lame excuse of borrowing a bit of milk. He just had soy milk, he said, because he's lactose intolerant.

"Me too," I said.

He looked at me funny, because what the hell was I doing borrowing milk if I can't even drink it?

"What do you really want?"

I stood just inside his door, the open hallway at my back, and shuffled my feet. He had a lot of cushions and blankets everywhere, like he wanted to be able to get comfortable wherever he felt like sitting down.

"Um," I said. He smelled very definitely of not-quite-dog, and under that was something else, something musky. Sexy. I looked up at him – quite a ways up because he was at least six foot four. More muscley than I like, but definitely appealing. Heat burned under my skin and I saw his expression change.

"I see," he said, and stepped closer.

"I…." I started to fish some logical explanation out of my brain, but was suddenly unable to think at all when he kissed me. It was forceful and toothy and scared the crap out of me, because I could feel exactly how strong he was. But the taste of his mouth made me hungry and I kissed him back, wrapped my arms around his neck and practically climbed his body to get my legs around him.

Then I realized what I was doing and pulled away. "Sorry," I said. "I didn't…." I backed towards the hall.

"I won't bite," he said. "Unless you want me to."

The attempt at humor stopped me. "That," I said. "Is the worst joke ever."

He smiled. "Yeah." He looked at me for while, then said, "If you didn't come to borrow milk or get laid – though I'm pretty sure we'd both enjoy that – why did you tap on my door?" His nostrils flared and he frowned.

I think he was trying to tell what I was. Human, he was probably thinking, but different. I wondered if I was a werewolf magnet the way I was a vamp magnet. Maybe that's why he kissed me.

"I heard you're a werewolf," I finally blurted out.

He was almost as fast as a vampire and had me pinned to the wall next to the door before I thought to react. I reached for my stake – I only had the one back then, and it was just bare wood without silver, but it was better than nothing – but stopped short of pulling it on him.

"Now why would you say that?"

I told him I was researching non-humans, and that a vampire – Reborn – of our mutual acquaintance had mentioned him.

"Liam," he said. "Bloodsucking asshole." There was a mental image I didn't need, and when I said as much, Magne laughed. He eased off on his chokehold – one-handed, no less, because he's got big hands – but didn't let go.

"And what do you really want?" he said.

I couldn't tell him I was trying to find out what I was. Or I didn't want to. Like Liam, though, he probably suspects the truth. So I made up some lame thing about growing up on legends of this and that and having family friends who were probably not quite human and now that my parents were gone I was trying to learn about their friends. Blah blah blah.

I could tell he didn't entirely believe me, but at least he believed I was sincere. Maybe werewolves can smell ill intent.

And that thing I said about the least probable being least likely to be real? Well, classic werewolves are pretty improbable. Actually a lot of werewolf lore and vampire lore are mixed up from way back. And the reality is, werewolves don't exactly turn into wolves. Instead, they have wolf-like abilities – hairiness, speed, strength, heightened senses – all the time. Something in them, in their genetic makeup, maybe, goes haywire at the full moon; they might even be the origin of the idea that the full moon drives people insane. Some of them hallucinate and start believing they are wolves. According to Magne, the older a werewolf is, the more the madness is under control, and the more they can use their wolf abilities to… well not exactly change shape, but alter their physiology to become more wolflike. Magne's even worse at explaining things than Liam, though I got the impression that he actually understands it better.

But yeah, I don't understand it, not really. I saw Magne once on full moon night, when I was out on the roof and he left on a midnight run. He sure looked more than halfway wolf to me. I've since learned that they don't need a full moon to change, either; it just makes them feel more wolflike and makes it easier, I guess, to get into the wolf frame of mind.

But I did say I learned that werewolfism, like vampirism, isn't passed on by bite (another bit of folklore that's wrong). And I still have a few scars from when I had to fight one off when I asked the wrong questions. Liam told me later lycanthropy is sexually transmitted, so I may have had a narrower escape than I thought. Maybe Liam was just jealous, but it was enough to make me mentally shift Magne from the "interesting" section of my brain's filing system to the "no way in Hell" section. Too bad, too, because despite his excess of testosterone, I do like Magne and I bet he'd be a fun lover, now and then.

We barely stop long enough at the loft to dump the boxes of books before we're back out and tracking down the address on Evgeny's license.

I'd prefer to go back for the rest of the books, then settle down with a pot of tea to go through them looking for references to Inari and foxes. But I also know how Evgeny must be feeling. Except his life is slowly coming back to him, memory by memory, while mine never has. It's like I didn't exist before I woke up on that bench. Except I had an expired driver's license and an old address, so I must've existed.

The street we end up on is in a decent neighborhood. Not expensive, but well-kept. There are a lot of older houses, mansard-roofed, turreted, widow's-walked, the whole nine, and most of them appear to have been divided into apartments. Evgeny's address is in a forest green house with burgundy trim, up in the attic at the top of a long flight of outside stairs. There's a light on in the window, which makes him hesitate. But then he fishes out a set of keys and goes to open the door. It's not locked.

He steps inside, cautiously, and suddenly there's a shriek.

"Evgeny!" From behind it's like a pair of skinny arms in stylish striped sleeves appears around his neck. He's a vamp, and still new, and the instincts of his symbiont are strong. Too fast to follow, he's got the girl turned around and pinned face-first on an island in the middle of the kitchen.

"What the fuck?" she yells. "Evgeny, you asshole. I thought you were dead."

"What are you doing here?" he asks. "Who are you?"

"I'm your girlfriend, you prick," she says, managing to land a pretty solid kick on his shin. He doesn't flinch, but my heart sinks – just a little – at the word "girlfriend."

"Um," I say. "I think it's safe to let her up."

Evgeny looks at me, then at her. "Oh," he says. "Yeah," and he lets her go. She tries to slap him and he grabs her hand. He doesn't even look – he's still looking right at me – just nabs her wrist. She snatches her hand back.

"Who the fuck is this?" she says, looking at me and sneering. "Is that where you've been? Off with some skinny chink?"

I blink at her. I didn't know anyone used the term "chink" any more, especially not someone as young as this girl. She can't be more than nineteen. And, I feel I should point out, she's significantly skinnier than I am. Like anorexically thin. My opinion of Evgeny drops a little, if she's his taste in women. Sure, she's pretty, and yeah, my language is probably not any cleaner than hers, but everything about her is surface. Her hair, her makeup, her clothes – it all looks carefully selected to appear a certain way, not like she actually likes any of it.

"I don't have a girlfriend," Evgeny finally says, turning to her. "I may have forgotten a lot of my life, but I do remember that."

"You have amnesia?" she says. "Poor baby," and she steps forward and puts her hand on his forehead like he's a kid coming down with a fever. Then her eyes catch the light and flare blue-orange and I realize the vamp smell isn't just Evgeny, and how did I miss that?

"She's Reborn," I say and he's got her pinned again before I can even take a step.

"Who are you?"

"Fuck you," she says.

He lifts her up and turns her around, holding her up by the neck, seemingly without any effort. His jaws unhinge and I have to look away. I don't turn my head quickly enough to avoid seeing Evgeny's fangs flip forward like the needle-teeth of a venomous snake.

"Who are you?" he says again, his voice taking on the higher pitch of vamp-speak. His words are slurred from the new shape of his mouth.

"Someone you shouldn't fuck with," she says. She moves to take something out of her pocket and I surprise myself by getting there first, stake to her chest.

"Don't try anything," I say.

"Who're you supposed to be?" she sneers, with effort, because it can't be easy to talk with Evgeny's hands clamped around her neck. "Fluffy the vampire sidekick?"

"What?" I say. I wonder how old she really is, and if she's messing up the pop culture reference on purpose.

Then she pulls her hand from her pocket and slaps it down on the kitchen island. When she moves her hand away, there's a brass pocketwatch there. I stare at it, then pick it up. It's smaller, and a little less ornate, but it matches the one I took from Papa Vamp.

"Tell me what it means," I say. I glance at Evgeny, then away. He's still all vamped out and just looking at him makes me want to crawl into the smallest cave I can find and stay there.

"It means," she says, struggling more visibly to draw breath to speak, "that you two fucks are going to be lunch for some very powerful Reborn unless you come with me." She stares at me, then licks her fangs. "Actually," she says, "you, geisha-girl, are gonna be my lunch. And this little newborn is going to come with me."

"Do not threaten her," Evgeny says, already more comfortable talking around his fangs.

She sneers again. "Made yourself a little human friend, have you?" she says. "Or were you saving her for later? Maybe we can share her. I could go for a nice long fuck 'n' feed." She licks her lips. "You're nice enough to look at, and she smells especially nice to feed on. What do you –"

I'm about to wave my stake in her face to get her to shut up when Evgeny makes a sudden sharp gesture and there's a loud "crack" and she goes limp.

I stare at her until he says, "I'm hungry. No sense letting her go to waste," and then I'm out the kitchen door and gasping for air at the railing. I try to ignore the wet sounds coming from inside, and I especially try to ignore the way the smell of her blood makes my stomach grumble.

I'm not squeamish about killing vamps, not when they're trying to kill me, but the way he can just kill her so casually, and so easily – snap! – that has me wanting to get away, far and fast.

Chapter Seven

WHEN I HEAR HIS FOOTSTEPS behind me – I'm pretty sure he's making the effort to be audible – I whirl around, stake ready. He stands very still, framed by the door and backlit.

"She threatened you," he says.

I sort through my thoughts, trying to find something to say, some reasonable cause for my actions. "She could have told us more," I say. "Now she can't tell us anything."

"We know there's a group of Reborn organizing for some purpose, and they want me," he says. I'm glad he reassembled his face before coming to the door.

"Yeah, but why?" I say. I stare at his eyes and see no evidence of vamp-glow. He looks human again. Completely. I try not to think how fast he moved. That vamp had to be way older, but she was like nothing to Evgeny.

He shrugs. "Perhaps the old one's notebooks will tell us." Then he frowns at me. "You're afraid," he says.

"Yeah." I want to look away, but I don't.

"Of me?"

"Yeah."

Something flickers across his face, like a spasm of pain. Is he hurt that I'm afraid of him? How could I not be?

"I will never hurt you," he says. "You're my friend. You helped me when I could not help myself, even though I was a danger to you. I will *protect* you."

I want to believe him. I want to step into his arms and let him take care of me. Except I'm not really one for being taken care of. And how can I trust him when every vamp I've ever met – even the ones I'm almost friends with – has admitted they'd be quite happy to violate me and drink my blood?

"How can I convince you that it's safe to trust me?"

I shake my head. I'm still pointing the stake at him, so I lower it, slowly, then holster it on my belt again. "Maybe you can't," I say.

He looks sad. Then my stomach grumbles, loud, and he laughs. "I might have food," he says. "I think I liked to cook."

"Well in that case," I say, "feeding me might be a good first step."

As he rummages and cooks, I have a good look at the vamp's watch. Evgeny's had the good sense to put her in another room and cover her with a blanket so I don't have to stare at her drained corpse. The watch doesn't have any crests or engravings on it. I pull out the old vamp's watch, that I've been carrying in my pocket so I can tell the time, and it's the same. On a whim, I get out my pocketknife and pry the back off the larger watch. Inside the back of the case are a few lines in Latin. I recognize the language and a few words are familiar but it's obviously not one of the languages I studied in depth.

Who the hell was I, anyway?

I pry off the back of Girl Vamp's watch and it's the same, but with different words.

"Do you know Latin?" I ask, when Evgeny sets a plate in front of me. It smells like ginger and garlic – crisp vegetables and thin slices of meat on a bed of jasmine-scented rice. I refrain from shoveling it into my mouth at top speed with difficulty, and thank him before picking up a fork and spearing a piece of broccoli.

He sits beside me and takes one of the watch backs. "I know a little," he says. "It's some kind of poetry, maybe. Something about domination and shadows." He studies it while I eat, absently plucking a green bean off my plate and chewing. He looks at the other watch back.

"From ruling over shadows, our dominance will emerge," he says. "Or something like that. And, 'Though the day star burns, we shall prevail'."

"Are they talking about wanting to be able to be out in sunlight?" I say around a mouthful of rice. Evgeny's a damn good cook, for a vamp. Hell, he's a good cook for a bachelor. "That seems like an awful big cliché."

"It is probably the only thing keeping them from taking over, or trying to," he says.

"Don't you mean 'us'?"

He looks confused, a bean sprout held halfway to his mouth. "What?'

"You said, 'the only thing keeping *them*.' The Reborn. Don't you mean 'the only thing keeping *us*.' You're Reborn, too."

He eats the sprout. "I didn't choose to be."

"That you remember."

Now he looks angry, but only for an instant. "I remember now," he says. "Being here, I'm remembering. I don't know why they chose me, but they must have followed me for weeks. When they grabbed me I was on vacation from work, my rent had just been paid. No one was expecting me to be anywhere, so I wouldn't be missed for a month at least."

"I wonder why you," I say, pushing my empty plate aside.

He just shrugs and takes my plate to the sink and washes it. I should do that, I'm thinking. I'm the guest. Instead, I wait till he's done and then I say, "So you really do remember that you don't have a girlfriend."

"No girlfriend," he says.

"Boyfriend?"

"No."

"Do you like women?"

"You already know I like you," he says. He's smiling, and the dimple's there on his cheek, so I get up from the chair and kiss it. Then I kiss his mouth. For a moment I picture him all vamp, jaw gaping and fangs extended and I almost pull away. "Please trust me," he says. I don't, but I can put that aside for now. He's remembered his life and it's like I can somehow absorb some of that remembering by kissing him, or at least share in it.

So I push aside the images of Evgeny the vamp and pull forward thoughts of the sweet young man from the dream, of the sexy fellow who stepped out of my bathroom earlier tonight. Then I remember how he told the girl vamp, "Do not threaten her," and even the vamp-face he was wearing can't stop the rush of heat in my crotch.

"Where's your bedroom?" I ask, and he takes my hand and leads me there. I don't even notice what the room looks like. I'm too busy discovering the feel of his skin beneath my hands. I pull off his t-shirt and trace the raven tattoo with my finger and again with my tongue. When I lift my head he kisses me, mouth hard on mine, then gentle. He touches my hair, finds the pins and elastics that hold it in place, and pulls them free so black strands cascade around my face.

He pulls away and says, "I was right, your hair *is* glorious." Then he takes off my t-shirt and finding no tattoo to trace, he plays with my nipples instead and the sensation shoots straight to my center. I push him back onto the bed and climb on after and he pulls me down to lie on top of him, rolls so we're side-by-side, holds me still.

"What's wrong?" I say.

He touches my lips with a fingertip, a smile tugging at one corner of his mouth. "Nothing," he says. But he blushes.

"What?" I can feel his erection through both our pairs of jeans, and I can smell his want, so I know there's no lack of interest. Does he want more time to mourn his family? To get used to remembering his life again?

He shakes his head. "I want…" he says, and I remember him saying – was it just yesterday? – that he didn't want to fuck, but to make love.

"To go slow?" I say.

He nods. So slowly I stretch out and kiss him, lingeringly, barely touching his mouth, and slowly I work my way down his neck to his collarbone, then down to a nipple, where the steel ring is warm against my tongue.

"Is this slow enough?" I say, and I trace his belly muscles with my tongue, and nibble the skin below his belly button, and pop the button on his jeans.

"Yes," he says, and it's more breath than word. I unzip him and he shifts his hips so I can slide his jeans off. His manhood pulses gently – it's ready for me, even if he's not. He strokes my hair and my name turns into a long moan in his throat as I slide my mouth over him. For a moment, he doesn't move as I tease him with my tongue, as I suck and very, very gently, bite.

Then he pulls me back up the bed, like he's afraid I'll break, or maybe he's just afraid he'll startle me. Then he rolls over, not on top of me, sensing maybe that pinning me down would make me nervous – and it would – but next to me, and he kisses me, kisses my breasts, tugs on my nipple with his teeth, and it's my turn to moan.

When he reaches my jeans, he undoes the snap and the zipper and looks back up at me. I reach down and push my clothes off myself. The first thing he does when I'm all naked is bury his face in my crotch and inhale, long and deep. When he looks back up at me, his eyes are half-closed and he looks euphoric.

"You smell so good," he says and for just an instant I think of his vamped-out state. But then he parts my thighs and flicks his tongue between my soft folds and I'm not thinking about much of anything any more. He licks and nuzzles and sucks until I want to come so bad I could scream. Then he finds my center with the tip of his tongue and I do climax, and it seems to go on forever. And I'm loud. I don't think I realized I'd be so loud.

Finally I push his head away and practically drag him up the bed to lie next to me. "I don't care about slow," I say. "I want you."

He smiles and nods and doesn't try to stop me when I climb on top of him until at the last minute he says, "Wait. In the drawer."

I have no idea what he's talking about until he twists away, digs in a drawer next to the bed, and hands me a condom. And then I feel like a complete idiot, because I should know better. Vamps and whatever I am may heal super-fast and we might even be immune to a lot of nasty things humans get, but that doesn't mean we shouldn't use protection.

I put the condom on him and he says, "Please hurry up and fuck me."

"You're the one who wanted to go slow," I say, but in an instant I've got him inside me. He doesn't last much longer after that, and damn does it feel good to be sitting on top of a beautiful man, making him moan. And he's loud too, I'm happy to say. Too many men try to muffle the sounds of their pleasure, but when those sounds are genuine, there are few things sexier. Consequently, by the time I roll off of him, I'm ready to go again.

This time, he uses his fingers, and they're just as clever as his tongue. He kisses me and I yell my pleasure into his mouth. After, we lie there, side by side, awake. His head rests on my shoulder and his hand is on my belly.

"I don't want you to be afraid of me," he says. Then he tilts his head to look at me. His eyes are startling blue under his dark bangs, against his olive skin. He's breathtaking – right now in a good way, but how can I forget what he is, what he can do?

"I can't help it," I say. "Even if you were an ordinary Reborn and I could kill you if I had to, you'd still scare the shit out of me."

"I would let you kill me," he says, muffled against my shoulder.

"What?"

He doesn't answer. He knows I heard him perfectly well. Finally, he says, "If you thought I needed killing, you'd probably be right."

"You're crazy," I say.

"I trust you," he says.

"Like I said, you're crazy."

Later that night, as morning draws closer, we're back at my loft. Evgeny's apartment is comfortable, and his bedroom even has heavy enough blinds that it could be made suitably dark, but if Girl Vamp was waiting for him there, then whoever the group of Reborn are, they know where he lives. They watched him there for weeks, too. And maybe they have non-vamp friends who could be paid to try to kill him during the day.

So we retreat to my place and sit sorting books into piles by subject until the sky turns grey. I was all for tackling Papa Vamp's notebooks first, but Evgeny insisted we look for information about foxes.

"I remembered," he says. "Now it's your turn. Tomorrow we can get the rest of the books."

"If Papa Vamp's goons don't get them first."

He thinks a bit, then shakes his head. "Wouldn't they already have gone there?"

"Maybe, but maybe they only just discovered you were gone. Maybe they thought you'd still be stupid and so they didn't bother to secure the old bastard's lair." Evgeny stares at the book in his hand, brow furrowed.

"What language is this?" he says suddenly. I take the book and flip it open.

"Korean," I say. I can even read a few of the words. Maybe not quite half of them. I put it in the pile of Asian books, with one in Chinese, one translated from Chinese into English, and a box set of two slick paperbacks translated into French from Japanese.

"When that Reborn who was in my apartment doesn't show up, they'll know something's wrong," he says.

"If they're that organized."

"Mmm," he says, and I look up to see him absorbed in a book. His black eyelashes, absurdly long, make a dark fringe on his cheeks. "This one looks promising," he says. "It's all about foxes in Japan."

I glance over at the little ceramic fox figure, the Inari fox. A Japanese mythological figure given to a Korean-Chinese girl by an old Chinese lady. It doesn't make any sense, except maybe Japanese, Korean and Chinese fox folklore all come from the same source. But what does it have to do with me?

"Maybe you're a were-fox," says Evgeny, passing me the book. It's a nice little volume, bound in heavy, nubbly silk that's faded to a soft orange. *Kitsune*, says the title. *Japan's Fox of Mystery, Romance, and Humor.*

"I've never turned into a fox," I say. "Or even believed that I did." But I look at the little ceramic Inari fox again and it almost seems to be smiling. Déjà vu hits again, not as strong as when I looked in the window of the Chinese shop, but still there, pulling at my memory. It was a figure like this one that caught my eye in that window, I think. No, two of them, arranged on either side of one of those bright red gates they have at Japanese temples. *Torii*, I think they're called. In the shop window, they're tiny, the foxes and the gate, and surrounded by a crowd of other figures from Japanese and Chinese mythology. But the memory that's pulling at me....

"I've been to Japan." I don't realize I've said it out loud at first, but the words echo in my ears. A tall red *torii* gate and life-sized white fox statues, one on each side. "No," I say then. "Not Japan. But a Japanese garden. Lace-leaf maples, bonsai in big concrete pots. A koi pond." I look at Evgeny and he's watching me, all vampire-still like he's trying not to be distracting. His stillness, once I notice it, is more distracting than normal breathing and fidgeting would be. Then the memory's gone and there's only the memory of a memory, if that makes any sense.

"When?" he says. "Where is it?'

I shake my head. "It looked like autumn. There were leaves on the ground and the air was cool. Almost cold."

"Recently?"

"I don't know. Maybe." I woke up with no memories in autumn. Maybe it was just before that.

"There's a formal garden out past Greenhill," he says. "Maybe they have a Japanese garden. There's a big Asian community not too far."

"Too bad I don't have a car," I say. I can't even rent one, because you need a credit card for that.

"Or a computer with an internet connection," Evgeny says.

"You don't have one either?"

He shakes his head. "I had a laptop, but I took it in for repairs, I think. Anyway, I didn't see it in my apartment."

"Maybe you have a receipt somewhere." So I guess he hasn't remembered everything, after all. Just most things.

Then I notice the light and mention that maybe he should retire to the bed. Vamps feel sunlight as heat, so it's mostly direct sun that burns them, but even filtered it can be uncomfortable. It's only when it's reflected by the moon that it stops bothering them.

"Come with me?" he says.

I'm still not so sure about sleeping next to him, though I'm getting used to the idea that he's maybe not going to eat me. At least not in the drinking blood or feasting on my muscle tissue sense. And *that* thought makes me blush.

He must sense my hesitation, because when he gets up he kisses my forehead and then heads for the bed, shedding clothes on his way.

"I hope you don't expect me to pick up after you," I say, and he looks embarrassed and sheepishly retrieves his clothes and puts them in a neat pile at the foot of the bed. He's down to his boxers and a t-shirt that fits snugly enough I can see the shape of his nipple piercings through the fabric.

"I'll be in there," he says, gesturing at the bed. I nod, and he turns and climbs between the curtains, giving me a very nice view of his backside with thin black cotton stretched over it. I almost get up and follow him then.

But instead I sit still, in the middle of the pile of books, and stare at the blank black cloth of the curtains. Red *torii* gates. I try to picture them in my mind again. Japanese maples. Bright orange koi. There are a lot of warm colors in the scene. A lot of reds. And blood. My blood. Suddenly, I'm terrified and I don't know why.

And then Evgeny is there – there's enough light in the room that he must be in considerable discomfort – and he puts his arms around me. He murmurs things in my ear that I don't really hear, but I can tell they're strong things, comforting things. And in a minute or two, I'm okay again.

"What happened, Su?" he says, as I lead him back to the bed. His skin looks blotchy and red.

"I tried to remember," I say. "Something happened to me in that garden."

"Something bad?"

"Yeah." I let him curl around me in the bed and hold me close. Just for a little while, I let him believe he's taking care of me.

"Su," he says, thoughtfully. "Are you sure that's Chinese?"

"I think so," I say. "Why?"

"Maybe it's not. Maybe it's Japanese."

"There's a syllable 'su' in Japanese," I say. "But I don't think it's a name. Not on its own."

"Maybe it's short for 'kitsune'," he says. "Fox."

"My last name's already Fox," I say. "Fuchs."

"Foxy Fox," he says, nibbling on my neck. "What does Panya mean? It's Korean, right?"

"I think it means 'midnight'," I say. "What does Evgeny mean?"

"Noble," he says. "My name is Noble Steadfast Son of Alexei."

"I couldn't find Panya in any books of baby names," I say. "But it's the name of a girl in a Korean folktale. She was killed and impersonated by a demon, I think."

He sits up a bit, as if to look at me, but it's pretty dark inside the curtains, and I don't think he can see me. "What kind of demon?"

"I can't remember," I say. "But 'Su' means 'plain' in Chinese. Or 'respectful,' depending on which character you write it with."

"What a terrible thing to name a child," he says. "It doesn't give them anything to strive for."

"And talk about a mediocrity complex."

He laughs. "You're not plain," he says. "Not at all."

Maybe he just likes Asian girls, because I look pretty ordinary to me in the mirror. Except for my crazy long hair, maybe. I guess you can't really call that *plain*.

Chapter Eight

I CAN'T SLEEP and it's not just because I'm lying next to a vampire. I keep thinking about foxes and names and my blood in a peaceful Japanese garden.

I don't think "Su" is short for "kitsune." Aside from the absurdity of having two names that mean "fox," I don't look Japanese. I at least look Chinese enough that the old lady in the Asian variety store thought I was through the busy glass window of her shop, and anyone who tells you all Asians look the same is either bigoted or really unobservant. I mean, Asians look like individuals, same as Europeans and Africans and everyone else, but because of strong cultural – and therefore genetic – isolation, you can tell Koreans and Chinese and Japanese and whomever else apart just by looking at them. To a degree, anyway. Like any generalization, it breaks down when you start finding exceptions, and there are always lots of exceptions.

So in my face in the mirror I mostly see Chinese and Euro. And yeah, I'm putting Europeans in one big group because there really hasn't been much cultural isolation in Europe, most of it, pretty much ever. Even in the Stone Age, Euro tribes were wandering all over the place, intermarrying and leaving children behind.

But I don't really think of myself as Asian or European. Just North

American, you know? Maybe I was different before I lost my memory. Maybe I was strongly Asian-identified, or maybe I thought about eyelid surgery to look more Euro. I don't know.

After a while, I'm worried I might wake Evgeny with all my tossing and turning, so I get up, make a pot of green tea, and sit on the couch with a stack of books next to me. I start flipping through the Asian ones, mostly looking at Papa Vamp's notes. Then, when I'm leafing through the Korean one, I catch sight of some familiar syllables – Korean has an alphabetic writing system but the glyphs are grouped together in blocks that look like separate characters, each representing a syllable. I see the symbols that spell "Panya." For all I know, I could have been called Panya before. It's my first name, after all. But "Su" feels more familiar, more comfortable, so that's the one I use.

In the book is the folktale I vaguely recalled. I'm not sure when I first read it. Maybe before. Maybe when I started researching non-humans. I try to read the story now, following along each line with my finger, but it's tough going. I know what sound each character stands for, but I don't know a lot of the words. I puzzle out that the story's about a girl named Panya and her father, and when it comes time for her to be married, every one of her suitors dies in their house. As usually happens with folk stories, a hero shows up to figure out why the house is haunted and saves the day. It turns out the girl had been dead for a long time, and the demon-ghost who killed her – as revenge against having herself been killed by the girl's mother because she was the father's lover (yeah, these stories are as complex as a soap opera sometimes) – has been impersonating the girl, and killing all her suitors by tempting them with sex. For most of the story, there are no notes from Papa Vamp. Then in one margin, he's written "symbiont?" with a line pointing to a word I don't know. *Kumiho*. I guess he's wondering if the demon refers to a symbiont, kind of the way vampire lore sometimes has the infected being demon-ridden. I wish Papa Vamp had included a few dictionaries in his library.

As far as I've been able to determine, most non-humans are either genetic mutations or inheritances – like witches – or in symbiotic relationships with another organism – like vampires. I've never heard of actual demon possession or anything else that might really be magic. And that's kind of depressing. Like, yay, the creatures from folklore are real but sorry, there's still no such thing as magic. So chances are, whatever I am is either a genetic inheritance, or it's caused by a symbiont. Either way, it doesn't seem to have taken, because I may have super senses and pointy teeth, and even a bit of extra speed and strength, but I'm still very much human. Much more than a vamp or were.

I wonder if it's possible to have a partial immunity to a symbiont, like when you get a mild flu instead of the whopper everyone around you gets laid out with. If that's the case, Evgeny must have the equivalent of the Black Death, because he seems to have ended up as a super-vampire. So maybe that's what drinking other non-humans does. Boosts the symbiont. Or adds more to the mix. I look speculatively at the fridge, where there's a bottle of blood labelled "lycanthrope" that Evgeny added to his box of books as we left Papa Vamp's lair. I wonder what would happen if I drank it.

I get to thinking about how werewolfism effects the body and decide to go talk to Magne again. If he's home.

He doesn't look too pleased to see me, but he lets me in. He's got leaves in his hair, and smells like blood and goats. I guess he was out hunting and some poor farmer will be one animal short in the morning.

"Busy night?" I say, and glance at the big clock on his wall. Not surprisingly, it has a moon phase dial that shows the moon is currently waxing.

"Social event," he says. "Did you know your new boyfriend is a bloodsucker?"

"He's not my boyfriend," I say. "And yeah, he's Reborn, but he's okay." I think about that and add, "More or less."

He flares his nostrils and gestures towards a pile of cushions. "Want a beer?" he says.

I shake my head and sit. I have a million questions, but I don't know how to frame any of them. Finally, I settle on, "Is lycanthropy caused by a symbiont, or is it genetic?"

He frowns and sits across from me. "You looking to create artificial wolves?" It takes me a minute to realize he's joking. He does deadpan so well I would have sworn he didn't have a sense of humor.

I smile. "No, just —"

"Research, yeah." He looks at me, dark eyes wide, like he's trying to read my mind. "It's none of my business," he says," but since you're poking around, I'm going to poke back. Do you think you might be a wolf? Because I can tell you you're not."

So he did figure out why I was asking him all those questions months back. I guess he's smarter than I thought, too. I take a deep breath. Not only do I not want to *need* to trust anyone, I just plain don't *want* to give anyone my trust. Maybe I'm anti-social.

"I don't think I'm a wolf," I say. "But…." It's hard to just admit I don't know.

"You know you're not quite human," he says, and I nod. "When a wolf is infected — and yeah, it's a symbiont, a close relative of the vamp symbiont." Which would explain why vamp and were folklore are more and more similar the farther back in time you go, until they're indistinguishable. "When you're first infected, it starts like that. You feel stronger — you *are* stronger. Your senses are heightened. Eventually, your body changes physically."

"I thought you didn't actually change shape," I say.

He shakes his head. "Not completely. At first, not much at all. But the older you get and the less you fight it, the more you do change. Some wolves change so much they can't change back. They stop being able to pass for human. It happens to all of us, eventually. But most of us change just enough that we can run on all fours comfortably. Our nails and teeth get longer, we get hairier."

He holds out his hand and flexes it and suddenly it's a different shape, like an elongated paw instead of a hand. He flexes again and it's just a large male human hand with hairy knuckles.

"Whoa," I say.

"It's not a transformation," he says. Then he gets a funny little smile and a dimple appears, reminding me of Evgeny and I try to stifle the flush that creeps up my neck. "Except maybe like those transformer robots." I must look blank because he says, "Don't you ever watch TV? The bones don't suddenly change shape. They gradually change the way they're jointed. I can bend them differently, arrange them differently, but they're the same bones."

"Like a vamp can unhinge its jaw," I say, getting the idea.

"Right," he says. "Bend and turn and fold and a human hand becomes a paw. All were transformation is like that. Combine it with the mental effects and you have a werewolf."

It begins to make a little more sense. Vamps and weres are two variations on a theme. Maybe whatever I am is another.

"Liam says vamps are reborn through an exchange of blood, but it doesn't work without a ceremony. I know from experience that it doesn't work just from being bitten."

"You were bit?" he says, looking at me with more respect.

"More than once," I say.

He frowns. Expressionlessness is not something weres share with vamps. "But you survived."

"I'm tough."

"I'll say," he says. "Even I wouldn't want to tangle with a bloodsucker." He runs a hand through his hair, finds a leaf there and plucks it out. He looks at it for a moment before setting it carefully on the wooden table between us. "The key isn't the *victim*'s blood, it's the… the parent's. For vamps, the symbiont takes over better when there's no resistance from the body. So basically, they kill the victim, nearly drain them, then infuse them with their own blood, already full of symbiont."

"Like a transfusion?"

"Right," he says. "If you study the folklore, you find that wolf and vamp lore start to diverge right around when science was gaining a better understanding of how the human body works. Best guess is that the vamp symbiont split off when some of the old stock decided to use science instead of luck to produce offspring, and now the vamp version can't survive well enough to be transmitted the wild way."

"And werewolves?"

He shrugs. "It's much more violent. The victim fights back, draws blood, it infects their wounds. And if they survive and heal, they begin to change, first slowly and then more rapidly. Because they haven't already surrendered to death like a vamp, the symbiont has to fight the person's immune system. Every now and then, it loses. Sometimes, the person dies.

But usually the symbiont wins, and it's extremely painful for the new wolf. Surviving the initial attack is kind of a measure of a person's worthiness to become a wolf."

"Okay, so if vamp and were are from different variations of the same symbiont, originally, are there other variants?"

He grins and gets up. When he comes back, he's got a thick book in his hand with the title *Changers* on the spine. "My family's been were for a few generations. Granddad wrote this." He hands it to me.

"I thought the symbiont made you sterile?"

He laughs at that, like it's the funniest thing he's ever heard. "Liam told you that?"

I nod.

"It makes bloodsuckers sterile," he says. "It's one of the weaknesses of the 'improved' symbiont. Wolves aren't sterile. Our lore says that once in a while, the symbiont even gets passed from mother to child in the womb, but I've never heard of it actually happening."

"He also said lycanthropy was an STD."

Magne laughs at that, too. "Ah, Liam. He's such a hilarious prick."

"It's not true?"

"Not unless you're tearing each other apart, literally, while fucking."

I look at the book he's handed me and it has chapters on all different kinds of weres. "All these exist?" I say. As I flip I see were-tigers in India, were-lions on the plains of Africa. Were-hyenas, too. Mostly big carnivores, but there are a few oddballs, like Romanian were-boars and Mongolian were-horses. From a quick scan of the table of contents, it looks like most of the shape-shifting creatures of world folklore, from Scottish selkies to North American Native animal people, are some variety of were symbionts.

Then I see a chapter on foxes. "Can I borrow this?" I ask.

"Don't let any humans see it," he says. "And keep it away from your bloodsucker friends."

"There's only one," I say. "And his name's Evgeny."

"Whatever." Then he sits next to me and leans over like he's going to kiss me.

"Hey," I say, starting to push him away.

"Trust me," he says, and he buries his face in my neck and inhales.

"Why is everyone saying that to me lately?" I ask.

"Because you're too suspicious," he says. "I'm trying to see if I can smell what you are. If you're some kind of a were, I should be able to tell."

"Being suspicious has kept me alive," I say, but I try to sit still as he bends over and smells my crotch.

"Fuck, you smell good," he says, and adjusts his jeans.

"Everyone keeps saying *that,* too."

He glances at me and grins. "If your vamp boy hadn't appeared suddenly, I was going to make a move on you."

I remember kissing him and suddenly I'm too hot. I know he can tell because his grin gets wider and the dimple gets deeper.

"If he's really not your boyfriend," he says, "I'd be happy to take a turn." He flicks out his tongue at me and I grab the nearest cushion and hit him with it.

He laughs. "Okay, I'm a pig. I'm a man, I can't help it."

"Fuck you," I say.

"I'd like to," he says, then immediately apologizes. Don't guys realize how creepy and icky they are when they say crap like that? I guess not, because they just keep doing it. Except Evgeny.

"Well," I say, shifting farther away from him. "Can you tell what I am?"

He shakes his head. "I don't know. You smell kind of like a were, but not exactly."

"Evgeny says I smell a bit like a wolf." Actually, he said "wet dog" but Magne doesn't need to know that.

He shakes his head again. "Canid, maybe. A little. But not a wolf."

"A fox?" I blurt out, without really thinking.

He considers that. "Maybe. Maybe fox. A bit musky, in a nice way. If I tasted your blood, I could tell if you were hosting a symbiont."

"No way," I say. "No blood drinking."

He shrugs. "Suit yourself."

When I get back up to the loft, the sky is getting dim and I realize I've hardly slept. If I'm going to go nocturnal, I really should try sleeping during the day. So I stretch out on the couch with Magne's book opened to the fox chapter, but before I can read more than the first line, I'm asleep.

I'm back in the Japanese garden and there are three little old Asian ladies staring at me. They have bright amber eyes, the same color as mine, and their hair is so long it trails on the ground behind them, like rivers of ink. When they get close, I can't understand why I thought they were old, because their faces are so smooth and unlined they're almost like masks.

One of them is dressed in a deep red silk cheongsam dress. Her feet are unnaturally tiny and she teeters like she's not used to walking. The second wears layers of silk kimonos in brighter, more orangey reds with blue flames picked out around the hem. Her feet, in tall geta sandals that make her almost as precarious as the first woman, just poke out from under her hem. The third is dressed in a snugly-fitting top and a roomy skirt in a red so dark it's almost black. Her feet are bare and her toenails are thick and black. She's carrying a pair of felt slippers in one hand.

They surround me, and I realize I'm naked, and blood streaks my skin, runs between my legs, seeps from my nose. I ache.

"Who did this?" says the first lady. She speaks to me in Chinese – not Cantonese or Mandarin, but a country dialect I can't put a name to. I shouldn't be able to understand her so clearly, but I do.

"Who?" echoes the second lady, in Japanese. It, too, has the sounds of a rural speaker.

"What is his name?" says the third lady, in Korean.

I'm terrified. Terrified of these three tiny women with their bright eyes and sharp teeth, and terrified of whomever raped me and left me naked in a formal garden in autumn.

"Vengeance," says the Korean lady.

"Or luck," says the Japanese lady.

"Or both," says the Chinese.

I can only shake my head. I don't know what they want. Then greyness covers my eyes and I'm falling. I can no longer see them, but their voices go on, closer now.

"She will have vengeance," says one.

"She is kind-hearted," says another. "She will not choose violence."

"Even the gentlest want their attacker to pay for a violation like that. She will take a middle way."

A feel a hand on my arm, then there's a hiss and it's suddenly withdrawn. Someone laughs.

"She already has something within," one of the women says. Their voices and their languages have run together in my ears and I can't tell them apart.

"A heritage?"

"Of us?"

"Like us, but not like us."

"It will fight us?"

"What do we do?"

The last voice fades away and I float in darkness. Slowly, light grows and I'm watching a sunrise from a mountain top. Only I'm not me. My center of balance is all off and I realize I have a penis and no breasts. I'm a boy, a young man.

"Evgeny," says a voice behind me, a deep, rough male voice. I turn – Evgeny turns – and the owner of the voice is there. David, his name is, and he's shirtless, pale and chiseled like a marble statue. He puts his arms around me, kisses me, reaches his hand into my jeans and cups my testicles, slides his palm over my erection. Then he's on his knees, blowing me, and my hands are buried in his blond hair. At the last second he bites me, hard, draws blood, but it's too late and I'm climaxing, pain and pleasure mixed. I look down at him and his face is covered in my fluids, white and red.

"Fuck!" I say and shove him away. But he's bigger than me, and he throws me down and pins me to the rock.

"I thought you liked it a little rough now and then," he says.

And suddenly he's not David, he's Papa Vamp, and I'm chained naked to a wall, bleeding from a dozen small cuts and Papa Vamp stands in front of me with a small knife and a large erection.

"Suck me," he says, and I try not to, but he's my – Evgeny's – parent vamp and I have to obey. Do weres have to obey their mama and papa wolves, too? I fight the compulsion.

"Suck me, you worthless whelp," he says, and lashes out with the knife, opening a cut above my eye. My vision is obscured by my own blood and my body leans forward against my will and my mouth opens.

I wake up yelling and Evgeny's yelling, too. We both fall silent at the same time. For a long while I can't breathe right, can't get the stench of Papa Vamp's unwashed genitals out of my nose. Then I pull myself together, climb off the couch and cross the room to the bed. For a moment, I hesitate. After a dream like that, he might not want me near him. But somehow I can tell it's okay – maybe I can smell his mood – so I get into the bed next to him and hold him while he shakes. After a while, he says, "Do you want coffee?" and I have to laugh at the ordinariness of it.

I wonder how much of the dream is actual memory and how much was nightmare. Did his beautiful boyfriend rape him while they were out camping? Or maybe he was joking and whatever really happened after he pinned Evgeny down was sweet and nice and mutual. I don't ask, though. I don't say anything. If he wants to tell me, he will. Then I wonder if he knows I shared the dream. He must have figured out I got the last part of it at least. He must have noticed I woke up yelling, and he must know it's why I got into bed to comfort him. But for now, I push those thoughts aside.

"Yeah," I say, uncurling and stretching. "Coffee would be good." Then I sit up and look at him. "You drink coffee?"

He shrugs. "I don't see why I have to change all my habits just because I have fangs and drink blood. Except for the avoiding sunlight thing. I guess I have to do that."

"I guess you do," I say. "Unless you fancy a Grade A sunburn."

"I used to tan," he says. "Brown as a nut." He sounds wistful.

"So much for sunbathing." I say. "I never really saw the point, anyway."

"At least I have a bit of natural color," he says. "So I don't have to be pale."

"I don't know," I say. "You've already got a bit of the goth thing going on."

He sticks his tongue out at me and then pokes his head out of the curtains. "I think it's safe to emerge," he says.

So we get up and make coffee and sit together sipping it, just like a normal couple in the morning. Except we're at the wrong end of the day.

Chapter Nine

WE DECIDE TO STOP by Liam's first to pay him and pick up more bloodbags. Neither of us actually says so, but I think we're both thinking that it's a good idea to get stocked up now, in case we run into any excitement at Papa Vamp's lair and don't have time later.

When we get to the market, no one's hanging around outside, but there are a few customers. They try to look casual and human when we walk in, like we might be human and they don't want to be caught buying blood. Because then the secret might get out. Personally, I think it's only the stubborn refusal of most humans to believe in scary things that's kept the secret so long. Vamps are actually pretty bad at keeping secrets. On the other hand, a lot of weird and scary shit is perfectly human, so it's not like believing in weres and vamps and whatever else is necessary to make sense of the violence in the world.

Evgeny sticks close beside me. This time, I'm not sure if he's nervous, or if he's protecting me. Maybe some of each. I don't think he's afraid of the other vamps, he just doesn't know how to behave around his own kind. I've described Reborn etiquette as best I can, but it doesn't seem to come natural to him.

The other vamps stare at us, then glance at Liam as if to see how they should treat us. I wonder if they can tell right off that Evgeny's a vamp and

I'm not. Liam seems to ignore their questioning looks.

"Su," he says. "And the new baby."

"Evgeny," Evgeny says.

"So you remembered your name, that's great." Liam speaks slowly and loudly, like some annoying adults talk to small children.

"Magne says 'hi'," I say, hoping he'll take the hint that we have questions and maybe encourage his customers to leave. "And I brought payment for the… uh… groceries."

He nods, but doesn't seem to be in any hurry. "Let me take care of my other customers, and I'll get you the rest of your order," he says. Then he ignores us. He writes down orders from the other vamps and disappears into the back room. Evgeny and I wander the aisles of the store, looking at the dusty displays. The state of the merchandise would give nosy people more of a clue that something was weird here than the peculiar customers.

The other vamps watch us while trying to look like they're interested in other things. Except one. A vamp that looks like he's been shriveling for years – possibly his unbrushed teeth keep him from getting laid enough to stave it off – stares openly at us. His hair is long, but in an uncared-for way, rather than in a too-nice-to-cut way, and his eyes are bloodshot. He looks like a junkie and I wonder if vamps have drugs. Or maybe they can be hooked on the same crap as humans.

Evgeny stares right back. He casually plucks a purple lollipop from a candy display, peels the wrapper off, and pops it in his mouth. I wonder how many decades old it is. The other vamps edge away from us, from Evgeny's calm stare, but the junkie moves closer. By the time Liam returns from the back room, the junkie's only one aisle away, staring at us – staring at me – across the brightly colored packages.

Liam doesn't seem to notice, or doesn't care. He's busy with the others, who take their goods and leave, glancing back over their shoulders as they go, like they're not sure what's going on, but probably don't want to be a part of it.

"I'll take *this* one," says the junkie, pointing at me.

"That one's not currently available," says Liam. There's just the slightest emphasis on "currently" that makes me glad I've never trusted him.

"I *want* it," says the junkie.

Evgeny steps in front of me, breaking the junkie's line of sight. To his credit, he doesn't try to put himself forward as my protector. Instead, he says, "She's not as palatable as you might think, friend. She carries a stake and knows how to use it."

The junkie blinks and refocuses on Evgeny. "But she smells like sex," he says, his voice coming out plaintive and lost. "I haven't wanted sex in forever, but I want her." Then he pulls out his penis and it's half-hard. "See." It also looks diseased and I feel sick. If I ever needed proof that condoms are a really good idea, even for non-humans, that's proof enough to last a lifetime.

"Put that away, you sick fuck," says Liam. "You know I don't sell anything live here. I've got your usual." He shoves a package in the junkie's hands and pushes him towards the door. "Go suck on that and you'll forget all your troubles."

When the door closes behind the shriveled vamp, even Liam looks relieved.

"I hate selling to that fuck," he says. "I don't even like dealing in that junk he buys, but it's all he'll drink and no one else will sell to him."

"He's sick," says Evgeny.

"He's sick, he's addicted to a variety of illegal and unhealthy substances, and he'd either die or reveal his true nature in about five minutes if I didn't keep him supplied."

I find it hard to feel sorry for Liam, or the junkie, though I'm surprised – in a good way – that he actually cares about another being. Unless he only cares to keep vamps secret. "I don't even want to know where you get whatever it is you sell him," I say.

"No," he says. "You really don't." Then he looks more closely at Evgeny. "So look who's not stupid any more. You recovered fast."

Evgeny just smiles and sucks on his lollipop.

"We need the rest of the week's supply," I say. I hand him the money.

Evgeny plucks the bills from Liam's hand. "It seems to me," he says, working the lollipop around in his mouth to better talk around it, "that a hundred dollars is a lot of money for only a week's worth of groceries for one person."

"Blood's expensive," Liam says, making a grab for the money. Evgeny's too fast, and Liam tries again, and fails. I watch Liam getting more and more angry and I think maybe I should intervene. Liam *is* a friend. Sort of. Well, not really, but he helped me when he didn't have to. But I'm also kind of enjoying watching Evgeny.

Finally, Liam bares his fangs and drops his jaw and lunges. And Evgeny simply isn't there when Liam lands. Liam stumbles into a shelf, almost brings the whole thing down, and wheels around.

Evgeny steps up close to him, nose to nose, and says, "I appreciate that you've helped us, but your prices are too high. If you don't give us a better deal, we'll pay only for what we've already used and take our business elsewhere."

Liam looks like he's about to explode, but he seems to realize he can't beat Evgeny. It's got to sting, since Evgeny's still newborn and Liam's got to be a century old at least. Finally he relaxes, lets his face return to its human configuration, and smiles. He straightens his shirt.

"Fine," he says. Then he looks at me. "Where the fuck did you find this child? He's not natural. No Reborn should be so fast."

I actually consider telling Liam about Papa Vamp's experiments – maybe he can offer some insights – but then I decide against it. Liam's got his own reasons for whatever help he gives, and simple kindness isn't likely one of them. "What do I know about the Reborn?" I say. "I found him at a bar, I gave him the blood you sold me, and this is the result."

On the other hand, if Liam was aware of Papa Vamp's group, he wouldn't be so surprised by Evgeny. I think. So I decide to take a small risk. "You heard anything about a group wanting to walk in daylight?" I say.

He doesn't look like I stumbled on some kind of secret. He just looks kind of blank. But then he's a vamp, and they tend not to react to much of anything, not visibly. "Isn't that every Reborn's dream? Not to catch on fire?"

"You tell me," I say.

He shrugs.

"What about Reborn wanting to come out of the shadows?" I'm thinking about the note I found in Papa Vamp's desk, that I haven't had a better look at yet.

"There are crackpots in here every month or so, spouting propaganda about taking our rightful place as rulers of the world. They don't tend to last very long."

Evgeny looks curious. "Do they try to reveal themselves? To humans?"

"Sometimes. Mostly they just annoy everyone until somebody gets irritated enough to dispose of them."

"So they're usually younger Reborn?" I ask. I take the cash from Evgeny and put it on the shop counter, but leave my hand over it.

"If any older vamps have delusions like that, they keep it to themselves," Liam says. He actually looks a little nervous, for a vamp, and I wonder what he's hiding.

I push the money across to him. "What do your other customers get for a hundred cash?" I say.

Liam looks sullen. "Two weeks' supply."

I nod. "Okay, then answer one more question and I'll give you the hundred for a single week. But next time, it's two weeks worth."

He scowls, but takes the money. I think he's unhappy not so much because he's being made to be fair as that he's not in control anymore. Not with Evgeny around. And it's got to rankle, being bested by a newborn. "What's your question?"

I take Papa Vamp's watch out of my pocket and I can see from the way his pupils dilate that he's seen one before.

"Fucking hell, Su. What have you brought me?"

"You tell me," I say.

He stares at the watch, then says, "Put it away." He paces behind the counter. "A few years back, there was a group. Elders, mostly. Real old Reborn. They decided we needed a ruling council to ensure our survival. Most of the basic steps we take to stay hidden come from them. They decided we should live on bagged blood, except in an emergency.

I wonder how long "a few years" is to a vampire. "So vamps – Reborn – do have a government. I thought you were anarchists."

"It's not a government," he says. "They showed up, handed out some rules, and they made sure we followed them, and made sure our progeny followed them. Then they disappeared. I don't think anyone's heard from them directly since."

"Directly," says Evgeny.

"There are stories. Reborn disappearing because they're too noticeable or too powerful." He looks right at Evgeny. "You might want to watch how much you show off that speed of yours."

"But you don't know it's them. The… council," I say.

"The stories often include a fancy brass pocketwatch being shown like it was some kind of token."

"So not so much a government as a… a secret society manipulating things from behind the scenes," says Evgeny.

"Through fear," I say.

"We're not afraid," says Liam, but his eyes keep shifting, like he's nervous.

"Sure," I say.

As we're walking to Papa Vamp's lair after dropping Evgeny's snacks at the loft, he takes my hand and laces his fingers through mine. This time, it's not for comfort – his or mine – but just to be touching, I guess. It feels absurdly intimate, somehow. Like that simple contact holds way more meaning than just hand touching hand. Like it's saying we're *together*.

I'm not sure I'm ready for that. I'm not sure I *can* be, with Evgeny. Sure, I can make a list a mile long already of all the ways he's so much nicer to be around than most guys in my experience. And sure, so far he seems determined to protect me. But so many things aren't what they seem.

Even if he was the most decent guy in existence as a human, all the extra bonuses the vamp symbiont gives can change a person. You know that saying about power? *Power corrupts. Absolute power corrupts absolutely.* It's like that, and Evgeny seems to have got a lot more power out of his symbiont than most vamps.

And the easy way he killed Girl Vamp, the way he handled Junkie Vamp, and the way he taunted Liam earlier – it was all emotionless. Cold. Chilling. How do I know he feels anything at all for me? But I don't pull my hand away. His touch is warm – not quite human-warm – in the cool of the night, and I guess it's just nice to be part of something more than just me for once, even if the togetherness is an illusion.

As we get closer, Evgeny walks slower and slower. At first I think maybe he's nervous again, full of thoughts of what Papa Vamp did to him in that lair. Because if he does remember all, or most, of his past, he's got to remember that. Maybe he's remembering the dream I caught part of, that we both woke from, yelling.

But then, a block before the building we're headed to, he stops. "Wait here," he says. "I want to make sure no one's going to ambush us."

"I can handle myself," I say. I hate being treated as weak. I hate being protected.

He looks at me, and something passes across his face, but I can't tell what.

"My sense of smell is better," I say. "My night vision. I walk more quietly." That last one's only true when he's not all super-vamp and scary fast.

"I know," he says. "But I'm faster." And he's gone. My fingers are still crooked from holding his hand, but the warmth fades quickly.

"Dammit," I say. As every hour passes, he's showing more speed and more strength and I know it should make me nervous – it should *terrify* me – but it's also so impressive. And I know he's probably right; I should wait for him to come back. But I don't take commands well. I do take care to be quiet – downright stealthy, in fact – as I make my way towards the building. I'm secretly pleased when he stops next to the shadow I'm in and moves on, back the way I came, without noticing I'm there. He gets almost all the way back to where he left me before he stops again.

"Su?" he calls softly.

"Here," I say. I smile at the surprise on his face.

"There doesn't seem to be anybody lying in wait." Before we continue, he kisses me; a long, hot one. "I apologize for treating you like you need looking after," he says.

I lean close to his ear, nibble on his lobe, and say, "You were probably right. But I won't play the weakling just because I'm a girl."

"Of course not," he says. "I'm sorry." He kisses me again, and I could just about go for a back alley fuck against the wall, but I do have a little more class. Besides, if there is some secret vamp society out looking for us – or for Evgeny, really – it probably wouldn't be a great idea to put ourselves in such a vulnerable position.

"Just wait till I get you home," I say. "I shall mete out an appropriate punishment."

"Will there be spanking?" he says, with an impish grin, and I swat his ass with the palm of my hand. His coat takes most of the sting out of it.

"Maybe," I say. Though really, I'm not a spanker. Or a spankee. But I'm pretty sure he's just teasing. I hope.

We both go serious when we get to the lair. I inhale carefully, trying to determine if anything's different. There might be a stronger vamp smell, maybe, and the dead thing smell has faded, and when we get to the big room, the vamp corpses are gone. The bottles of blood are still there, but Evgeny eyes them dubiously.

"You think they spiked them?" I say. The vamp smell is definitely stronger, recent, but not like anyone's still lurking. Though it's such a faint smell anyway, that it's hard to say for sure.

"Maybe. It would be a good tactic."

In the small room, the desk is on its side and books have been thrown around, like someone got mad when they didn't find what they were looking for.

"I bet they wanted the notebooks," I say. "The ones with the experiments feeding you different stuff recorded in." The notebooks we've barely looked at.

He nods, then grabs a box, tips out its contents, and fills it with books. There are books mixed in with files and the possessions of dead vamp progeny, so it takes longer to stuff two boxes full, but in the end I think we get every volume. I poke through the other things as I go and find a few things I can pawn, a bit of cash. I also find a wallet. I take the cash and look at the ID. It shows a handsome young man with soft-looking dark skin, brown hair and glasses. "Papa Vamp didn't like girls, I take it." Evgeny looks over my shoulder.

"I remember him," he says.

"You knew him?"

"No, not as a human." He rests his chin on my shoulder, tilts his head sideways to rest against mine. "He was one of the other progeny. I think –" He steps away to look back into the big room. "He was chained next to me.

When I got hungry, when the old one didn't come back… I ate him first." There's no emotion in his voice, but I think maybe that's because he's very carefully keeping it at bay, rather than not feeling it in the first place. "He made me strong enough to pull free." Then he ate the rest of them.

I try not to think about how those newborn vamps were thinking, feeling beings, confused and scared and unable to flee. Evgeny wouldn't have been thinking at all then. He wouldn't have been himself. In that moment, he had already ceased to be Evgeny the nice human boy and hadn't yet become Evgeny the seemingly-still-nice vampire. He was only the symbiont added to the most basic need for survival.

I also try not to think about how, if I hadn't killed Papa Vamp, those other young men might still be alive.

He turns back around and his eyes are glowing faintly, purplish from the fluorescent tube in the ceiling, bluey-orange where they catch glints from the bulbs in the other room. He looks terrifying, and he looks lost.

"Let's get out of here," I say. So we each take a box and leave without looking back. Outside, Evgeny closes the doors, making sure there's no garbage blocking them. He checks that the latch is secure. It's not to keep anyone out – the lock is broken, anyway. I think it's just symbolic. A final closing of a door he'll never have to set foot through again. Then he hefts his box and we set off, heading for the loft. I'm thinking about a long shower – maybe shared with a pretty vampire – and tea and something spicy to eat. I don't know what Evgeny is thinking, because he's quiet.

"I wonder if we should take a different route," I say. "Just in case they have bloodhounds, or something." I don't really imagine vamps use bloodhounds, but maybe they have some way of tracking people, and I don't fancy having them know where I live.

We step in under the trees in the park, and Evgeny's drawing breath to answer – I can hear the faint sound of him inhaling – when he suddenly goes still. I hear them, too. Then he sets his box of books down on a bench, takes mine and puts it there, too. And I catch their scent, just a hint on the air. Vamps, all around us in the woods. I can't tell how many, but we're definitely outnumbered. I can't tell if they're our enemies, either, but I can guess that they don't have goodwill in their slow-beating hearts.

I pull out the stake holstered at the small of my back and then the one in my boot. I guess tea and spicy food will have to wait. I put my back to Evgeny's and relax into fighting mode. Kung Fu Su. Evgeny's so soundless I almost can't sense him there.

He touches my hand with his briefly, and doesn't need to say anything. Together, we wait.

Chapter Ten

NOT FOR THE FIRST TIME, and probably also not for the last, I wish I could summon up that part of me that's kept me alive through several vamp attacks and a couple of fights with weres. I wish that extra speed and strength I sometimes call Angry Su because it kicks in when I get beyond fear to anger, was mine all the time.

But just terror can't call it up, and neither can clear-headedness. I have to get so close to dying that I'm no longer afraid, I'm just pissed that some lousy bloodsucker's about to take everything. Maybe if I could just skip right to the anger, I could call up the superpowers. I think I might even have just about done that with Papa Vamp, but it's not consistent enough to rely on.

But as I stand there back-to-back with Evgeny, waiting for the lurking vamps to decide to strike, I try to work myself up to anger anyway. I'm definitely annoyed. I'm hungry, and I want a hot drink to drive away the autumn chill. And I want to read about foxes and figure out what Papa Vamp was up to and then I want to crawl into bed and fuck my boyfriend.

Well, not my boyfriend. My lover, let's say. And not *fuck*, as Evgeny would say. *Make love.* I've finally found someone I like enough to make love *with* and now these vamps are going to try to take him away. But I just can't seem to get beyond irritated and inconvenienced to really, actually angry.

We wait and the temperature drops and the moon dips below the treetops, leaving only the uncertain, spotty lamplight. Maybe the vamps think it will hamper us, being in darkness, so their greater numbers will give them an even bigger advantage. But I can see just fine, since I'm not the human they assume I am, and Evgeny killed three vamps (one with my assistance) in near-blackness before he even had his memories back. I don't doubt he's even better at it now.

When the last sliver of the moon is out of sight, they step out of the trees. I can see six, and there must be more behind me, facing Evgeny. I can't tell if there are still vamps lurking in the woods.

"You've been causing a lot of trouble," says one of the vamps I can't see.

"I've been minding my own business," says Evgeny.

"You kill your father and slaughter your brothers and that's minding your own business?" The vamp's voice slides up the register in disbelief, and he finishes his sentence in vamp-speak.

"I didn't kill my… maker," says Evgeny, deliberately choosing not to call the old bastard his parent, and keeping his voice in human range. Maybe he's doing it to refuse to acknowledge their kinship. "As for the others, I was not in my right mind."

A vamp laughs, one of the ones nearer to me. "How could you kill them, newborn? Who is helping you? Tell us his name."

Evgeny doesn't turn, doesn't move at all. "I had no Reborn help." He says "Reborn" like he's spitting out filth. I wonder if he hates what he is – and there's a nice pop culture cliché for you – or if he just hates the ones like his vamp father. Or maybe he thinks the pretension of calling themselves "Reborn" instead of "vampires" is stupid.

"Tell us what happened," says the first vamp. "Come with us to the council, and we'll let your little human go."

"Hey, Claudio, you said we could eat her," says one of the vamps facing me. He looks a little shrunken, like he lives on the leavings of others. And he looks hungry.

"Eat her and *fuck* her," says the vamp next to him, a scrawny little thing who appears similarly undernourished. I've begun to notice there are a lot more male vamps than female, not just in this crowd, but everywhere. Weres, too. It is because men are more bloodthirsty and therefore more likely to want to become vamps? I don't think I buy that, though, it smacks too much of prescribed gender roles. Maybe the symbiont just takes better to men. Or men only like to recruit other men.

"Shut up, goons," says another vamp, the only woman I can see in the bunch.

"He promised," says Scrawny.

"Do not threaten her," says Evgeny, and a shiver runs through me at the tone of his voice. I hope I never, ever hear that tone directed against me. It's colder than cold, but perfectly even and calm. The tone of a sociopathic serial killer about to dismember a victim alive.

"You like your little pet, do you?" says the first vamp, the one who's acting like the leader. "What if we take her? Will you follow us then?" I guess he makes a gesture to the minions, because they move in closer. The female vamp knocks Scrawny and Hungry aside and gets to me first, to walk right into a kick in the gut. Even without Angry Su in charge, I'm still not a total pushover.

Then there are vamps everywhere, and my kung fu training kicks in and I'm just holding my own as Evgeny becomes a blur of motion and one by one the vamps stop moving. I take out one, Scrawny, with a stake in the back after I evade his attack and trip him on his way past. Then Hungry's on top of me, bearing me to the ground with his weight. He lands with an elbow square on my wrist, which seems to hurt him as much as it does me by the way he grimaces.

My stake drops from numb fingers, but it's only my left hand and I still have my bigger stake in my stronger right hand. He makes the mistake of fumbling at my clothes, maybe thinking he'll memorialize his dead friend by raping me like Scrawny wanted to. It gives me the time, and the leverage, to get him off of me. And I'm getting *really* pissed off at how men can't seem to think or talk about anything to do with me without sex being right up front, and that gives me the energy to throw all my weight behind the stake.

Then there are other hands on me and I strike out only to find I've dug the silver point of my stake into Evgeny's throat. It must hurt, but he doesn't seem to notice.

"Are you all right?" he asks, and I feel the anger drain away. I nod and look around. There's only one vamp left standing, and he doesn't look like he's in very good shape. I count bodies. Fifteen. More than I thought, then. A lot more. I only got two, which leaves thirteen for Evgeny, plus the one who's barely standing.

"You've made a big mistake," the injured vamp says. It's the leader vamp. "The council will have you, even if they have to fetch you themselves."

Evgeny gestures around. "It seems to me that you are the one who has made the mistake."

Leader vamp spits a glob of blood and phlegm on the ground. Lovely. "The elders all feed on nothing but Reborn children," he says. "Any one of them is more than a match for you, little boy." His contempt is genuine, but so is his fear. I wonder if he's more afraid of Evgeny or of going back to his masters and admitting failure.

"I have no quarrel with your council," says Evgeny. "But I will have if they don't leave us alone."

Leader vamp scoffs, then limps into the darkness. Evgeny lets him go.

I clean my stakes and stow them away. Evgeny watches me jam the smaller stake into my boot. "That looks uncomfortable," he says.

"It's not so bad."

"I can make you one that will fit better. You'll have to do the silver work, though." I remember him telling me his father – his human father – taught him to make things out of wood. "I'd like to make you something," he says, and the sweet shy boy is back in his voice.

I can't just leave all those pockets unpicked, even though every moment we're here is another we could be discovered, either by other vamps or by some hapless human. But I go through every pocket and as I finish each one, Evgeny drags the body away from the main pathway. I don't ask if he feeds, but it would be the practical choice. When I'm done I've got a nice wad of cash, a pocketful of coin, and some assorted odds and ends I can pawn, and Evgeny looks sleepy. I don't find any pocketwatches on the dead vamps – and I'm keeping special lookout for them – so I guess none of our attackers are in the inner circle, or even in the main group of enforcers. Hired thugs, I think.

Some of the newly acquired money goes towards Chinese takeout. I get enough to share, in case Evgeny is hungry for something besides blood. We sit in the bathtub, eating with our fingers, and then we just sit. I've got one of those huge clawfoot tubs that I don't use that often because it takes so long to fill up, but right now it's perfect. The taps are in the middle, too, so we can each sit at one end and pass the containers back and forth.

Evgeny doesn't eat much. Mostly he watches me and dozes in the hot water. He wakes up when I slide down the length of the tub and into his lap.

"Mmm," he says, as I recline against his chest. He reaches for the bar of soap – tangerine scented – and begins to wash me. He's slow and gentle and seems determined to touch every bit of my skin with his slippery hands. He begins with my neck, washing and rinsing. Then my shoulders, and my arms one by one. He pretends to ignore my hard nipples as he washes my chest. But once he's set aside the soap, he returns to them, cupping one breast in each hand and running his thumbs over them.

I wriggle back against his chest and feel him hard against my back. He mumbles something into my neck that even my ears don't catch.

"What did you say?" I ask. I grab the soap and wash his legs. Like the rest of him, they're lean with smooth muscle and I run my hands over them, kneading.

"That feels good," he says.

"That's not what you said."

"I can't tell you," he says.

"Why not?"

"I'm not ready yet."

And how many things are there that a man can be "not ready yet" to tell a woman? But it's too soon for that, anyway, isn't it? I barely know him.

Then he tweaks my nipples between his fingers, which I'm pretty sure is meant to distract me, but I don't care because the sensation twinges all the way to my crotch, making me arch my back. Then he slides one hand between my legs and I push against his fingers, wanting his touch. I feel swollen and hot. He slips two fingers inside me and I gasp.

"Okay?" he says.

"Fuck, yes," I say, so he pushes them farther in and I open my legs to help him. In and out his fingers slide and then he moves his other hand down to tease me and I don't last much longer after that. The sound of my voice echoes on the tile of the bathroom coming back at me even louder.

When I'm done I lay against him for a moment. I can still feel his hardness against my back. So I slide away from him, sit up, and turn around. I soap up my hands and dip them under the water, sliding over him.

"Mmm," he says.

I keep one hand wrapped around him, sliding up and down, slow, then fast, then slow again. I watch his face. He brow wrinkles, like he's thinking. With my other hand, I squeeze his testicles, gently, feeling the round softness through his scrotum. Then, curious, I slide one soapy finger farther back, to his ass. I'm not interested in anal sex myself, but I've heard some guys like a finger up there now and then. And Evgeny's bi, so maybe he likes it more.

His eyes fly open, wide and surprised. Or maybe not. I move my finger away.

"It's okay," he says. "But just one."

So back my finger goes and I push it inside him, not very far, and he seems to like it. His hips push against each stroke on his hardness, so I go faster and faster. Soon he's gasping, his hands clenched on the side of the tub and then he goes still and I watch the white fluid spiral into the bath water.

When he relaxes, I let go, gently slide my finger out, and start to get out of the tub. He takes my hand. His eyes are closed.

"I know it's stupid," he says. "And I know it's way too soon." He stops and I wait. Then he opens his eyes and they look even more impossibly blue than usual. "But I said… earlier. I said, 'I love you'." Then he closes his eyes again and lets go of my hand and I feel like I need to sit down.

I can't answer him, not yet. Maybe not ever. I get out of the tub and wrap myself in my bathrobe and head out to the kitchen. The sky is going grey and it'll be light soon. I hear Evgeny get out of the bath and dry off, and I don't turn around when his footsteps leave the bathroom. He pauses, then continues to the bed and climbs in. When I finally turn around, the curtains are closed tight and I can only barely hear the sound of his breathing.

I didn't mean to reject him. But I hardly know him, despite having shared a few deadly encounters and some great sex. He's a vamp. And even though he may not be like others of his species – and maybe I'm being unfair to the species, but they really haven't shown me their best side – he's still a bloodsucker. He's an especially fast and deadly bloodsucker.

But he's also the only person I've really opened up to in the past year. And whatever else he might be, he's the only guy lately who's actually been not-creepy to me. The only guy who hasn't constantly made comments about wanting to fuck me. Even Magne, who seems a decent enough man, can't resist sexual innuendo. Maybe it's whatever I am that makes guys, especially vampire guys, go all sexual predator on me. But Evgeny hasn't been like that.

And I *like* him. But love… no. Yeah, maybe I'm falling for him. Maybe I'm even a little *in love* with him. But I don't know yet if I want more. I think I need to know what I am before I can figure out what I want with someone else.

Finally, I sit on the couch and read Magne's grandfather's book on weres. The chapter on foxes. And that's when I learn that China, Korea and Japan all have stories about fox demons that can possess human women, or that can look like human women, and I remember that in the story of Panya, she was possessed by a demon called a *kumiho*. Magne's book says *kumiho* means "fox demon." The book also mentions European lore about trickster foxes and speculates that maybe some of those were based on were-foxes. But it seems Magne's grandfather never met any fox non-humans. *Others*, he calls non-humans. It seems they're rare, if they exist at all.

And that's all it says on foxes, so I put the book aside and stare brooding at the bed curtains. The sun comes up and hits the couch and it's so warm I want to be as close to it as I can get. I stow a stake in the pocket of my robe, then I say to the curtains, in case Evgeny's still awake, "I'm going up on the roof for a bit." Then I climb the stairs and stretch out in a pool of sunlight, glad I'm not a vamp and wondering what the hell to do about having a vamp in love with me. If he really *is* in love with me.

I wake up feeling better rested than I've felt in what seems like ages, but is probably only a few days. The sun is already low, just about to dip behind the tall buildings to the west. I feel bad that I walked away from Evgeny, left him alone in bed all day, right after he said he loved me. But that was kind of heavy, and I really do feel better for a good sleep alone. I don't even remember any dreams, which is a welcome change considering the kind of dreams I've had lately.

I should go back in, get some coffee on, and make sure Evgeny's feelings aren't too hurt. But I feel good, just lying on the roof doing nothing, thinking about nothing, or trying to. I can almost pretend it's life as usual, except I don't exactly have a usual life, even under the best of circumstances. I watch the last of the sunlight bleed from the sky, to be replaced by the hazy glow of the city. Only directly upward does the sky really look dark. One by one the few stars I can see this close to urbanity appear, biggest and brightest first. I can make out the main stars of Orion and it gives me an odd sort of comfort. I wonder if the constellation had some kind of special significance to me before, because I feel glad every time I see it.

I hear the faint whir of the elevator inside the building and smile. Magne must be out for another midnight foray as the moon gets closer to full. He seems to get more nocturnal around the full moon and I wonder how he explains it to his boss at work. I wonder what his job is. I imagine something like construction, but maybe that's just because he's big and always dressed casually. I imagine him in a business suit and it makes me giggle.

Then I think about Papa Vamp and his feeding experiments and I decide it's time to set aside research into foxes for now and figure out what those vamps – the so-called council – are up to. There will be lots of time to figure out what I am after we're not in danger of getting killed by Papa Vamp's buddies anymore, and that means finding out what their plan is and… well… stopping it, I guess.

I wonder if we're going to have to kill the whole council, just to be safe again. I wonder if we *can* kill them all. I don't like the idea of all that killing, even if it's life and death. It smacks too much of extermination. Genocide, even, though I don't think we need to kill all vamps, just the ones that want to kill us. Still, it's an uncomfortable thought. They may be generally nasty, but they're thinking beings. Intelligent. I think of Scrawny and Hungry from last night, and of Liam's junkie friend. Well, most of them are intelligent.

And that niggles at my mind. Why would the council use minions like that to catch Evgeny? Sure, they might assume he was weak still, like the usual vamp newborn, but those two were so incompetent I was able to stake them without Angry Su really kicking in at all. Unless maybe *I* was their assigned target in the first place. But they were so stupid they blurted out that I was their reward for catching Evgeny when leader vamp was trying to convince him that they'd let me go if he went with them.

Maybe it's nothing. Maybe good vampire minions are hard to come by. But I'll mention it to Evgeny anyway. Maybe he'll have some ideas.

So finally I get to my feet and stretch. My robe falls open and the night air feels good on my naked skin, though rather too cold for comfort. I wrap it back around me and tie it firmly, then I go in.

At first I think Evgeny isn't awake yet and I have the kettle filled with water and turned on before I notice the curtain is all rucked up on one side, caught up on the edge of the bed instead of hanging to the floor beside it.

"Evgeny?"

I part the curtain and look inside. He isn't there. I put my hand in the hollow where his body had been and there's no heat left. Not that he generates much, most of the time. I look over at the bathroom door. It's open and the room is empty.

Then I remember hearing the elevator earlier. Had it been Evgeny leaving and not Magne? I look around for a note. He'd have left a note if he went out, wouldn't he?

But last night he had told me he loved me and I had practically fled from him. And I hadn't spoken to him after that. He'd have woken up to find me gone, because he probably *had* been asleep already when I'd said I was going to the roof. And *I* hadn't left a note.

It's possible he's just gone out to scout around and make sure were hadn't been followed. Maybe my rejection doesn't have anything to do with it. I mean, I'm not so fabulous a woman that any self-respecting man – especially one as beautiful as Evgeny – would be all that crushed by me walking away from a declaration of love. But I think about how I would feel if our circumstances were reversed. It would sting. Maybe even make me mad.

Mad enough to take off without explanation? Yeah, probably.

Damn.

Maybe it was too much, too soon – and Evgeny even admitted as much – but that was still no reason for outright rejection. Which is how he'd see it, even if I hadn't meant it that way. I'd only meant to be on the roof for an hour or two. Then I was going to curl up in bed with him. That's what I had meant to do.

So what now? I finish making coffee and drink a cup while picking at the remnants of yesterday's Chinese food. Then I get dressed and sit back on the couch with Papa Vamp's notebooks. But the messed-up curtain catches my eye and I have to get up and straighten it. And I trip over Evgeny's shoes, which he's left next to the bed.

He left without his *shoes*. And then I realize what it was that bothered me about Scrawny Vamp and Hungry Vamp last night. They'd had that same glassy look, vacant and stupid, that the junkie in Liam's shop had. And Evgeny almost certainly fed off the vamps we'd killed.

I feel cold. I could be wrong – I *hope* I'm wrong – but I can't shake the idea that the vampire council would drug their own minions in order to drug Evgeny. But what if they had? He wouldn't go without his *shoes*. Would he? And they couldn't have taken him by force – not without making a giant mess of my loft, or at least leaving behind traces of their scent. But they must have taken him somehow.

And now how the hell was I supposed to find him?

Chapter Eleven

I SIT ON THE BED, in the hollow Evgeny left when he slept there yesterday, and I try to figure out what to do. If the vamp council drugged him, and somehow kidnapped him, I have no way to know where they took him.

My nose is good enough that maybe I could track them, but probably not very far, what with all the sense-dulling smells in the city. And besides that, they almost certainly had a car. Carrying a drugged person through the city streets is not a good way to be inconspicuous, even at night. I try to remember if I heard a car and I might have, but this is the city and who notices a car driving away when it happens every five minutes? And besides *that*, there are no lingering scents in the loft that I could track them by. Just Evgeny's.

So I think about my options. I can go on with my life and assume Evgeny can take care of himself, and oh well, so sad if he can't but that's vamp business. And what good can I do against an entire council of vamps that Evgeny couldn't do, even drugged? But how can I just leave him to his fate? The same tendency that wouldn't let me leave him to survive or not when I first saw him in the bar won't let me just do nothing.

But what can I do? I can try to find them, and find Evgeny, and hope an opportunity to help him arises. And I figure I have three, maybe four possible sources of information. There's Papa Vamp's lair, which might have an address or other information somewhere in all the business paperwork. That seems to be the likeliest option, so I'll do that first. Then there's Liam, who said he didn't know much, but who almost certainly knows more than he said. Liam has connections everywhere. It's one reason I kept going to talk to him even after he turned out to be an ass.

Then there's Magne, who probably doesn't know much, not being a vamp, but he knows a lot of the people Liam knows, so he might have an idea about who to talk to. Plus, he seems to actually like me, and only partly in a creepy way. I'll talk to him if Liam won't give me anything I can use.

And of course there's Papa Vamp's notebooks. I hop off the bed and find the books where I left them on the coffee table earlier. *This* is where I'll start.

I can't sit still, so I pace back and forth across the loft while I flip through the books. There aren't any dates on the entries, but he's recorded where he found each non-human and how much blood he drained from them, and which of his progeny he fed it to. He doesn't call any of his offspring by name, but uses the numbers 1 through 7 instead. When one dies, he replaces them, and uses the same number of the dead one, but with an additional number to indicate which one in the sequence he's referring to. So there's a 1, a 1-2, a 1-3, and so on. It seems much more cumbersome than names to me, but I suppose it's a way of distancing himself. Of depersonalizing them.

Most of them die when he decides to drain them fully, though a few seem to have died from a reaction to whatever he fed them on. Curiously, he's also kept notes on the ancestry or geographic origin of each of his children, as if he's maybe trying to combine some aspect of genetic heritage with the vamp nature. Each number corresponds to a region, too, so vamp 1 is always of East Asian ancestry, 2 of Middle Eastern, 3 African (which seems like a ridiculously large region to me), 4 Australian Aborigine or Māori or Polynesian, 5 European, 6 North or South American (another stupidly large category, but maybe the regions are also an illustration of Papa Vamp's prejudices). Number 7 is from one of the countries formerly in the USSR. Evgeny is 7-7, because that one in the notes is listed as

"Russian (+ Greek)."

I can't imagine what Papa Vamp was trying to accomplish with his geographic categories. They're either too big, or too genetically mixed (or both), to be any use I can see. But maybe it's got something to do with the Reborn's sort-of scientific approach to procreation – what made vamps and weres split in the first place. Maybe just the appearance of science is enough to make the vamp council feel like they're doing something significant.

I study the notes on how Papa Vamp fed his boys (and they are all male). Most of the progeny were fed on other vamps. The 7s must have been Papa's special favorites, because they got fed other non-humans most often. They also died the most often. There's nothing in the notes about making them service him, though he does note when he allows them to taste his blood, and when he feeds on them.

The final entry for each number 7 shows them fed *hexen*. Witch, it seems, doesn't go down so well, because every one of them dies of it. Except Evgeny. Papa Vamp reports feeding on the dead offspring himself and feeling at first extra strong and invigorated, and then extra ill. It's then, it looks like, that he kills one of his other progeny by draining them. Probably in an attempt to heal himself of the ill effects of the witch blood.

The final entry in the last notebook shows all of progeny 1 to 6 in good health. Number 7 had just been fed *hexen*. He's sluggish, and Papa notes that he's going to bring back a human, to see if it dilutes the witch blood better than vamp or were, to see if it will help number 7 recover. I guess I was supposed to be that human.

Evgeny must have recovered all right, but on his own, and stronger than ever. And finding itself ravenous and chained to a wall, the symbiont had used that new strength to reach the next newborn vamp over and drain him, which gave him enough strength to get free and drink the others.

He must have burned through whatever sustenance they gave him quickly, trying to metabolize the *hexen* blood, because Evgeny had drained all six of his vamp siblings. And he must have done it fast, because it wasn't so long after I killed Papa Vamp that Evgeny stumbled into the bar. And was hungry again.

For a long time I stare at Papa Vamp's last entry. The details are sketchy, but it looks like Evgeny would have been exactly what Papa was trying to achieve. The ultimate food source for Papa himself. Presumably, he'd have kept Evgeny alive to produce more blood, maybe to keep processing *hexen*, if Papa could find a steady supply to feed him. Though Liam says the death of a victim adds an extra boost. It's a good thing, I'm thinking, that I killed Papa Vamp when I did, and not just for Evgeny's sake. No good could possibly come from a nasty vamp like that with abilities like Evgeny's.

I flip through the notes one more time, but quickly. There are no mentions of any other vamps or of a council. No hints about where I could find them. Then I remember the paper that was in the drawer with the notebooks. Where did I leave it? My jacket?

I dig through my jacket pockets and it's not there. I try to remember what I'd done after we brought the books back. I'd had Papa Vamp's fountain pen and ink bottle in my pocket, too. I look around and spot them on a little table across the room. The note's got the ink bottle on top of it like a paperweight.

It's as cryptic as I remember, but I smooth the paper out and puzzle through it. It looks a bit like a manifesto, all stuffy language and declarations of coming victory and the like. At the bottom there's a spot for a signature, and there's Papa Vamp's old-fashioned brown ink and fountain pen. It might be something like "Iolo Pendennis," his name, but it's a bit of a scrawl compared to his precise notes. Welsh and Cornish, I think. Which doesn't explain his obsession with feeding Russian vampires German witch blood.

There's nothing on the paper that will help me find the council, or Evgeny. I tuck the page in the front of one of Papa Vamp's notebooks, because I should read it again later and see if I can figure out what this group of vamps actually wants. But right now I just want to find Evgeny.

The lair, then, is my next stop. I take the bus, catching it at a stop a few blocks from the loft and changing buses once. It takes nearly as long as walking, but it means I don't have to cut through the park, and I'm not likely to be ambushed by vamps on public transit. I have no way of knowing if they're even interested in me. And it's only then that it occurs to me to wonder how they found my place. *If* they found it, because there are no signs of anyone else having been there. Despite my assumption that

Evgeny was drugged, maybe I just want to believe that because it means he didn't leave because I hurt him. But if he wasn't taken, if he left on his own, why did he leave his shoes? And if he *was* taken, why couldn't I smell anyone else's lingering scent in the room? Not that much time passed between when I heard the elevator and when I went inside.

Maybe they had a drug that would somehow let them call Evgeny from a distance once he was under its influence. But how? Psychics? I'm not sure I can believe in psychics. Sure, some things – like witches – can influence perception, but that's not really the same thing, is it? Or maybe it is. And what else would you call the way I'd shared Evgeny's dream, not once, but twice?

Damn. There's just too much weirdness to keep track of. Hell, ordinary human life is complicated enough without all the extra, non-human stuff.

Just before my bus stop, traffic gets really slow and soon I can see the flashing red-and-blue lights of police cars. A fire truck goes wailing by. I don't even have to get off the bus to see that there's a fire in the building where Papa Vamp's lair was. Smoke billows out and I hope everyone in the restaurant upstairs got out okay.

For a few minutes, as the bus inches its slow way towards the stop, I think about ways to slip past the police and firefighters into the lair to see if there's anything useful left intact. But even before I get a look down the alley and see that the worst smoke is coming out of the basement doors, I've decided there's no point. I don't know if the vamps set the fire to destroy any evidence of their existence that might have been left, or if it was an accident, but I'm not likely to find anything useful there. Even if the uniforms let me by, which is unlikely, everything that might have an address or a hint on it was paper, and almost certainly burned to ash.

So I just stay on the bus for a few more blocks, then catch a different route heading back towards my part of town. I'm still leery of going on foot, just in case anyone's keeping an eye open for me. I'm not even sure I want to go home, though realizing it's unlikely anyone actually came and *took* Evgeny makes me feel a bit less exposed. I *think* home is still safe.

Liam's market is empty when I get there, though since the door's unlocked he's got to be nearby. I loiter around by the counter and when he still doesn't appear I lean over and press some buttons on the cash register. It's the only thing that's not grimy or dusty, so I know he must actually use it. The key's still in it, and the drawer pops open with a "ding."

There's a lot of money stuffed in there, but I'm not even tempted to take it. I lean farther and slide the drawer closed, then push a button and pop it open again. I'm about to do it one more time when I hear the door to the back open.

"Get the fuck away –" Liam starts to say, but I cut him off.

"I thought that might get your attention." I smile sweetly as he opens the register and examines the piles of bills. "I didn't take any," I say. "I'm not stupid."

He scowls, an exaggerated expression that doesn't look quite real on his face, and slams the drawer shut. "What do you want?" Then he realizes I'm alone and his expression goes all smarmy. "Where's your pretty pet?"

I ignore the question, though I find it interesting that Evgeny's the pet, when the other vamps refer to *me* as the pet. "Tell me more about this council."

"What? Why? They don't really do anything," he says. He walks around the counter, sliding one hand on its surface as he does, and leans against it, as close to me as he can get without leaving its support. He smiles and he's almost good looking. Not so long ago, I'd have thought he was sexy – I *did* think he was sexy – but then I was sexually frustrated. Which I'm going to be again if I don't find Evgeny.

"I need to find them," I say. "They took something of mine, and I want it back."

He stares at me, face blank, then something makes his pupils dilate, like he's suddenly remembering something, or making a connection between two things he'd thought were unrelated. He's one of those vamps who can only mimic human facial tics, though, so his surprise doesn't register on his face. If I hadn't been looking him in the eye, trying to seem forceful, I'd never have caught it.

"What do you know?" I say, putting command in my voice.

"You're too cute to be intimidating," he says.

That annoys me enough that I have my stake at his throat before he can grab my wrist, but once he does grab it, he forces my hand away easily. If he's surprised at how fast I am, he doesn't show that, either.

"Pretty Su," he says. "You can't threaten me."

"You're afraid of them," I say. "The council."

"Not really," he says, but I think he might be lying. "But there are advantages to cooperation."

I bare my teeth. I don't do it often, because normally I'm trying not to draw attention, but I can't think of any way to make Liam tell me anything.

He laughs. "Those are some impressive pearly-whites you've got," he says. "But you're still only human." He steps close. "Though I'll admit, you're an especially delicious human."

An idea occurs to me. A repulsive, unpleasant idea, but it just might buy me the information I need.

"If you tell me what you know about the council," I say. "Everything you know, including where I can find them, I'll…." I hesitate. I really don't want to do this. But what choice have I got? "I'll let you have some of my blood."

That surprises him. His face is vampire-still, but I catch a whiff of excitement and I know my gamble will work, as long as he doesn't just decide to *take* what I've offered. I'm pretty sure I can kill him if I have to, if he hurts me enough to wake Angry Su, but if I kill him, I don't get the information I need.

"Aw, and here I was hoping you'd offer me your sweet ass," he says. Why did I ever think he was a decent guy?

"That'll never happen," I say.

"And what's to stop me from taking it, and your blood, too?"

I lean against the counter facing him, forcing myself to be casual, "You won't," I say. "Because if I'm willing, there's always a chance of more in the future. And besides, Magne's looking for an excuse to kick your ass." I don't now if that's true, though it seems plausible. And maybe Magne's enough of a friend that he *would* avenge me.

"Magne doesn't scare me," he says. But I wonder how much of that's bravado.

I shrug. "Do we have a deal?"

"How much?"

"Tell me everything, and you can have two pints. I need to be able to function when you're done." I know the usual donation amount for blood is only one pint, but I figure I'm tougher than the average human, and I need to make it enough he won't argue.

"That's not very much."

"I need to be able to walk out of here," I say. "And if your information's good, I'll consider giving you a bonus, at some later date."

He scowls.

"You know I always pay up," I say. I have needed to buy information from him before, though it's always been for cash.

"Yeah, until your newborn pet decides he doesn't want to pay for his meals."

"You were cheating me," I point out. "And you're still getting a fair deal on that."

"Fine," he says. "But blood first."

I shake my head. "Information first."

Now he shakes his head. "I tell you something, you give me a pint. I tell you another something, you give me another pint. Then I tell you the rest."

"All right," I say, and follow him into the back. I try not to look at the chains and other weird things in there. I just perch on a cold steel countertop. He puts a couple of empty bloodbags, some tubing, and a needle next to me. It's all in sterile packaging, so I least I don't have to worry about catching something.

He looks at me. "I was asked to provide a cocktail of drugs – something like what my junkie friend Frederick gets. I didn't ask what it was for and they didn't tell me."

"Who asked for it?"

He picks up the needle and opens the package.

"Put gloves on for fuck's sake," I say. He scowls his fake scowl, but he puts on a fresh pair of latex gloves. And he gets some alcohol swabs and cleans a spot on the inside of my arm. I clutch my jacket in my lap and try not to look nervous.

"Who asked?" I say again.

"It came from a guy I know as Jonesie. He's a minion, though, for a council Reborn. Samuel Charleston."

"Sounds like a fat rich white guy."

Liam laughs as he slides the needle into my arm. "He *used* to be a fat rich black guy. Now he's a skinny rich black Reborn." He attaches the first bloodbag to the needle and I watch my blood begin to run into it. Liam watches it, too, and licks his lips. "I can hardly wait to taste this," he says.

"Well, wait till I'm gone," I say. "I don't want to watch."

"I'm getting a stiffie just thinking about it." He adjusts his pants and I want to gag.

"Where does this Charleston fellow lurk?" I say.

He gives me the name of a big fancy office tower downtown that the council Reborn owns, where he figures their lair probably is. "It'll be guarded," he says. "He's a popular boss for thugs looking for a master to play minion to."

"What about the rest of the council?"

He detaches the first bloodbag and hooks up the second. "I expect they'll be nearby. I don't know who most of them are, though I have some ideas. As far as I know, though, Charleston's the only one who owns his own building. Most of the other elders tend to me more… inconspicuous."

"So that's the best place to look?"

"Only place I can think of."

"This drug cocktail you made, what does it do?"

"Mmm," he says. "He's staring at the bloodbag, and at the tube running into my arm, watching the blood. "It makes most people feel good. Happy. It makes them suggestible. Biddable. And sleepy. Sleepwalking is a common side effect."

"What else?"

"They wanted a lot," he says. "And they had me dope six minions right then and there."

"When?"

"Last night."

"Did they say why?"

"I assumed it was a reward. Though most of the boys I doped didn't look like junkies." He looks at me speculatively. "I'm guessing that's not what it was for. I'm guessing...." He pauses to leer at me. "That the idea was to poison the well, so to speak. To feed the drug second-hand to someone they couldn't give it to first-hand." He leans over me and licks my neck. "I'm guessing they sent those poor dumb fucks after your pretty boy and he fed on them. Just like he was supposed to. And later he fell asleep and dreamed the loveliest dreams and sleepwalked right into their waiting arms."

As he pulls the needle out and sticks a bandage on my arm, it occurs to me that he could have told them where I live. He doesn't know the exact address, but he knows it's in the same building as Magne, and there are only three lofts in there. But I'm pretty sure he didn't tell them. Maybe it just didn't occur to him to volunteer the information without them asking. And paying. Or maybe, just maybe, he's slightly more decent a guy than I gave him credit for.

Chapter Twelve

MY FIRST IMPULSE, when I walk out of Liam's vamp market, is to head downtown to storm the building of Samuel Charleston. But of course, that's a stupid idea. I'm lightheaded from the blood loss, so unless I want to suddenly go all weak, I'd better eat something first. And arm myself with everything I can lay hands on that might hurt a vamp.

And it might not be a bad idea to talk to Magne one more time. If nothing else, he might be able to lend me a nice big knife or two. So I turn my steps homeward, though I do take a circuitous route to get there and pay close attention to see if anyone's following me.

Magne looks rumpled when he answers the door, like he just woke up. He's wearing jeans, but no shirt, and his feet are bare. He's hairier than I like – a side effect of being a werewolf, I suppose, and the poor were-women must be hairy too – and over-muscled, but he's in good shape. And he has a definite appeal. Faint white scars crisscross his chest and belly and when he turns to lead the way into the living area there are even more scars on his back. I almost want to reach out and touch them. Under other circumstances, I might even have dared to do it, to trace them with my tongue the way I traced Evgeny's tattoo. I wonder if Magne would react the same way.

"Your boyfriend left you," he says and he stops and turns so suddenly

I walk right into him.

"He's not my –" My words are cut off by Magne's mouth. He's surprisingly gentle, especially compared to last time I kissed him, and it catches me off-guard enough that I don't stop him until he's pressed full-length against me with his hand up the back of my shirt, hot on my skin. He pushes his hips against mine and I just manage to catch myself before I push back against his hardness.

"Wait," I say.

He pulls back, just enough to look at me. "Too soon?" he says. "Damn. I didn't think you were that attached."

"I'm…." But I'm not sure what I am. "I can't," I say and I step away. He lets me go, but reluctantly.

"Too bad," he says.

Yeah, I think. Too bad.

"I need your help," I say. I tell him what's happened, what I found out. Not all of it, and not in detail, but he gets the idea. Hell, I don't know if I can trust him, but right now I'm not sure how trusting him could possibly make anything worse.

He sits on a pile of cushions. Sprawls, really, and watches me. And damn if he doesn't look sexy. But I think of Evgeny, and thoughts of sex fade. I must really have fallen for the vampire boy, if he can even distract my overactive hormones from what's right in front of me. Sure, I still want sex, but now I want Evgeny, and he's not here.

Magne watches me. He shifts his weight on the cushions, holding my eyes while he adjusts his jeans to fit more comfortably around his erection and for just a moment I think he's going to take it out and jerk off in front of me. But maybe I should give him a little more credit. The next thing he does is grab a t-shirt off a nearby chair and put it on.

"What do you want me to do?" he says.

"I don't know," I say, and I finally sit down, too. I'm still uncomfortably damp between the legs, but I ignore it. "Give me some advice, maybe."

He sighs and leans his head back against the wall. "I don't like it," he says. "Vamps have always thought they're better than anyone else, but they've never really been *organized* before. Not that I ever heard of."

I tell him about the weird note signed by Papa Vamp, and the pocket watches, and Papa Vamp's notes about Evgeny. He whistles, a long one.

"Trying to create a super-vamp," he says. "Damn." He ponders, rubs his face. "But the extra-powerful progeny isn't the final goal."

I shake my head. "No. They're the… the magic pill to make the old vamps, the council, stronger."

"It's clever," he says. "A lot of non-humans aren't palatable to other non-humans. I guess for survival reasons. But if you *could* make them digestible, maybe you could absorb some of their abilities."

"But the aim seems to be to use Evgeny to… to sort of distill the *hexen* blood, the witch blood, to filter it through him so Papa could consume it."

"Right."

"But why *hexen*? Witchery is genetic. It's not transmissible. And it only expresses in women anyway."

He sighs. "Good points, but the truth is, no one really knows that much about witches. There are so few of them left. I've never met one and I'd wager Liam hasn't, either."

"So we know generally what these vamps are trying to do, but not why, and not the specific effect they hope to achieve."

"And if they've got Evgeny, you can bet they'll have sampled his blood, to see if he's done his job and made the witch blood edible for other vamps." He gets up suddenly, starts pacing.

"So he's probably still alive," I say.

"Almost certainly, but who knows what state he's in."

"What do you mean?" I think I know exactly what he means, but I can hope I'm wrong.

"They could have him drugged. They could be feeding him even more witch blood, which could make him sick. Most likely, they'll at least try to drive his human memories back into dormancy while they do whatever they're doing."

"Because the symbiont's stronger unhindered by human thought."

"Exactly. But it's also ungovernable."

"So he'll be chained," I say. "Locked up."

"And probably very hard to get to." Abruptly, he sits down again. "I can't give you as much help as you need," he says.

"What do I need, do you think?"

"A fucking army."

I should forget the whole thing, just walk away and live my life. I could crawl into Magne's lap right now and we could both forget vamps exist for a few hours. But I can't abandon Evgeny, and if the vamp council ever takes over the world, I'd feel shitty for not at least trying to stop it.

Then Magne sits up straight. "But maybe," he says, "one small, stealthy, not-quite-human could be even more effective than an army."

"How?"

"I can't give you any soldiers," he says. "Even if I was pack leader. I couldn't ask my brothers to die for someone they don't even know. But I can ask them to poke around a bit."

I frown at him. "Poke around how?"

"I know some people. I might be able to get you enough information to get into the building undetected. Getting back out, though, will be the problem, especially if your pretty vampire isn't himself."

"You would do that?"

"I don't want the bloodsuckers to be any more powerful than they already are," he says. "And besides, I like you. And not just as a potential bedmate."

"I don't have any way to repay you."

He waves his hand at my words. "You can owe me a favor," he says.

"How long will it take, to get this information?"

"Give me a day or two."

"I don't know if Evgeny has that long." I fidget. Mostly I don't know if *I* can wait that long.

"They won't kill him outright," he says. Then he leans forward and takes my hand. "Poor girl," he says. "You really do like him, don't you?"

I open my mouth, but nothing comes out. I don't know how to answer that.

"In the meantime," he says. "You should try to figure out what that not-quite-human part of you is. You'll need every advantage you can get, and maybe that will give you one."

I haven't told him yet about the déjà vu. The Asian women, the garden. So I do now, but I leave out a few details, like being raped and left naked. And I tell him about the folk stories I've been reading.

He considers. "Foxes," he says. "Now I can see why you asked about being a were-fox. I don't think that's it. But foxes, somehow that's the key."

I hesitate, then say, "You said you could taste the symbiont in my blood, if it's there."

He blinks in surprise. Weres can do still pretty well, but not like vamps. That and not being burned by sunlight (though they do feel some discomfort on very bright days) makes it a lot easier for them to pass as human. "You want me to taste your blood?"

I nod. Some weres like to drink blood, though most of them prefer raw flesh. I'm not going to let him take a chunk out of me.

"Hold out your arm." For some reason, I expect him to bite me, like a vamp. Instead, he makes a shallow nick on my wrist with a very sharp pocket knife, then gently squeezes my skin until a little blood gathers. Then he leans over and licks it away. My nipples stand up at the touch of his tongue, but then I see his face.

He grimaces, walks quickly to the sink, and spits several times. He rinses his mouth repeatedly.

"What?" I say.

"Remember what I said about some non-humans being unpalatable to *others*?"

"Yeah?"

"You're way beyond unpalatable."

I wonder if I should be relieved or insulted. "Well, I guess we know for sure I'm not human. Could you taste a symbiont?"

He shakes his head. "If there is one, it's nothing like the were-vamp symbiont." He leans over and spits again. "Jesus."

A though occurs to me. "If I taste bad to you, how would I taste to a vampire?" I've told him how I seem to attract vamps, and he knows I've been bitten.

"I can't imagine you taste any better."

"I wonder why they always want to bite me, then."

He looks thoughtful, then he grins. "You have a very strong sexual allure, for me," he says. "Probably for other wolves, too. But vamps always have to mix up feeding and fucking, so probably they feel the pheromones and think you'd taste extra-good. You probably make anyone who likes women horny, regardless of whether they're were or vamp or something else."

That idea – that I have some sort of super sex powers – reminds me of the Panya story. The fox demon, the *kumiho*, trapped Panya's suitors with sex. Is that what I am? A sex-wielding demon fox? But then shouldn't I be able to turn into a fox, too?

"That old Chinese lady, the one who gave me the ceramic fox, she said I was unfinished, 'still sleeping'."

"So whatever you are isn't awake yet. Maybe it happens slowly, like lycanthropy."

"And…." I frown, trying to puzzle it out. "In the dream, in the garden. They said I already have a heritage, one that might fight… them… fight whatever…." I stop and stare at him. "Whatever they did to me."

"It sounds like you need to go back to that garden," he says.

I think I've known that since I first dreamed about it, but to be honest, I've been afraid. When it comes down to it, I'm not so sure I want to know what I am. What if it's something really terrible? But I nod. "I guess that's what I'll do while your people are scouting out Mr Charleston's building," I say.

"You want company?"

Yes, I think. *Evgeny's company.* But I shake my head. I watch him rinse his mouth again, this time with a swig of bourbon. As he spits it into the sink a much more amusing thought comes into my mind.

"I traded two pints of my blood to Liam for the information he gave me."

Magne pauses in the middle of raising the bottle to his lips. Then his eyes crinkle at the corners and he takes a long swig and swallows. "Oh, he must love you now." He grins and his dimple appears.

I grin back. "I really, really hope he takes a great big first sip."

Magne, it turns out, has a computer with an internet connection, and he lets me borrow it to look up the formal garden. As Evgeny thought, it's out past Greenhill, which is not exactly close, but at least there's a bus that runs that way pretty regularly. I'll have to wait for daylight, though, because the buses don't run there at night and the garden's not open anyway. I don't know how much security a fancy garden would have, but I'd rather keep things simple.

My bed's my own for the first time in several nights, and at first it's luxurious. But I can't sleep, wondering what state Evgeny's in. Then I wonder if maybe there's a way to deliberately connect with his dreams, like maybe we can communicate that way. So I make myself lie still and concentrate on him. But of course, thoughts of Evgeny rapidly become lustful and I picture him naked in my bathtub, beautiful and glistening. I think about touching his tattoo, about the way his nipple piercings feel cool, then warm on my tongue. And I think about the way he tastes and smells, salty and musky, and the velvet feel of the skin of his hardness as I suck on it. And next thing, I've got one hand roaming my bare skin, copying the way he touched me, so strong but so gentle, and then my other hand is between my legs where it's wet and slippery and I squeeze my eyes shut and imagine it's his fingers sliding between the folds, his tongue teasing me until I push my hips up against my fingers over and over. I turn my head and bite the pillow to keep from moaning out load. It shouldn't matter, since I'm alone, but I don't want to be heard right now.

After, I lie in the dark, night air cold on my skin, until I crave warmth, so I pull the blankets up to my chin. And then I can think about Evgeny lying quietly next to me, sleeping. I imagine the sound of his breathing, the small movements of his body, because even in sleep he's not vamp-still unless he wants to be. And I remember the way he smells, not when he's musky with sex, but when he's sweet and sleeping. Soap and night air, that's what Evgeny smells like. And the faint tang of vampire-scent that on him is spicy.

I try to remember what it feels like to dream his dream. It's not like regular dreaming, because I'm aware I'm dreaming and I'm aware it's not my dream. I try not to concentrate, because it seems like the sort of thing you can prevent from happening by trying too hard. Instead I just aim to replicate the way it feels different from sleeping, from dreaming my own dreams.

And something shifts, suddenly, subtly, and I'm not exactly asleep, but neither am I awake any more, and I'm no longer inside my own head. I don't know if it's an ability of mine, from whatever non-human, whatever *other*, I have in me, or if it's something Evgeny got from Papa Vamp's experiments. Or maybe it's the rare coincidence of both that lets us connect this way.

At least I think I'm in Evgeny's head, because this is not my own perception. It's dark, but there are faint lights at the end of a hall. If I was seeing from my own eyes, those red exit signs would be enough to let me see clearly. I'm in a cell – I can just see the gleam off the bars and the blacker lines they make in the darkness where they block the dim light.

The air is cold, and I'm naked, but the manacles at my wrists and ankles are colder. I'm chained on my back on a metal cot – it's cold, too – my wrists above my head. There's a strap across my forehead and another across my chest and a third across my hips, so tight I can't move. My breathing sounds harsh in my ears, and too fast for a vampire.

The inside of one elbow aches and something burns there – a cold needle, maybe. Everything metal stings with cold, seems to suck my meagre body heat away. I can't even shiver, the bonds are so tight.

Oh, Evgeny, I think. No one deserves to be treated like this. At least they could have given him a blanket.

I see through his eyes – not that I can see much besides the black bars and the dim light, even by straining to look in different directions. I feel what he feels and hear what he hears. But in none of the dreams have I been able to know what he thinks, beyond a vague impression of his emotions.

I focus on that, block out the externals, and try to sense what's going on inside his head. I can't feel anything. It's just grey and dim and empty, like there's no one home inside him. But I have no way of knowing if that's a limitation of this dream connection, or if I should be worried.

Then there's a sound in the hallway and every muscle in Evgeny's body is suddenly tense. And I feel his fear. I can just see dim movement, then there's a sudden blinding-bright light and the clanking of the cell door opening.

"Hello, scum," says a voice. It's female, derisive, with a burr like someone who's smoked too many cigarettes for too many years.

"Don't talk to it." A male voice, smooth and deep. Like James Earl Jones, but cruel.

The woman chuckles low in her throat and steps into view of my – Evgeny's – straining eyes. The fear deepens. The woman runs a hand over my body and her skin is cold, even for a vamp. She pauses at my penis and laughs. "Poor thing's all limp," she says and takes it in her hand. I feel Evgeny's body begin to respond and want to sever the connection with him. This is not something I should witness. This is not something I want to know.

But the fear suddenly becomes hate. Intense sick-making hate like I've never felt. Like I didn't know it was possible to feel. And my – Evgeny's – jaw unhinges and I hiss and the woman takes an involuntary step back. My member flops against my leg, already going soft.

Now the male vamp steps into view, pushing the woman aside. "Don't play with the food, you stupid cunt."

I hate people who use that word to refer to women. It denigrates both women and cunts. Cunts are nice. They're soft and they feel good. They taste good. But use the word to insult a woman and it becomes filthy. I don't like that.

Evgeny hisses at the man, too, and the other smacks him, hard. Blood trickles from my mouth and my jaw cracks. I have to put it back into human configuration to align it properly again. The man is thin, but very strong, and in the contrasty light in the cell he looks literally black instead of just dark brown.

"Can we eat him yet?" the woman says.

"Do you want to die of *hexen* poison?"

Hexen poison? They know it well enough they can refer to it so casually? How long have vamps been trying to feed off witches? And why?

"Of course not," she says.

"Then we finish the testing." He steps away for a moment and returns with a glassy-eyed minion. He takes a sharp knife from somewhere outside my view and cuts Evgeny, a deep jab in the upper thigh, and forces the minion's head down. Evgeny hisses again, this time in pain. The minion tries to turn away at first, but then begins to suck eagerly at the cut.

I can just see then minion's head bobbing down there, like he's giving head, and I want to look away, but Evgeny won't let me.

Just as I start to feel faint, the vamp – it must be Samuel Charleston himself – drags the minion away from Evgeny by his hair and holds him up. We all watch: the woman, Charleston, and Evgeny, with me inside. The minion hangs limp, looking dopey. Then he revives and his eyes blaze.

"Fuck, yeah!" he says. "Oh, fuck, give me more of that shit!" He twists in the vamp's grip, catches sight of the woman, and leers. "Hey, baby, I could give you the best fuck of your life after that snack."

She moves to hit him, but Charleston blocks her with his free hand. His gaze never moves from the minion.

"It burns, man," the minion says. "It burns so good." He jerks open his pants and his penis springs out, engorged. I don't know if he's just really big or if it's an effect of Evgeny's blood, but the guy is *huge*. When Evgeny closes his eyes, I'm grateful. I can hear the skin on skin of the minion jerking off, hear his moans and his sharp breath, and I'm so glad I don't have to watch, too.

His moans get louder and louder and there's the splat of his jism hitting the floor and suddenly he's screaming and Evgeny looks and I see gushing blood. The poor bastard, I think. His eyes are crazed and he's tearing at his own skin and I realize he's trying to eviscerate himself.

"It burns!" he screams and somehow I tear myself free of Evgeny's mind and almost don't make it to the toilet to puke.

Chapter Thirteen

THEN I PACE until the sun comes up. I get dressed, walk to the bus stop, and pace some more. At the terminal where I change buses I have to wait an hour for the right one, so I force myself into calm. I buy a cup of coffee at the station coffee shop and think of how a vamp can be so still he doesn't seem alive, how a were can stand unmoving, watching. And I put myself into that frame of mind I use when I practice kung fu. You can't fight if you can't find that calm place, so if you're ever going to be good at a martial art you have to be able to call it up at will. So I will, and it works. I'm calm.

The thoughts are still swirling around in my mind, but for the moment my consciousness rests in a bubble of nothingness in the middle of the storm. I have to gently deflect those thoughts around me, keeping them from intruding, or they'll carry me away with them again and I'll be up and pacing before I even realize what I'm doing.

Finally, the bus pulls up and I get on, and have to practice calm again as it sits at the exchange, waiting for a connecting bus. And practice some more as we follow the meandering suburban route, stop for people to get on and off, pause longer at a terminal in Greenhill and then, at last, the bus pulls up at the gates of Chesterly Formal Gardens.

There's a tour-bus-load of Asian tourists waiting – Hawaiian Japanese,

I guess, from their mix of languages and their tans. I have enough money in my pocket to pay the entry fee, but it's a ridiculous sum – typical overpriced tourist gouging – so if I can avoid paying it, I will.

The tour guide is a skinny white kid with bleached-and-dyed blue hair and a nose ring. He's in that awkward age where he seems to be all limbs and acne, but he has a nice smile and actually seems to be enjoying himself. He doesn't see me get off the public bus, and he doesn't notice when I slip into the crowd of tourists.

To me, I stand out like a parrot at a penguin park, and the tourists know I don't belong, but the guide hardly glances at me. Just one more Asian in a yellow crowd, I guess. He herds us all through the gate, and then starts passing out little plastic buttons to each tourist, to show they've paid for access to all areas of the garden as part of their tour. I slip away before he gets more than a few handed out – he'll notice me when he comes up one button short – and no one pays any attention to me leaving. It'll be awkward if I get stopped and I don't have a button, but I suspect no one will bother to check unless I try to go somewhere that requires staff supervision, like the butterfly house. So I won't go to the butterfly house, and I'll see if I can avoid running into any staff.

I don't dare stop to consult the map at the entrance, in case tour-guide boy notices I've left his flock, and I don't have a brochure, so I'm not sure where I'm going. I smell the air carefully, and head in the direction that has the strongest smell of water. And a fishy taint. I'm hoping it's the koi pond.

I'm guessing the garden will soon be closing for the season, because now only the hardiest flowers are left and in the native plant area only the latest-blooming plants are still showing color. But they've done a good job with the plantings; though the variety is limited, the arrangements are nice and there are lots of reds and yellows and blazing oranges from a backdrop of shrubs and trees with their autumn leaf colors in full glory. It's peaceful, once I leave the tourists behind, and I can't help but relax a little bit.

I wonder if that's how I was caught by whomever had nabbed me that autumn day – was it only a year ago? Maybe I was so absorbed in the beauty of the place that I didn't notice some creep sneaking up on me. I'm not likely to be surprised like that again; with my heightened senses even vamps have a hard time sneaking up on me. Except Evgeny.

From somewhere ahead and to my right an echoing sound catches my notice. It's familiar. I tip my head to one side to hear it better, and choose paths that look like they'll take me in that direction. It's a wet, hollow "thunk" repeated at slow, even intervals. As I get closer, I recognize that the accompanying sound of running water changes regularly, too, as if the noises are connected. It sounds like a fountain at first, like a spout of water filling up a vessel, then running over. Then there's a faint "whoosh" and a spill of water splashing on rock, and finally the "thunk" and it starts all over again. I know that sound. It permeates my memory of the Japanese garden, so regular I didn't notice it in my dream, though it's loud enough that I should have.

The twisting paths of the garden seem calculated to lead me astray and I take several wrong turnings before I come upon a grove of small maples with deep red leaves, just changing to orange at their edges. There are no other plants growing around the maples, just a deep carpet of moss so bright green it seems to glow. It's so quiet even the regular "thunk" seems muffled. I feel like I'm caught in my dream again, though this specific setting isn't one I remember. But it *feels* the same. So silent and full of waiting. Of *expectation*.

The gravel path has given way to stone, irregular flat shapes in a mosaic of grey, each crevice between pavings populated by the green moss. It's like fairyland.

The path leads me to a tiny bridge in a high arch, almost a half-circle. It's painted red. This whole scene is red and green and grey. The bridge spans a stream, steep, swift and rocky. As I cross, the "thunk"s become louder, as if the sound follows the stream, and then is muffled again by the trees on the other side. Then I am among bamboo and if you think of bamboo as a thin reed, then you've never seen it all grown up. This bamboo is a forest, paler green than the moss, and turning gold at the edges. Individual stems are thicker than my arm – some much thicker – and they tower over the maples.

Amid the bamboo is a little hut – a pagoda? – with benches and a table. I could imagine sitting and drinking a cup of tea there, surrounded by the bamboo, like giant grass, and feeling like Alice when she met the caterpillar. I am insignificant here, so I hurry my steps.

I leave the bamboo and emerge on a lawn that leads down a slight incline to a pond, the koi pond from my dream. Huge orange and white and black fish dart among the smaller reeds in the shade of more delicate maples. Willows lean over the banks. And the path leads to a red *torii* gate with a white fox statue on each side of it. I stop and stare. Here, right here, I stood in my dream, in my memory. Naked and in pain, violated, I had paused on this grass and three small women had approached me.

Where had they come from?

The path splits here. One branch curves around to the pond and a wooden deck where there are places to sit and look out over the water, and then it winds back into the bamboo forest. The other branch turns uphill, between the pillars of the gate. I can just see that the path beyond is lined with concrete pots holding ancient bonsai trees like little old men, twisted and bent with time and wisdom.

I head that way. I can't resist pausing to put one hand on the nose of the right-most white fox. The autumn sun has warmed it, and it feels almost alive. "Wish me luck," I say.

I follow the path upwards. The hill is planted with maples and pines and I've almost forgotten the sound I was following until the ground levels out and there's a fountain. Perhaps the geography of the hill deflected the echo. The water runs from a bamboo pipe into a larger upright piece of bamboo which fills, then tips over and spills. When it's empty, it rights itself, because it's balanced and pivoted to tilt just so when full, just so when empty. And righting itself is swift and sudden and the bottom end of it hits stone with a loud wet hollow "thunk."

Next to the device, in the center of the fountain, is a bronze statue of a boar. There's an inconspicuous sign there, to explain it all, but I remember now. It's a boar-scare, a deer-scare. Bamboo and stone and running water arranged specifically to make a sudden loud noise. They're used in traditional homes, gardens, and hot-springs in Japan, to scare off beasties that might eat the plants. Or attack the guests, because boars can be as dangerous as wolves.

It's clever and lovely, and I could watch and listen to it all day. But it's not why I came here. The path continues on the other side of the fountain, through another red *torii*, past another pair of Inari foxes, farther up the hill.

I want to be alert and ready for anything, but this place is so dreamlike it's difficult to even think of it as real. The group of tourists I snuck in with might as well be on another planet. It's so calm here, I just want to sit and linger, but there's a sense of urgency deep in my guts, and I have to go on.

I feel I should hurry, run even, but I force myself to walk slowly, around the left side of the fountain, under the gate, and up the hill. I flare my nostrils and catch a smell I can't put a name to, but it's familiar as the taste of my own tongue. It's something alive, slightly musky in a pleasant way, warm.

I take another slow step up the path, and another, and emerge again. There's one more *torii*, one more pair of foxes, and a stone-paved area at the top of the hill, surrounded by trees. Immediately ahead is a tiny Shinto shrine, and to the left, looking down on the garden, is a gazebo. And at a table in the gazebo, sipping tea from tiny earthenware cups, are three small Asian ladies, dressed in red.

At first, I just stare at them. They don't seem to notice me, so I take the time to look. From this distance, they look old, and I wonder if they'll look younger up close, like they did in my dream. This time, their clothes are different. Still red, still silks and wool, but they look like traditional men's costumes, instead of traditional women's dress. All three of them have bare feet – I can see them clearly because they've got their legs stretched out beneath the table so their toes are touching. All of them have long, narrow, bony toes with dark pointed nails. Beside them on the benches are weapons, bows and short swords, like they've been practicing, or like they're setting off for war. Their glorious black hair is twined and pinned and tied up in elaborate hairstyles.

They speak quietly, each in their own language, and they smile a lot, flashing long canines – longer than mine, and even longer than Magne's. There is mischief and humor in their bright eyes. One of them shifts her position and I see she's got a fox tail hanging from the back of her belt. Then it twitches and I realize it's not an ornament, it's real. It's *her* tail, protruding from a tidy slit in her trousers.

I must have made some noise then, because they all turn to look at me. There is mild surprise on their faces, but also welcome.

"Daughter," says one, in perfect unaccented English.

"Come sit with us," says another, in the same language, just as perfect.

"We've been waiting for you."

I suppose this is what I've come here for, though I can't say it's what I was expecting. I didn't think the women from my dream, my memory, would be literally real; I suppose I thought they were some kind of metaphor. But for the past year I've ben living in a world of vampires and werewolves, witches and fairies and who knows what else. I should have known better.

So I sit with them, and accept a cup of tea. The view is beautiful and for a while I just enjoy it.

"You must have questions," says the Japanese woman, finally. Next to her on the table is a beautiful mask. An animal mask, painted white with red and blue details. She sees me looking at it and smiles. She picks it up and holds it over her face and suddenly her face is a fox's, white-furred and pointy-eared, red tongue lolling out. She laughs with a human voice, then takes off the mask and her face is human again, except for the long teeth.

"Do you like it?" she asks.

I'm not sure what to say, so I nod.

She pushes it across the table to me. "Then you may borrow it. But do not wear it too long, or your face will be stuck that way." She laughs again, a peculiar barking laugh that's full of merriment.

"Now," she says. "Ask me a question."

"Wait," says the Chinese woman, holding up her hand.

We sit as the tour group flocks up the hill, "ooh"s and "aah"s over the shrine and the view, then bustles away again. They don't seem to notice us at all.

"A fox is unseen when she wishes to be," the Chinese woman says, and I think about hiding from Evgeny in the shadows of the alley outside Papa Vamp's lair.

"Indeed," says the Japanese woman.

"What are you?" I say, and she smiles.

"*Kitsune*," she says. I know it means "fox," but in her voice it means more than that. Like when an Indigenous North American says "coyote." It's trickster, spirit, fairy, and animal too. Sometimes benign, sometimes dangerous. It's joy and sorrow both.

"*Huli jing*," says the Chinese woman. The term is more specific. Demon fox, spirit fox, fox fairy. There is more danger in her name, but still delight. She is also trickster and imp, but she is bloodshed, too.

"*Kumiho*," says the Korean woman. Her name, too, is demon fox, fairy fox, but there is much less humor. She is anger, vengeance, terror.

All three of them are beautiful. Up close, they are only old in wisdom, in their amber eyes. Physically, they're young, and I find myself looking from face to face, studying them. Their lips are beautiful, sensuous, sexy. I'm blushing; I can feel the heat under my skin.

The Japanese woman reaches up to her hair, pulls out pins, and it falls around her like a curtain. She reaches out to me and my hair falls down, too.

"Such a pity you cut it," she says, stroking my hair, my face. She leans closer, and kisses me. She's unbelievably soft. Her cheek is velvet under my hand, her lips pliant against mine, and I start to forget everything else. Then our teeth bump together and I remember. I pull away.

"Evgeny," I say.

"It must be love," says the Chinese woman, the *huli jing*. "If your charms don't work on her."

I stare at the table, blushing furiously. The Chinese woman touches my hand.

"Don't be ashamed," she says. "Beautiful women are called 'foxy' for a reason. Even you can feel our power, because we are seduction."

Then I realize what the warm, living smell is. It's them. And they smell like me.

The Chinese woman draws a pin from her hair and it falls down around her. She suddenly turns and throws the hair pin and it impales a bird in mid-flight. She gets up, fetches the bird, and sits back down. As she brushes against me, I feel heat between my legs. I try not to imagine what it would be like to spend an hour or two in bed with one of these women. I remind myself that, from far away, they are old.

The *huli jing* twirls the hair pin in her fingers. It's beautiful and deadly.

She sees me looking. "Do you like it?"

I nod.

She removes two more from her hair and passes them to me. "Then you must borrow them. But don't rely on them too much. Each time you throw one, it will become less accurate.

"What am I?" I ask.

"You are many things," says the Japanese woman, the *kitsune*. "You are human." When she says "human" her voice conveys warmth, intelligence and vitality, but also weakness, fragility.

The *huli jing* traces shapes on the back of my hand. "You are a little of us. Of *kitsune*, *huli jing*, and *kumiho*. We gave you our blood and our tears to make you stronger. To save your life. To give you vengeance, if you want it."

Then the Korean woman, the *kumiho*, speaks. "But you are more. Deep in your genes, you were already something more." She flares her nostrils. "Something like us, but not us. You are *fuchs*."

Fuchs. Fox. My surname. But what is that?

Then she smiles, but it's grim. She slides closer to me, whispers in my ear and I shiver, half in fear, half in desire. I picture Evgeny naked, and maybe she knows what I'm thinking, because she laughs. Then I realize what she's said. "You are vengeance."

She unwinds a silk scarf from her neck and brushes it against my face. It smells of an intoxicating perfume that makes my nipples stand up and my nether parts go warm and moist.

"Do you like it?"

I nod.

"Then borrow it. It can turn anyone's head, make them desire you. But take care not to overuse it, because desire can become possessiveness and that can be dangerous."

Then she leans back and I can breathe again.

"Ask your final question," she says.

"Why am I unfinished? Why hasn't the… the fox awakened in me yet?" It comes out more plaintive than I meant it to, and I feel childish. But the women look on me kindly.

"Your heritage," says the *kitsune*. "It manifests slowly, it seems."

"And our gifts are hampered by it," says the *huli jing*.

"You must awaken it yourself," says the *kumiho*. "I think avenging your violation will do it."

"We don't agree on this point," says the *kitsune*.

"We agree but little," says the *huli jing*.

"It was…." I hesitate. I've had my three questions, and I don't think they'll allow me another – if this works the way European fairy tales do – but I still want to know what happened to me here. I still want to *remember*, as awful as it might turn out to be. "I have no memories, before waking up in the park. Except fragments of this garden."

The *kitsune* nods. "We found you here, and left you there, with clothes and money."

"We hoped you would find your way."

"We are uncomfortable in the city."

"We did not know you had forgotten everything."

"We only meant for you to forget the trauma."

I puzzle over what I do know. "I came here. For whatever reason. I was here and then someone…. I was beaten. Raped."

The three women look at me, faces full of sorrow. "If we had found you sooner, we would have stopped him."

"We were busy elsewhere."

"We didn't see until too late. He was gone."

I feel tears burning behind my eyes, but I refuse to cry. I dare another question. "Did you… Do you… Who was he?"

"That is buried in your memory."

"But it happened here, in our garden."

"That much, we can show you."

Each of them reaches out a hand to touch my forehead and my vision starts to grey out, like in my dream, and then even their voices are gone.

Chapter Fourteen

I WAS AT THE FRONT gate of the Chesterly Formal Gardens, selling tickets in the office. I worked there, and though I found it tiring to deal with people all day, I liked it because my last task before going home was to walk the pathways to make sure everyone was gone who shouldn't be there. It was a lovely way to end the day, and I looked forward to it.

An hour or so before closing, a man came in. He was kind of good looking, if a bit beefy for my taste. A bit hairy. He leaned over the counter and asked if he could have a discount, since it was nearly the end of the day. His breath was minty, like he'd just finished sucking a strong peppermint, and his teeth were very white. He smiled and it made him look younger.

"Sure," I said, and gave him half-off the admission.

"What time do you get off?" he asked, and I mumbled something about working late. He seemed okay, and he wasn't repulsive, and I was single, but I had my eye on one of the apprentice gardeners. I hadn't yet had the courage to ask her out, but she always smiled when she saw me, and her "hey" always seemed a little bit breathless.

Half an hour to closing, I had to leave the front office to relay a message to one of the managers, so I left the rest of the front desk staff to get ready to close and headed out back. I delivered my message and swung by the main greenhouse – which was almost on my way back, anyway – to see if Alex was still there. That was her name, the red-headed gardener's apprentice. Before I got to the door, half-off guy stepped in front of me.

"Hi," he said.

"Hi," I answered. I looked at my watch. "We close in fifteen," I said. "If there's anything else you want to see, you should do it now."

It was getting on to twilight, and the lamps along the paths came on, making shadows that shifted and moved as the plants swayed in the breeze.

"I'm looking at what I want to see," he said, touching my arm. "Maybe you could show me around."

I smiled, tried to be pleasant. "Sorry, but I still have to work."

"There's gotta be someplace… private, where your boss won't notice you slacking off." His touch on my arm became a grip and he leaned close. I tried to pull away and his grip tightened. He grabbed my other arm and pressed himself against me. I could feel that he wanted me and it freaked me out.

I wasn't a prude. I liked sex, and I'd had a few boyfriends and a few girlfriends. But I liked to get to know my partners first, and I sure as heck didn't like to be pressured.

I wasn't scared, not really, because we were right outside the main greenhouse and I knew several of the gardeners were still in there, working. We were winding down for the season, but there was still plenty of work to do to prep for overwintering the plants. I could have screamed and people would have come to my rescue.

But I didn't have to, because suddenly Alex was there, and she was tall and strong and even guys bigger than her got nervous around her. She was like a Celtic goddess, all flashing dark eyes and a voice like poetry, if storm clouds spat sonnets instead of lightning. She made my knees weak.

"You have some business with my girlfriend?" she asked, and the guy looked flustered.

"Your girlfriend," he said. "What a waste." Then he let me go and walked away.

"Thanks," I said. I knew I was blushing fiercely, but I hoped she couldn't see it in the uncertain light.

"Any time," she said. Then she headed for the greenhouse door.

"Alex?"

She stopped and turned, something on her face, like hope, maybe.

"You want to maybe… have coffee or something?" I knew it was lame, but it was all I could think of.

She laughed, but not like she was laughing at me, like she recognized my awkwardness and found it cute. Instead of answering, she walked back over, touched my cheek, traced my lips with the tip of one finger, and kissed me.

I kissed her back. Of course I kissed her back, and she was wonderfully soft, but hard, too, with lean muscle and sharp bones. I opened my mouth so she could kiss me deeper and she slid her tongue in and I wanted to faint into her arms.

I forgot where I was and put my arms around her, felt her arms around me, her breasts pressed against mine. And I could feel her nipples poke against me and I knew she was as aroused as I was.

Finally, she pulled away. "Wow," she said.

I remembered that I was at work. "I have to go walk the rounds," I said. "And make sure everyone's gone."

"You want me to come with you? In case that creep's still here?"

I said yes, and she let her boss know and then we walked around the paths and didn't see a soul. Finally, we sat on a bench looking over the koi pond and held hands.

"How long till you have to lock up?" she asked. I was usually the last one out, so I did the final locking up. My manager said she wanted me to replace her when she retired, which would put me in charge of the whole public programming section. I wasn't sure I wanted that, but it was years away, anyway.

I checked my watch. "About thirty-five minutes."

Then she kissed me again and somehow we ended up lying on the deck under the stars. It was chilly, but I didn't feel it. She leaned over me. "You're beautiful, Panya," she said.

I reached up for her and pulled her mouth to mine. Suddenly I was so hungry for her. I put my hands inside her jacket, right under her shirt and her skin was like silk. She wasn't wearing a bra and I dared to move my hands around to her front, to touch her small, perfect breasts, feel her erect nipples on my palms.

She gasped and kissed me harder and put a hand inside my shirt. She had to fumble with my bra, but her hands were clever and it was soon out of the way. She smiled mischievously, then ducked her head, lifted my shirt, and took a nipple in her mouth. I felt like I could melt away into nothing, or burst into flame and fly away like ashes on the wind. I buried my hands in her hair.

She switched nipples, bit gently, sucked, and then her hand was on my thigh and sliding up my leg under my skirt.

"Alex," I said. She lifted her head to look at me. "Are we going too fast?"

"You've been giving me shy looks for six months," she said. "How long do you want me to wait?" But she moved her hand away. I took it in mine, and put it back on my thigh.

"I just don't want you to think I'm a slut."

"Do you really like me, or do you just want to fuck me?"

"I really like you." I was blushing again, from her language, and from the intensity of her look. She smiled.

"I don't think you're a slut." She kissed the end of my nose. "And I've been thinking about doing this for *ages*."

"Really?"

Instead of answering, she kissed me again, and as she did, her hand found my crotch, tugged my underwear down. I arched under her touch.

"Yes," she finally said. Her breasts were warm under my hands, and I wanted to put my mouth on them. She let me roll her over, and moaned quietly when I touched a nipple with the tip of my tongue. When I started to suck, she slid her hand between my legs, and her fingers parted my folds and I felt a rush of heat.

When she took her hand away I wanted to weep, but she lifted it to her mouth to taste my fluids and I must have stared because she grinned.

"Your cunt tastes so good," she said, licking her fingers. And that was the first time I heard the word "cunt" used in a nice way. It was the way I'd use it from then on.

I smiled and turned my attention back to her breasts, felt her fingers on me again, slipping between my folds, teasing me. And I fumbled with her cargo pants – fortunately they were loose-fitting because I wanted to touch her so badly I couldn't seem to make the zipper work. She shifted her hips so I could reach her and then we lay face to face, kissing, stroking each other, pushing our hips against each other. I was the first to come and she kissed me, hard, so I couldn't cry out. Then she came – I could feel how hard and swollen she was against my fingers – and kissed me again. We lay catching our breath and she said, "If we weren't in a public place, I would never have stopped you from making noise."

I smiled.

"There's nothing sexier than a beautiful woman screaming her lungs out from pleasure," she said.

I blushed again, but looked into her eyes instead of looking away. She was lovely, but she made me feel beautiful. Then my watch beeped and I realized I had to get back and lock up.

She looked at her own watch. "Shit," she said. "I shouldn't have stayed gone so long."

"You go ahead back," I said. "I'm going to sit here a minute." I wanted to collect myself before I went, just in case one of my co-workers was still there when I got back.

"You sure?"

I nodded, so she kissed me one last time, quickly, adjusted her clothes, and set off. She was almost to the bamboo forest when she turned and called back, "I still want to have that coffee sometime."

I was so full of joy I wasn't aware of anything else.

"Well, that was a nice performance," he said.

"The garden is closed," I said. "You shouldn't be here." I got up and started for the path that led back to the entrance by the quickest route.

"Oh, but I'm a paying customer," he said. He pulled a wallet out of his back pocket, took out a few bills, and tossed them at me. I walked faster and he kept up easily.

"Don't go," he said. "You forgot your money."

"Leave me alone," I said. I was just about to break into a run when he grabbed my hair – it was long and loose down my back – jerked me backwards, and I tripped and sprawled on the ground.

I scrambled backwards, but a kick in the ribs doubled me up and then he was on top of me, breathing hard and not from exertion. His hand went up my skirt, and I was still wet from Alex's touch, and he smiled.

"See, baby," he said. "You *do* want me." I drew breath to scream and he hit me backhanded across the face. I felt blood drip from my nose. Then he licked his fingers, tasted my fluids, and smiled. His teeth were too white, and too big.

I fought. I really did. I knew kung fu, and I was good at it. I fought hard when he hit me, but I was only human and he was strong. Too strong. He held me down while he ripped my clothes off of me, leaving welts when the cloth wouldn't tear easily, yanking off one piece of clothing at a time, down to my last sock. He kept one hand clamped over my mouth so I couldn't scream, though by then everyone had probably gone home and there wouldn't be anyone to hear me.

Then he opened his fly, pulled out his cock, and that was when I started to cry. But I still fought the whole time he was inside of me, and maybe that was why I was bleeding between my legs by the time he was done. He pulled out before he finished, wrapped a handkerchief over himself, and spurted into it.

"Fuck yeah," he said, "Oh fuck yeah," over and over. He was so heavy on top of me I could hardly breathe.

Then he did himself up, still one-handed. And he let go of me, just long enough to hit me so hard I blacked out.

When I came to, I was alone, bleeding, aching. Something felt wrong inside. Tears and snot and blood mixed on my face. I was on the lawn below the Shinto shrine, and as I got to my feet, I saw three women come down the path. There was sorrow in their eyes, and pity, and deep, rending anger.

"Help me," I said, "He —" I choked and vomited and the women surrounded me, comforting me, stroking my hair, saying calming things.

I passed out to the sound of their murmuring voices, arguing gently with each other. I drifted in and out of consciousness, got vague impressions of more blood, weeping, and pain, but also of gentleness, warm water, soft cloth. And when I finally woke at last, completely, I was not sore or bleeding any more. I was whole and healthy, but cold. And I didn't remember who I was.

I come to at the table in the gazebo and a tall, willowy girl with curly brown hair and velvety dark skin is looking at me curiously. "I'm sorry, miss," she says. "But we close in fifteen minutes."

I smile sheepishly. "I guess I fell asleep," I say.

"It is so peaceful here," she says.

I get up and start down the hill, but then I turn back. "Do you know if Alex Holz still works here?"

"I'm sorry, the name's not familiar. Do you know what area he was in?"

"She," I say. "She was a gardener. An apprentice. Tall, red hair."

She thinks, then her face brightens. "Oh yes," she says, and for a moment I'm filled with joy at the thought of seeing Alex again, though I have no idea what I'll say to her. I still don't remember anything beyond what the Asian women, the fox women, showed me.

Then the girl frowns. "She left, oh, almost a year ago, I think. I heard she got some great offer from one of the national gardens. She's really good, I guess."

"Oh well," I say. "Thanks."

"Someone told me," she says, then hesitates.

"What?"

"Well, I don't like to gossip, but the story was all over when I started working here."

"What is it?"

"Well, a woman went missing, just before she resigned to take the new job."

"Missing?" Something feels cold in my guts. I wonder how they took my disappearance.

"That's what they say. They found her clothes in the gardens, all torn up, like a wild animal got them. And she never came back to work. Your friend Alex was all broken up, I guess. Blamed herself, or something. So when she got the chance to go somewhere else, she took it. That's all I know. It was before I started here."

"Thanks," I say, and make my way off the hill. *Like a wild animal got them.* "Motherfucker," I growl under my breath. "That prick was a fucking werewolf."

All the way back home on the bus I can't stop thinking that I was raped by a werewolf. I've been thinking vamps are bad, and yeah they keep trying to suck my blood and they keep saying they want to fuck me, but none of them actually *have.* No, before I was strong enough to defend myself, kung fu or no kung fu, a goddamned were forced himself on me.

I can't decide if I should tell Magne or not. On the one hand, I don't want to admit I was raped, especially now that I remember it, now that it's not just an abstract concept. I understand now why so many women don't report rapes to the police. It's humiliating. Humiliating to have it happen in the first place, and humiliating all over again to have to tell someone about it. Especially a man. A man in authority, who's stronger than you. But on the other hand, I'm pissed. I don't think I've ever been so angry. It burns through me, in my veins, under my skin, until I half expect to see heat distortion from my own breath. One part of me wants payback, and Magne might be able to tell me who the guy is, so I can tear off his cock and stuff it down his throat.

But I'm also terrified that I can be so angry. It makes me feel strong, like Angry Su is right there with all her superpowers, like I *am* Angry Su, all the time, and not just when I'm in danger of dying. I feel barely in control of myself, like if I tip over that edge, just a little bit, I'll go on a rampage and kill every man who's ever looked at me with lust in his eyes or said a sly thing about how good I smell. And that would include Magne, who I think might be my friend. It might even include Evgeny.

It's not the thought of killing that bothers me so much, though I don't really like that either. It's the idea of not being in control. Being strong and on a rampage isn't that much better than being weak and pushed around by everyone else. Either way, its not you choosing your actions.

In the end, I don't have to decide whether or not to tell Magne because he's sitting on the front doorstep of our building when I get there and as soon as he looks at me, he's got to know something's up.

"You look scary," he says.

I stare at him, wondering what to say.

"And you smell really angry. How about I make you something to eat?"

It's such a considerate thing to do that I feel the anger ebb, just a bit, so I nod and let him lead me to his loft where he makes me a nice rare steak and fries with the potato skins still on.

He talks about inconsequentials as we eat, then he hands me a beer and says, "Drink. You're wound tighter than a... an overwound something-or-other."

We both laugh, and I sip at the beer. It's not my drink of choice, but it actually helps.

"Have you got any info about the vamp council's building?" I ask and he shakes his head.

"Should be soon," he says. "Don't worry. Now tell me what's really bothering you."

So I do. Not all the details. I leave out most of the sex and reduce the rape to a flat statement, but it's enough for him to understand.

"Jesus," he says softly. "You want another beer?"

I'm not even halfway through the first one, and I have no intention of getting drunk. It's nice to relax with a drink, but it's a bad way to solve your problems – or avoid them, rather – especially when you're as prone to deadly hangovers as I am. So I shake my head, but I don't pull away when he sits next to me and puts his arms around me. There's nothing sexual in it – I can tell from his scent – but just one friend comforting another. If it was the least bit suggestive I might have ripped his throat out with my bare hands right then.

Then he gets up and paces. "Describe this wolf again," he says.

I give him all the details I can remember.

"Was it a red handkerchief? One of those Western, cowboy ones with the white patterns on it? A bandana?"

I think about that. I don't want to, but I make myself remember the scene, the guy lying on me, hand clamped over my mouth, twisting away to spurt into a cloth. Red cloth.

"Yeah, I think it was." I shudder in disgust.

"Shit," he says. "I know who it was."

"Who is he?"

He shakes his head. "Not someone I know well. But I know what his name is, and I know how to find him."

"Tell me."

He smiles a grim, humorless smile. "You wouldn't be able to get near him."

"I'm about to infiltrate a whole building full of vampires, and you think I can't handle one were?"

He laughs, a short bark. "Well put. But this is different. Wolves have a better sense of smell than vamps, better hearing, and he's got a pack."

"Fuck," I say.

He puts a hand on my shoulder. "Look," he says. "Right now you worry about getting your bloodsucker boyfriend back."

"He's not –"

"Fuck that," he says. "You just don't want to commit. Of course he's your boyfriend."

That shuts me up.

"Get him free, deal with this vamp problem. You live through that, I'll bring you the wolf, and you can deal with him any way you like."

"You'd do that? Give up a fellow werewolf?"

He makes a sudden gesture with one hand, a chopping motion. "There are things you just don't do," he says. "Things no wolf will let another wolf get away with." He looks at me, and his dark eyes are almost blazing in the light from the fixture above his head. "Wolves don't kill in cold blood, we never harm children, and we do not rape. Not women, not men."

"So werewolves have a government, too." I'm teasing, just a little.

"It's not government," he says. "It's basic decency."

Chapter Fifteen

NIGHT COMES and I know the vamps will be doing their tests, feeding Evgeny's blood to their minions, feeding witch blood to Evgeny. I wonder if they're going to try to feed him so much *hexen* that the effects of drinking his blood don't wear off so quickly, or if they'll try to dilute it by feeding him other things so it doesn't make them tear their own skin off.

I wonder how they know what to do without Papa Vamp's notebooks. Maybe Papa Vamp wasn't the only one working on the project. Maybe Papa Vamp was even a rogue, working without his council's permission. He had his own lair, after all, did his feeding experiments away from them, like maybe he was plotting to take over, to cast down filthy rich Samuel Charleston and take over the council himself.

I consider trying to dream my way into Evgeny's head again, but after the last time, I'm not sure I want to. I feel bad, that he's going through torture all alone. Maybe if I thought he knew I was there with him, I might try, just so he would know there was someone with him. But I don't think that he does know I'm there. I don't think the human part of Evgeny is aware of much of anything.

So I pace around for while, pick books up, put them down. I take a shower, but cut it short because I have no patience for anything. I know fretting is no good, there's no point, I'm just burning energy, but I don't *want* to be calm.

Losing your calm will get you killed. The sentence suddenly echoes through my head and I stop moving. I stand in the middle of the room. It's a memory, I think. *Losing your calm will get you killed. Centre your mind, Angry Su. Let the rage flow around you.* And I smile. The speaker was a middle-aged Chinese man, an inch or so shorter than me, but so fast. He worked through the series of moves he wanted me to copy so quickly I had trouble following, and forgetting several in the sequence is what made me frustrated. When I first started to study kung fu, I was so full of anger all the time. "Angry Su," he called me, and the name stuck, even though I guess I went by Panya back then, going by the memory of Alex in the garden. After a few years of study, I didn't get angry so often.

The memory ends, but it leaves me smiling. I can't even remember my teacher's name, but he was so kind to me, to the messed-up teenager I was went I first marched into his class (but why was I messed up?), that even after the first lesson I knew I was going to be all right. And now his first lesson is more valuable than ever.

Anger can be a source of strength, when you think you have none left, but you mustn't let it overwhelm you. You mustn't let it make decisions better left to reason.

So I take a deep breath, sit on the floor and let calm buoy me up from the center of my being. All the anger, fear, uncertainty, I let swirl all around, there but not touching me. And when I feel my calm is unassailable I stand, and stretch, and go through that sequence of moves I remembered my teacher demonstrating. First, I go slow, feeling out the order of kicks and strikes and lunges. I practice silently. Some martial arts include yells, called *kiai* in Japanese, but my teacher never required them. It's good, because I don't like having to raise my voice. I'm more efficient when I control my breath, let it out it short bursts and hisses between my teeth.

Once I'm comfortable with the sequence, I start to go faster. I'm glad I left a big open space in the center of the loft, between the bed and the living area. It gives me room to really move, to spin and leap and strike. And soon I'm moving faster than my teacher ever did, faster than any human could.

It feels glorious, but eventually I have to stop. I'm shaking from the exertion, and sweaty, but now I'm genuinely calm. I can set aside thoughts of the rapist werewolf, and worries about Evgeny, and sharp pangs of missing Alex whom I've only just rediscovered knowing.

This time when I get into the shower, I have a long hot one, scrub myself and shave my legs, and lather my hair. It's gotten longer, just in the past couple of days, I'm sure of it. It's past my butt now. I could braid it into a garrote and use it as a weapon. Or get caught by it.

Then I sit by the window for a long time, just staring at the dimly-lit street, and the streak of reddish sky. I don't think of anything at all. And finally, I'm pretty sure I can sleep, so I get in bed.

I wake late in the day to a knock at my door. It's Magne, and he has a pile of papers in his hands. He looks at the empty space and says, "Nice décor."

"Ha, ha," I say. But I'm not feeling like banter. I'm still full of last night's calm.

He looks at me. "You seem different."

I shrug. "Coffee?" He agrees and so I put on the kettle, then duck into the bathroom to get dressed. I put on black. Black jeans, black t-shirt, black sweater. Then I braid my hair, coil it on my head, and pin it. Reaching for a last bobby pin my hand instead encounters something long and sharp. I look at the shelf below the mirror and there are the Chinese fox woman's three silver hair pins.

I blink stupidly at them. I'd forgotten all about them. I glance in the mirror at the back of the bathroom door, and there, hanging on the hook where I usually keep my robe, are the *kitsune*'s mask and the *kumiho*'s scarf. I leave the items where they are for now. I don't remember bringing them home, yet I must have done.

Magne's sipping coffee when I leave the bathroom, and he hands me a cup, like we're in his place and not mine.

I nod at the sheaf of papers he's put on the counter. "Is that some good news?"

"Well, it's info," he says.

"Tell me."

He must sense that I'm not in the mood for smalltalk. Seeing the foxes' gifts – borrowed items – has disturbed my calm, and I can feel the negative thoughts creeping back in. I need action so I don't have to think.

"It seems," says Magne, "that if Liam was going to send you into Mr Vampire Charleston's office tower, he was intending you not come out of it again."

For a long time I just stare at him, sipping my coffee stupidly. Then I muster a few brain cells and say, "Liam wants me dead?"

"Well, I don't think he so much wants you dead as out of the way so you can't tell his bosses he ratted them out to you."

"I'm confused. How is sending me straight to them keeping me out of the way? And Liam is working for the council?"

"He's not actually a minion." He says "minion" the way you might talk about a dog turd you just stepped in. "He's more of an independent contractor. He knows everybody, so he keeps tabs on them, and now and then he does jobs for the council. And it seems this council has been around in some form or other for hundreds of years."

"He told me a few years."

Magne snorts. "Technically, this version of the council has probably only been around for a few years, but it seems some not-so-elder upstarts took it over, started threatening vamps to do what they said, and then carried through on the threats. Word is, as long as they don't endanger the secret existence of Reborn kind, the real elders can't be bothered to make them stop."

"How did you learn all this?"

"I told you, I know a few people." He grins.

"I thought you meant werewolves."

"Wolves, vamps, a few other non-human types. Most of us had lives before we became *other*. Friends, lovers, family. I also know most of the same people Liam does, but they like me better. I'm not such a dick."

I have to laugh at that. "So what do I do about Charleston's building? Do you think Liam would tell them I'm coming?"

"Thing is, that may be where most of the minions are, but it's a red herring. I have it on good authority that's not where the action goes down."

"The action?"

"Whatever they're getting up to."

"So they want anyone who might be poking around in their business to go to the office tower and walk into a trap, and even if they avoid the trap, they don't learn anything because there's nothing to learn."

"Exactly."

"Do your sources say why Evgeny's papa vamp was working on his own?"

"He was a bit of a kook. A mad scientist type. No one really thought he'd have any success, but they kept an eye on him anyway. Then one of his progeny got super-strength, killed him, ate the rest and escaped. So they wanted to catch said progeny to add him to their collection."

"Evgeny didn't kill his papa," I say.

Magne grins. Maybe he's guessed who did, because I don't remember telling him. "They don't know that."

"I think Liam suspects. I didn't tell him, but I said Evgeny being orphaned was my fault." I thought about that. "But I don't think he knew until recently who Evgeny actually was."

"The good thing about our Liam," Magne says, "is that he seldom does anything without being paid. It makes him useful to the council, but less dangerous to us."

"They don't even know to ask."

"Exactly."

Then something else he said twigs in my mind. "What did you mean, 'add him to their collection'?"

"Supposedly, they have other... test subjects. It's just friend-of-a-friend info, but it makes sense."

I shudder to think of all the people that might be kept captive, just so a few old vamps can get stronger. Maybe that's where Papa Vamp got his witch blood, though where they found witches these days, who knows?

"So if they don't have Evgeny at the office tower, where is he?"

"Did you know," he says, a mischievous look in his eye, "that many buildings extend nearly as far underground as they do upwards?"

I raise my eyebrows. I wish I could just raise one; it's so much more effective. "And...?"

"What's the tallest building you can think of?"

"Hadley Towers." It's a monumental office tower, even bigger than Charleston's building.

"Think tall, not big."

Then I have it. "The Standard Comm Tower." It's a communications tower and a tourist attraction. I think it was the tallest building in the world – if you can really call it a building – for all of five minutes after it was completed. There's a monstrously long elevator to a big revolving viewing platform at the top, and all sorts of arrays and antennas all up and down it.

"It's got a multi-level parking garage under it, and below that, several levels of so-called R&D labs, leased to an S.E. Charles."

"And S.E. Charles is the current *nom de plume* of one Samuel Charleston, vampire."

"The same."

"He really tried hard to hide his identity with that pseudonym."

"He's like all bloodsuckers – cocky."

I sit on a stool by the counter and set my coffee cup aside. "What kind of security does it have?"

He picks up the pile of papers and shuffles through them. I see a cross-section of the tower, and pages of small text. He finds what he's looking for and hands the sheet to me. It's a work order for a private security company, listing an assortment of locks, keypads, cameras, and motion detectors. None of it looks particularly innovative, but I'm just a pickpocket, so it's going to be a challenge for me just to get through the most basic locks.

Magne taps the page I'm holding with his finger. "A good friend of mine works for the security company. It's owned by vamps, but most of them are decent. And it just so happens that they equip every lock they install with a master override. Just in case."

I don't ask, "Just in case what?" Instead I say, "And are these vamps you know good enough friends to give you the override?"

His smile is so broad his teeth show. Unlike a vamp's fangs, which fold back into concavities in the roofs of their mouths, like a snake's fangs, werewolves have heavy canines that are big and pointy all the time. They can be made to protrude a lot more though, but even withdrawn, they're huge. It's rather unsettling.

"They're not such great friends, except the one guy, but they don't like other vamps – especially these ones, apparently – trying to intimidate them into obedience. They were happy to give me the master code." He flips through the sheets and gives me another page. "They specifically said they don't want to know why I wanted it."

"You kept your name out of it?"

"Of course. But in a week, they're going to scramble the master during routine testing, so that's how long you've got."

"I only need a day," I say.

"Don't be in too much of a rush."

"If I don't do it soon, I'll either go nuts from the tension, or lose my nerve altogether."

"Okay, well, there are some basic floor plans here, but things have probably changed. They built the place with a lot of moveable walls so the space could be reconfigured."

"Moveable as in flimsy?"

"You should have such luck. More likely, they'd be even stronger than standard wallboard-type walls. Metal frames and panels, steel track to slide on, that sort of thing."

"Great."

"Yep. Great engineering."

"What about cameras?" That's a different problem entirely. You can break them, block them, shoot them out, but the very fact of them being obscured is sure to get someone to check out what's wrong.

"There are lots, and two separate guard rooms."

"So if I want to be unseen, I have to take out a lot of vamps."

"It might be better to be seen, but look like you belong."

"How am I supposed to do that?"

He considers, pours himself another big cup of coffee and gulps the hot liquid, seemingly impervious to scalding. "Go at night, when vamps are more active."

"And more apt to be run into in the halls."

"Maybe." He shrugs. "But the alternative is to be obviously *skulking* in the halls."

"What else? I guess vamps don't necessarily look any particular way."

He looks my black-clad self up and down. "It's supposed to be a research facility. Charleston's big in pet food, among other things."

"Pet foods? You've got to be kidding me. He made his pots of money selling dog kibble?"

"Very expensive dog kibble, I guess. Anyway, there will be labs. So wear a lab coat, carry a clipboard. See if you can pinch a name tag."

I don't think I've ever told Magne I pay the rent by picking pockets, but from the look he gives me, I think he might know. "Okay. Lab coat. Clipboard. Name tag."

"And walk around like you belong there."

"How do I do that, if I don't even know where I'm going?"

"Be the new girl. Ask dumb questions."

"Great. I have to be inconspicuous by being noticeable as the bumbling newbie." I sigh and rest my chin on my hand. I liked this plan better when I was going to sneak in like a cat burglar.

"You'll be fine," he says. "Getting in should be a piece of cake."

"Right, it's getting out that'll be a sonofabitch."

"If anyone in either of the security stations hits the panic button, the whole place will lock down and you'll be trapped until the all-clear is given."

"No master override for that?"

"If there is, my associates didn't see fit to provide it."

"Fantastic."

"Good luck. You should get some rest while you can."

"No way," I say. "I have to go buy a clipboard and a lab coat. And maybe glasses."

"Vamps don't need glasses."

"Right. No glasses." If this is how clearly I'm thinking, I'm in trouble.

I'm there just after sunset, across the street. I watch the last of the late-season tourists trickle out of the Standard Comm Tower and the lights go off in the ticket window. The young man who was selling tickets leaves in a group of other Tower employees, and then it's quiet.

I adjust my lab coat – I decided to leave my jacket behind even though it's cold, because I won't have anywhere to stash it once I'm inside, and walking around with a jacket over my lab coat would just look dumb, and draw attention. I watch, and try not to shiver.

Then a light comes on over a side door and I notice a sign on it in fancy brass. Even from this far away I can pick out the lettering. "Charles Industrial & Feed," it says, and under that, "Research and Development."

A few at a time, people arrive and go through that door. Some of them have lab coats on, like me, and others are wearing heavier coats. It will be winter soon. At first, I count the employees, and try to figure out which ones are human and which ones are vamp. I can't tell for sure, but I think almost all of them are vampires. I wonder why they don't have a day shift of humans. It would look more natural to have a 24-hour R&D lab than one that operates only at night. But then, there's so much weirdness in the world that not many people would do more than think, "Hunh, only at night. Weird," and go on with their lives. Because as far as they're concerned, vampires don't really exist.

I'm about to step into the street, to cross it and open that door, when another person leaves the shadows and walks over. I quickly melt back into my patch of darkness and watch. Sooner or later, I'm probably going to have to bluff my way past a vamp, but it's not just the fear of meeting anyone and revealing myself that stops me. It's also that she's familiar. It takes a moment to sink in, but just before she opens the door, she turns slightly and I see her face clearly and remember where I've seen her. It's the vamp from Evgeny's cell. The one who touched him, who called him "scum" and then started to give him a handjob. I wonder if she's on her way to him now. I wish she was heading into a forest or a tangle of back alleys. I have no doubt I could follow her easily there. But she's going right into a building I know almost nothing about.

I can either dash across the road and hope to catch the elevator with her, then hope she doesn't ask me who the hell I am and what the hell I'm doing there, or I can wait and try to pick up her trail later, and risk losing it. And then go back to plan A and wander around the complex with no clue where I'm going.

I smooth my lab coat, make sure the fox hair pins are firmly in place, and the scarf is twined around my neck, and the mask hanging down my back where it looks odd, but is at least out of my way. Then I take a deep breath, and sneeze. I'm wearing Evgeny's dirty t-shirt under my white coat. It's a little ripe, but it also smells like dirt and grave and vampire. I hope it's enough to make me inconspicuous.

Then I step out onto the sidewalk and cross the street like I know where I'm going. I pull on the door and step into a little lobby. There's a security door and I hold my breath while I punch in the code. It seems to take forever, but then the little light goes from red to green and there's a beep and then I'm in.

And there's the elevator, and the vamp woman. She turns as I enter, looks at me disdainfully, and says, "Good evening."

I smile tightly, pretending to be nervous at coming face to face with a higher-up, when really I'm terrified of what I've got myself into. "Good evening, ma'am," I say, and stare at my clipboard.

Then the elevator doors slide open and we get on. When they close, I feel like I'm being sealed into a tomb alive.

Chapter Sixteen

THE VAMP WOMAN presses a button on the elevator wall and looks at me funny. I stare at the glowing circles and try not to panic. The M button at the top is green – because it's where we are – and below it are six lights with no buttons, labelled P1 through P6. Then there are three smaller buttons labelled A, B and C.

The vamp woman pressed C. I give out a fake giggle and press A. "I just started," I say. "I keep forgetting where I'm supposed to go."

She looks down her nose at me, and since she's not much taller than I am, it's quite a feat. "Sign in on floor A," she says. "They'll tell you where your assigned station is." Her voice is full of condescension and I know it's affected – which means she very definitely wants me to know how far beneath her I am – because vamps have a limited range of vocal expression that they use automatically. Kind of like their facial expressions; they have to work at it to sound much of anything besides flat. She also flares her nostrils as she inhales, maybe to let me know I smell less than freshly-washed, or maybe just to pull more air in to see if I smell like a vamp. I guess I pass muster well enough because she turns and faces straight ahead, watching the digital display count down the floors as we descend. There are six levels of parking garage to go past, and the elevator is one of those super-high-tech-looking, but extra-slow models so the numbers flick on and off slowly.

If she smelled my nervousness, she must have figured it was new job anxiety. I have to make a choice now. Either I go to floor A and try to somehow get the people who sign in the new employees to give me the appropriate clearance to get wherever I need to go, or I follow this vamp woman to the lower floor, which is more likely to be where Evgeny is being kept. Maybe I can even follow her right to him. If I can think of an excuse to not get off when the door opens for floor A.

And that's going to happen any second. I start to feel panic edge in again and I take a deep breath – long and slow so I won't draw attention – and I sneeze again.

But it's not Evgeny's dirt-and-grave smelling t-shirt that's bothering my nose. It's a faint whiff of perfume from the scarf around my neck. And then I have a terrifyingly pants-wetting idea. I glance at the vamp woman and she's still pointedly ignoring me, so I unwind a length of the scarf from my neck, just about a foot of it, and waft it gently in her direction. She sniffs in disdain, but then her face softens from vamp-still to... I don't know, relaxed, maybe? A hint of a smile pulls at the corners of her mouth and turns her severe face pretty.

"That's a lovely scarf," she says.

"Do you like it? A friend gave it to me." I step closer and waft it again, then tuck it around my neck securely. I don't know for sure this will work, and I have no idea how much of the scent to waft at her, but I'm keeping the *kumiho*'s warning about too much love firmly in mind.

The vamp woman steps closer and nuzzles the side of my face. "Lovely," she says.

"Will you do something for me?" I smile and tuck a stray lock of her hair behind her ear. I hope I sound genuinely lovey and not like I really want to puke, which I do.

"Anything, darling," she says, and kisses my temple.

I glance at the digital display on the elevator wall. Almost out of time.

"Come with me to the sign-in," I say, then I pout. "They won't give me full clearance without authorization." Something shifts in her eyes, like maybe she's becoming suspicious, so I slide my hand to the back of her neck and pull her face into the scarf. When I let her go, the suspicion is gone.

"I'll get you every clearance it's in my authority to give," she says.

"Thank you, darling," I say and she smiles. As the elevator dings and the doors begin to slide open I say, "One more thing."

"Anything, my love." She starts to kiss me and I push her away gently, though I really want to knock her across the elevator with my boot.

"They can't know you're my…." I hesitate.

"Lover?" she says, voice husky.

"Right. They have to think you're still just my boss. It… we would be… frowned on. They'd make you leave me." I have no idea if any of this rings true, but I can't have a lovesick vampire woman hanging off me, especially if she's supposed to be a higher-up.

I hope I've guessed correctly that she *is* a higher-up.

"Of course," she says, and by the time the doors are open all the way she's looking at me disdainfully again and for an instant I'm worried that the scarf's scent has worn off, but then she surreptitiously reaches out and pinches one of my butt cheeks and I know it hasn't.

"Ma'am!" I say under my breath, pretending to be bashful and flattered.

When we get off the elevator I'm really glad I didn't opt for coming here on my own and bluffing my way through things, because I have no idea where to go.

You'd think the sign-in would be the first thing you see when you leave the elevator, but she leads me through several turns of the hallway before we get there. They could at least have put up signs. There's a blocked-off elevator door across from a glass-walled room labelled "Administration" and I realize we've come all the way around to the other side of the elevator shaft.

Vamp woman sees my glance and says, "They were supposed to install an elevator with doors on both sides, but ordered the wrong one. It'll be replaced next week, but until then we are inconvenienced. The new one, I'm assured, will also be considerably *faster*."

Her contempt for the people who installed the wrong elevator is obvious in her voice, and I have to admit that she's good at mimicking tone. I'm glad for the mix-up, though, because it gave me enough time to come up with my desperate plan on the ride down.

Vamp Boss Lady ushers me into administration and leans over a skinny young man in a sweater vest who's pecking at the keys of a computer like he's not quite sure what they're for.

"We have a new employee," she says.

When he sees her, Computer Boy sits up straight and says, "Yes Ma'am. What's her name?" He presses a few keys and I can see by the color of light the screen throws on his face that he's opened a new window.

Crap. Name. Obviously I can't give my real one. But *any* name is going to be the wrong one, because I'm not really a new employee. But I also can't say nothing. They're waiting for me to answer.

"Lily Cheung," I say. I look Chinese; I might as well sound the part.

The boy types and says, "There's no record of your hire." Naturally.

I step behind him and lean over him, letting the end of the scarf tickle his nose. "Oh," I say and point to the screen. "It's L-I-L-Y. Only one 'L' in the middle."

He types some more. "No," he says. "It's still not here." But he looks at me, mouth slightly open, like he's hoping I'll turn and kiss him.

"There must be a mix-up," I say. Then lower, so (maybe) the others in the office can't hear, "Surely you can fix that. You look so… capable." I suck at flirting, especially when my heart is very definitely not in it, but it seems to work anyway. He starts up a different program, opens a new document, and begins to fill out the form that appears on the screen.

When he gets to "FIRST NAME" he types carefully and says "L-I-L-Y" under his breath as he hits the relevant keys. I give him phony contact info and make up some truly crap-sounding previous employment that anyone with half a brain can probably tell are not only fake, but were thought up by someone who has no idea what sort of previous employment a lab monkey in pet food R&D would have. But neither Computer Boy nor Boss Lady seem to think any of it's weird. Finally, he gets to the credentials, and Boss Lady waves her ID in his face.

"Full clearance," she says.

"I'm sorry," he says, "but the system requires a security code from the Big Man himself for that." He actually does look apologetic, or rather like a puppy unable to do what its master is asking.

"Well, as much as my security level can give her, then."

So he types some more. I lean over him again and say, "Surely you know the secret code," and I nuzzle his ear. Boss Lady looks miffed at that so I back off. No sense in starting a lovesick vampire fight. That would obviously draw a lot of attention.

"I wish I did," he says. "I really do. But you got the next best thing to full clearance. Only one level down."

He gets me to stand in front of a white wall and snaps my photo with a digital camera, then I sign an electronic tablet, press my fingertips to a fingerprint reader — I don't remember *that* in the specs Magne got for me — and the next thing I know I've got a brand new staff ID with an embedded chip holding my security clearance info. And I didn't even have to steal it.

Before we leave the administration office, I glance around. There are several other employees in the office — all staring at their computers and tapping at keyboards. Out the glass wall on the far side I can see a grey hallway and a door marked "Security A-1." That would be one of the two security stations. I wish it had windows so I could see inside.

Out of view of the office, Boss Lady links her arm in mine. "Only Samuel himself and his closest associates have higher clearance than you now."

"Are you one of those closest associates?" I say. I don't like that her arm is through mine, and not only because I don't like her. Remembering how she touched Evgeny makes my skin twitchy. But there are also security cameras everywhere and it probably looks odd to have this usually frigid, stiff woman walking so intimately with some inconsequential employee. But I don't want to upset her, either.

Now I have to figure out what to do with her.

"I am," she says, smiling. "Which means I can get into more places than you. *Secret* places."

"Maybe you can take me with you." I try to make my voice sexy. I had planned to get rid of her somehow, after getting my fake ID — I like to skulk around alone, generally — but it could be worthwhile to stick with her a little longer. At the very least I should be able to get her to tell me where Evgeny is.

"Maybe," she says, and leans over to kiss me.

"Wait," I say, and she stops. "Someone might be watching." I indicate the closest camera with a jerk of my chin.

"Of course, you're right," she says.

Then the elevator door opens and we get on — fortunately, there's no one else in it — and as soon as the doors close she's pinned me to the wall and has her tongue in my mouth. I pull away. "Wait," I say again.

"No cameras on the elevator," she says. "They decided not to install them, since they have to replace the elevator anyway." And she kisses me again. I try to go along with it, to pretend I'm into it, but I really want to bite off her tongue and spit it back in her face.

After a moment she pulls away and giggles. It's a horrible sound, coming from her. She pats her hair into place and adjusts her uncomfortable-looking, but very business-stylish, suit jacket. Her movements attract my eye to a gold watch chain running from one button hole into her jacket pocket.

"You've got me all flustered," she says. "Thinking with my pussy." I hate the word "pussy," and I don't want to think about hers. At first glance, "pussy" seems less offensive than "cunt," but equating genitals to animals creeps me out. And yeah, I know a cock is a rooster, but for some reason it doesn't weird me out the way "pussy" does.

"Which floor?" I say, to change the subject.

"Do you want to see the deep dark secrets?" she says in her breathy-rough smoker's voice. She leans over me to breathe on my neck.

"You know I do," I say, and I lick her cheek, trying not to gag. I don't want to touch her this intimately. I don't want to touch her at all. Hell, I want to be as far from her as I can get. But I have to keep her on my side as long as I can, so I pretend like she overwhelms me with desire.

"Then it's down to C floor, and then on to the other elevator."

The *other* elevator? Does that mean there are more floors? I'm beginning to think Magne's information is woefully incomplete.

She presses the C button and the elevator begins its sluggish decent. It stops at B and the door slides open and there are three people waiting. My stomach feels like it's trying to crawl up out through my throat.

"Up?" one asks, hopefully, though surely there's an indicator arrow out there that they can see. If not, then the elevator installers really *did* do a lousy job.

"Down," Boss Lady says, all her contempt back in her voice. I smile apologetically – I'm behind her so she can't see – and one of the group gives me a little grin in return. So maybe not all vamps are bad. Then the door closes and we descend some more.

"How many levels are there?" I ask. I might as well get as much information as I can, while I can.

"Three more below C," she says, turning to look at me. "X, Y, and Z."

"And what's in them?"

"My, but you're curious."

I stare into her eyes, looking for any hints of suspicion creeping in, wondering if I should use the scarf again, but there's nothing that I can see. "I just want to know all about your work," I say. "All about you." I lean close and whisper that last bit into her ear. A slight flush spreads over her cheeks.

"I would very much like to remove all your clothing and explore your body with my tongue," she says and I try not to let my revulsion show. "I'll bet you have the sweetest, tightest little pussy." And she slides her hand to my crotch and rubs. I very nearly elbow her in the teeth, but instead I step back.

"Soon," I say. "We're at floor C."

"Too bad," she murmurs, then leads the way off the elevator. "The lower floors," she says, "are where we do R&D on Reborn sustenance." I'm glad there's no one else around to hear her spilling secrets to me.

"How exciting," I say. "What kind of sustenance?"

"This must never get out," she says, and I mime zipping my mouth shut. "But we have a variety of *others* that we've been…working with to develop new sources of blood. New… flavors. New benefits for the Reborn drinker."

"*Others* like werewolves?" I follow her through the maze of hallways. Some of the rooms have large windows through which I can see people working at various tasks. There is all sorts of equipment – very shiny and expensive-looking – that I have no idea of the purpose of.

"Weres…" She says the word like a human might say "roaches."

"Fairies, even –" her voice drops conspiratorially – "witches."

"Witches," I say, filling my voice with awe. "I thought they had died out."

She smiles and her fangs pop down. She giggles and puts her hand to her mouth. When she takes it away, her fangs are folded back again. "Oops," she says. "You got me all excited."

I smile, wishing I could just find Evgeny and get away from her.

"We've been collecting witches for years," she says. "Decades. Though you're right, they are terribly scarce. And we can't even drink them. Not yet anyway. But they have other uses."

I don't think I want to know what those "other uses" are. "Not yet?" I ask.

She smiles slyly and says, "That's the biggest secret of all. One of our… associates discovered there may be a way to filter *hexen* blood through another non-human so we can partake of it." Now she looks uncertain, as if she's starting to realize she's said too much.

I touch her hand, lean close enough for her to catch the scent of the scarf and say, "How *exciting*."

And then we round a corner and there's another security station with a full-body scanner and the other elevator beyond it. I wonder if silver shows up on their scanner. The three knives I borrowed from Magne sure as hell will.

"They won't know you," she says. "So let me do the talking."

So I wait while she goes into the security station – this one has a big window. I wonder if I should duck around the corner and remove the knives and stakes from my body, stash them somewhere. But if I'm going to need them, chances are I'll need them on the lower levels, because once I find Evgeny, I may well have to fight my way back out. On the other hand, attempting to get them through the scanner is going to attract way more attention than I need. I look around, hoping a solution will present itself. The only other doors in the hallway are two washroom doors across from the security station, one on this side of the scanner and one on the other. Both are marked "Staff Only," with no little stick-person-in-trousers or stick-person-in-a-dress symbol to indicate male or female, just an icon of a toilet and sink. Probably they're both one-seaters, so it doesn't matter who uses them.

I glance in the window of the security station and see Boss Lady is waiting impatiently to talk to a burly man. His attention is on his telephone, and the other person in the room, an equally burly woman, is doing something complicated-looking with the wiring on a computer and ignoring Boss Lady entirely.

As I push open the door of the closest washroom, I realize the absurdity of the "Staff Only" sign. Who else could get this far into the complex?

Inside, I lock the door. As I guessed, it's just a single room with an impeccably clean toilet and a sink with a dripping faucet. There's really way more room in here than they need. They could easily have fit at least three toilets in a row on the back wall.

Now what? I had vague ideas of stashing my weapons in the toilet tank. Yes, I'd rather have them on me, but I can't think of any way to get them past the body scanner. Unfortunately, the toilet is the kind that doesn't *have* a tank, like the ones they have in shopping malls. The garbage can?

But then I notice an air vent high on the wall above the toilet. I stand on the lid – luckily the toilet isn't also the lidless kind – and peer in. I was hoping I would look right through to the other washroom. No such luck. But I pry the grate off anyway and stick my arm inside as far as I can, which isn't that far since it's still above me on the wall. Through the wall and to my left, my fingers encounter another grate. Excellent.

So I climb back down, strip off my lab coat, and pull off all the knives, stakes and pointy objects I've got hidden on me and slide them into the vent. Then I pop the grate back in, put my lab coat on, and flush the toilet.

Just then there's a knock at the door. "Lily?" says Boss Vamp's voice. "They're ready for you."

For a moment I have no idea who "Lily" is, and then I remember she's me. My fake name. I look in the mirror and see my amber eyes are wide and frightened-looking.

"Be right there," I say. I stare at myself, breathe deep and quickly wash my hands and dry them on a paper towel. I concentrate on calm until the freaked-out look on my face fades and vanishes, replaced by careful stillness.

"Okay," I say, barely vocal. "Here goes." And I step back into the hall to face the vamp security detail.

"Sorry," I say, pressing a hand to my lower belly. "I must have eaten something that disagreed with me."

"They often do that," says Boss Lady, with what passes for humor in vamps, I guess. "Until you break their necks."

Chapter Seventeen

THE BURLY SECURITY GUARD stands on the other side of the scanner, looking bored.

"Come on through," he says.

So I step into the arch, stop when he says, wait while he checks his screen, then step the rest of the way through. I stand still as he checks places that show up with metal on them – my boots (aglets, metal-tipped laces, and steel toes), my belt (buckle and studs), my hair (bobby pins and the *huli jing*'s hair pins), and my clipboard.

"ID," he says. Talkative fellow. So I hand over my card and he scans it, then scans my fingerprints. My stomach is roiling and I'm glad I didn't eat much during the day. The sound it makes lends verisimilitude to my story about something I ate not sitting well, which is good, because I'm about to make use of it again.

"New girl, eh?" he says. "You must come highly recommended." He hands back my ID, touching my hand as he does. He licks his upper lip with the tip of his tongue.

"Why do you say that?" Any more of this nerve-wracking inspection, and I'm not going to have to *pretend* to need the washroom.

"Most employees here have to work their way through the ranks to get to the lower floors."

"She's very good at what she does," says Boss Lady, and Security Vamp immediately steps back.

"Of course," he says. "You're all clear." As he heads into the security station he smirks at me and wiggles his eyebrows like he knows I'm fucking the boss lady and that's how I got my job. Except of course I'm not. I just made her fall in love with me by waving a pheromone-laced scarf under her nose.

I guess Boss Lady did the whole security thing while I was in the washroom, or else she's so high up she doesn't have to, because she just walks through the scanner and toward the elevator. I follow her, and just as she's pushing the button I clutch my belly and groan softly.

"I'm so sorry," I say. "But I'm going to have to hit the can again. Whoever I had for breakfast is really not sitting well."

"Take your time, dear," she says. "And consider switching to Charleston Reborn meals. All the unfortunate additives humans put into themselves are filtered out."

She sounds like a walking advert. And I'm not going to take too much time, because I don't know how long it will take for the *kumiho*'s scarf to wear off.

So I stumble into the washroom, lock the door, and slip off my lab coat. And then I see a problem. The other grate is there, but it's just far enough to one side of the toilet that I won't be able to reach it by standing on the seat.

"Shit," I mutter, and look around. The only other possibility is the garbage can, and it doesn't look very sturdy. But what choice do I have? So I lift the peaked lid off and pull the bag out – no sense in dumping trash all over the floor. Then I upend the can under the vent and climb on. It tips and I nearly tumble off backwards. Wouldn't that be grand, I get this far and then crack my head open on a bathroom floor? The can creaks alarmingly, but it holds, so I reach up, pop the grate off, and reach inside. I have to hold the grate between my knees and stick knives and stakes in my belt, which almost sends me to the floor again. But I manage.

Just as I get the grate back on the garbage can splits down one side and starts to buckle. I jump clear and land so hard my ankles ache. But I've done it. I redistribute my weapons on my person, put the garbage can back together – I turn the split to the back so no one will see it when they come in – and put my lab coat back on. Then I actually use the toilet because I might as well pee while I have the chance. Who knows when I'll get another opportunity?

When I go back into the hall, Vamp Lady has a hard look in her eye and she keeps shooting me weird glances, so as soon as we get on the elevator I step close and give her a whiff of the scarf.

"Careful, lover," she purrs. "The lower level elevator does have a camera."

"Oops," I say, in my best cute girl voice, and step back.

"Once we get to my office, I'll ravage you properly," she says, staring ahead at the door and pretending to look severe.

I certainly hope that never, ever happens. But I make myself giggle and say, "Oh, I hope so. But first you'll give me a tour, right?"

"Of course," she says.

We get off on floor X. I still don't know where Evgeny is, and Boss Lady has decided to give me the full tour. She turns aside any more questions with, "Just wait and see, darling. Just wait and see."

So I follow. Level X is more labs like the floor above, but instead of a mix of vamp and human technicians, these ones seem to be all vamp, at least as far as I can tell. Every one I look at has eyes that flare purple when they catch the fluorescent lighting. Some of them even seem to be working with their fangs hanging out.

Boss Lady laughs when I mention it, drawing a few stares. "It's hungry work, dealing with blood all the time. Some of the younger whelps aren't so good at controlling themselves."

Do they ever, you know… sample?" All the blood is in vials and beakers and bottles. Not a bloodbag to be seen.

"If they do, they're immediately terminated," she says. "Not all the work we do here is… healthy."

I think about how they drugged Evgeny. But that wasn't an in-house recipe. They got that cocktail from Liam. Maybe she doesn't mean drugs. Maybe she means something else. Something worse. Biological warfare for vamps? I don't quite dare ask.

Then I wonder what she means by "terminated." Maybe they're not simply fired.

"All our employees are well fed in the cafeteria," she says.

After what seems like an hour of wandering up and down corridors and looking in lab windows – plus a stop at said cafeteria where I refuse a snack (this gets me a piercing look, but then I smile cutely and she seems to forget) – I put on a pout.

"This is all very interesting," I say. "But it's nothing I haven't seen before. I was hoping for something more… exciting."

She looks exaggeratedly disappointed, and puts on a pout of her own. "But I'm getting to that, darling," she says. "I want to set the stage, build *anticipation*."

"Oh, of course," I say. "But the sooner you give me the grand tour, the sooner you can… show me your office."

Her eyes brighten and she looks like a vulture, eyes hooded with desire, predatory gaze, sharp beak, and all. "Oh, *yes*," she says, holding the "s" for far too long. "Level Y should whet your appetite." She leers. "And if you like a little… depravity, it'll wet your pussy, too."

I roll my eyes at her back as she leads me to the elevator again. Does she really think that was sexy? Or funny? Because it just made me want to vomit.

Floor Y turns out to be much more promising. Beyond a row of offices arranged along a grey corridor – she points to hers and licks her lips as we walk by – there are more labs, but these look like they're part of a veterinary surgery, but for really big dogs.

The technicians in these labs wear heavy gloves and lucite face masks – a few even wear chainmail shark suits – and the "patients" are *others*. Non-humans. Weres, mostly, as far as I can see, but there are some I can't tell what they are by peering through the lab windows at them. There are other vamps there, too, eyes glassy and jaws unhinged. I stare at each one, hoping to find Evgeny, but none of them are him.

In one lab, empty of technicians, a little girl huddles in a cage. She looks barely conscious.

"You have children here?" I ask.

"*Hexen*," she spits. "Barely more than an animal."

I try not to shudder, because I don't want to arouse any suspicion, but

I wish I could free the poor child. There is way more nasty stuff going on here than I had at first thought. How can I possibly leave here with just Evgeny? But I'm only one small not-quite-human. How can I save them all?

I can't turn away. But then a technician enters. He's got extra-heavy rubber gloves on and some kind of science-fiction hat all covered in electrodes and wires.

"To shield his mind," Boss Lady says. "*Hexen* are poisonous to the brain." She laughs. "Poisonous to the belly, too. But if we could drink them, ah, then we could control the mind, too." She sounds excited. Elated.

As I watch, the tech opens the cage and drags the girl out, then puts manacles on her wrists and a bag of some shiny substance over her head. When he's snugged it shut at the neck with a drawstring, he takes off his bizarre headgear and pulls the girl out the door. We turn and watch them go by.

"Where's he taking her?" I ask.

"The kennels," she says. "We keep all the curs safely locked up on Z floor." She smiles and her voice goes hushed. "And our greatest prodigy is there," she says. She sounds like she's having a religious experience.

"What's that?" I say.

"A newborn who can metabolize *hexen* blood," she says. "He can consume any *other* blood too, but he's the only one we've ever found who can eat witch and live."

"And then you can drink him?" I say, trying to fill my voice with awe. Really I'm terrified and sickened.

Her elation fades. "Not quite yet," she says. "He's not as toxic as an actual witch, but he still sickens us, kills the weak. We're working on getting the right proportions of various bloods and drugs to feed him. We're close. So close."

She's grabbed my hand as she's speaking and now she pulls me along. At first I think she's taking me to the elevator, to show me floor Z, but instead she pulls me into her office, pushes me against her desk, and starts trying to take off my trousers.

"Wait," I say. "You haven't finished the tour."

When she looks up at me, she's gone vamp, jaws unhinged and fangs unfolded. "Fuck the tour," she says. "I'm hungry."

"I thought…" I stammer. "We were… lovers."

"Oh, I'll fuck you," she says. "I'll lick you until you scream, and you my dear will lick me. But first I'm going to drink a little of your blood. Your thighs look especially tasty."

Maybe I should have waited, waved the scarf under her nose again, tried to get her to show me the lower floor, but sheer terror takes over me and I break the first rule of martial arts as I learned them – I let my fear decide for me. When she turns back to my crotch and bends over, I pull out one of the *kumiho*'s hair pins and stick her with it.

It slides in like a toothpick into an oven-hot cake – I have a sudden unsettling memory of my mother testing the done-ness of a birthday cake by sticking a wooden toothpick into it – and she collapses to the floor. I wouldn't have thought a thin sliver of metal like that would be so effective. But even though I didn't throw it, maybe it still has the *huli jing*'s accuracy, maybe it hit her heart just right and being silver did more damage that its size would suggest.

I pull it out, wipe it on her suit jacket, and then put it back in my hair. I take her pulse – a vamp's heartbeat is usually slow and weak, but still detectable, but she was excited so hers should be more obvious – and I can't feel anything. I should probably cut her head off to make completely sure she's dead, but I can't bring myself to do it.

"Fuck," I say. Then I take her ID badge and her pocketwatch and stash them in my own pockets. And maybe I've seen too many spy movies, but I think about fingerprint scanners, and feeling really icky the whole time, I slice off her index finger with one of Magne's knives and find an envelope in her desk to stash it in. It doesn't bleed much, thanks to vamp physiology, but it's still pretty grisly.

Then I drag her body behind the desk, where it won't be so obvious from the door, and head for the elevator again.

It takes forever for the elevator to arrive from wherever it took its last passenger – though it could only be one floor in either direction. I'm terrified the whole time. The jolt of fear I felt when Boss Lady looked up at me all fanged out hasn't gone away, and it's getting stronger every moment. I breathe deep and try to find my way to stillness. I've just about got it back when the lift arrives and the doors slide open and I'm face to face with the biggest werewolf I've ever seen, halfway to wolf form, saliva dripping from his jaws like a B movie monster.

I think I make some kind of squeak as I jump back, followed by, "Jesus!"

The skinny lab tech next to the were – the same one who dragged the witch child away not long ago – laughs. It's a thin sound, like he doesn't use it very often. "Don't worry," he says. "This guy's so full of juice he's harmless."

By "juice" I assume he means some kind of sedative or behavior-modifying drug.

"I was just startled," I say, forcing my breathing to slow, then slower still, so I'll seem more like a vamp.

"You must be new here," he says.

"Just started today."

"Well, I hope you do okay. We tend to have a high turnover of newbies." He leads the werewolf down the hall.

"Thanks," I say to his back and he raises a hand in acknowledgement.

I get on the elevator and press the button for floor Z. Under the buttons is a slot, like a card reader, and a tiny fingerprint scanner with a minuscule numberpad below it. I didn't notice them on the ride down from security, or from floor X, because Boss Lady took charge and stood in front of the buttons. I think about her card and her finger in my pocket and wonder. But right now I need to see if Evgeny's down here.

I step into the hall and there's no buffering row of offices between me and the "kennels" as I was expecting. There's just a long row of cells – cages – extending in both directions. It's not exactly noisy – I don't think anyone occupying any of the cages is conscious enough to be noisy – but there's a low murmuration of labored breathing, moans, and even weeping. It's the last that damn near breaks my heart. Somehow, I'm going to have to get all these people out.

Like a kid in grade school, I look around for a fire alarm. I don't see one, but I bet there is one somewhere. And then I wonder what they'd even do in a fire. I haven't seen any stairways and there's just one elevator between X and Z floors and one between C and the surface. Even if one assumes they'd abandon the menagerie to a fiery death, how do all the employees get out?

I look up and down the hall. Aside from the prisoners, there doesn't seem to be anyone around. I suppose the staff only come here when they need to retrieve a specimen. I have to pick a direction soon, or some security monkey on the other end of that camera feed is going to notice. So I glance at my clipboard as if I'm checking the location of a prisoner and begin to walk. I go left first, not because it looks any more promising, but just because I happened to get off the elevator closer to that side.

I look into each cell as I pass. They're furnished identically, with a bunk, a toilet, and a shelf with a pitcher of water and a plastic cup. The bunks look hard and uncomfortable, but I don't think any of the occupants are in any state to complain. I wonder how the vamps can think they're doing science when the specimens are so drugged up they must surely contaminate the samples.

Each of these cells contains a vampire. Most of them are skinny, even for vamps, and look like they haven't had decent exercise in years. I find myself feeling sorry for them. The poor things thought they were gaining eternal health when they were reborn, and instead they're kept like cattle – worse than cattle – by their own people. It's a mercy, I suppose, that they're too out of it to know.

I turn the corner at the end of the hall and see more rows of cells. If Evgeny is their "prodigy" they've probably got him stashed somewhere away from the general rabble, and judging by the dream contact I had with him, it's somewhere dark and quiet – and not just drugged-prisoner quiet, but really and truly silent.

I know he's probably not in this main block, but I can't help but walk down another row, and another. I make sure to keep glancing at my clipboard, so I'll look sort of like I'm doing something productive, and every now and then I stop and pretend to make a note.

I walk down a row of weres – mostly wolves, but there are a few others. Some of them are in human form, but the mind-blanking effects of whatever drugs they're kept on have reduced many of them to the animals vampires say they are. Under other circumstances it would be interesting to observe the different stages of lycanthropy present. None of them is so old they look completely wolf-like, but otherwise they range from mostly human but looking wrongly-jointed, to standing on all fours like it's their natural state. If Magne had known the extent of the vamp council's "collection," he might well have mustered that army for me.

There are rows of less identifiable *others*, though I do see one I'm pretty sure is Papa Vamp's *síog*, the Jinny Greenteeth, or another of her species. Her cell is different from the others because she's got a bathtub instead of a bunk, and she floats in it on her back, her hair spread out around her and looking an awful lot more like pond scum than you'd think possible. She seems less drugged than the others and she watches me pass with bright green eyes. I shudder and hurry on.

Finally past the rows and halls and corridors of cells – I don't even try to calculate how many non-humans are kept here – there's a dark grey wall with three doors in it. The first I come to says "Maintenance" on it, and I assume they keep all the food for their captives there, and all the cleaning supplies and things. It has a simple card reader on the door and I'm tempted to go in just to see what's there.

The second door says "High Security" and it has a card scanner and a fingerprint scanner. I wonder if my security clearance will get me through it, because that's probably where Evgeny is. But because I want to be thorough and not make any mistakes, I move on to the third door. It says "Warning: Wear Mind-Blocking Headgear at All Times." *Hexen*. I think of the weird hat the tech had worn, and I think I maybe should have borrowed it.

I put a hand on the door. I should just go and get Evgeny out and get the hell out of here before somebody suspects something. There's an itching between my shoulder blades like someone's going to shoot me there any minute. Or like someone is staring intently. I glance up at the security camera and down at my clipboard. I tap my finger on it. I should get Evgeny. I start to turn away, but then I remember the witch child, dragged away with a thought-blocking bag over her head.

"Damn," I mutter. I can't just walk away.

I pull out my card and slide it into the reader. It seems forever before the light turns green and I can pull it out. Then I swipe my finger over the print scanner. The red light goes amber and blinks and I don't know what to do. What does it mean? Is it a signal to security? Desperately, I swipe my finger again and the amber vanishes. I almost panic, but then the light goes green and the door unlocks with a "click."

I hesitate, hand on the door handle.

"Oh, fuck," I say, and pull it open and step inside. For a long moment after the door closes it's completely silent. Then their thoughts hit me all at once.

Chapter Eighteen

I LOVE MUSIC, but I can never play it very loud for long, because after a while even my favorite tunes start to feel like a physical assault. It's weird, and it's probably one reason I don't play an instrument. As much as I love the sound – and I really do – I can only take it for a short time. Crowds of people kind of feel the same way.

And that's what it's like when I step through the door of the witch area and it closes behind me. The voices in my head hit me exactly the same way as that point in listening to music when I just can't take it any more and I have to shut it off. Like the sound waves are bashing against my grey matter and creating a throbbing not-quite-headache. Except the witches aren't making any actual sound; it's all inside my mind. And it's way stronger than loud music.

And even though it's not physical, it still slams me back against the wall. Or maybe I slam myself against the wall, trying to get away from it. And it fills my head so full I can't make out any individual voices. It's an almost unbearable pressure.

And I realize, finally, that it's a pressure with *direction*. An attack. I've walked in acting like an employee of this horrible place, unprotected, and they're striking out. I think they're trying to beat me into submission, in a way. Squash my free will, so I'll do what they want, which is probably to set them free.

I find myself trying to claw my way backwards through the wall, or trying to bash out the back of my own head. Or both. As my shoulders hit, the fox mask jabs into my back and, desperate, not really thinking – because I can't think – I yank it around to my front and clap it into place on my face. And instantly there's silence.

Three heart beats. Four. Then a voice, a physical, sound-producing voice, says, "*Fuchs.*"

"I'm here to help you," I say, and I really hope no security guards are looking at their monitors just now. My voice sounds weird in my ears. Muffled, sharper.

"Take it off before they see," says the voice, echoing my own apprehension. "Put on the shielding hat so you won't be noticed."

Gingerly, I take the mask from my face, afraid of the voices, but they've stopped. I look around, conscious of my surroundings again, and spy a mad-scientist hat on a nearby table, so I put it on.

Then, finally, I can look around. I hold my clipboard up, pen at the ready, so I look like maybe I'm actually doing something like work, in case anyone checks the camera. I see only a single one, high in the corner at the end of the row of cells, and it's aimed at the door. I guess they're more concerned about who comes in than what the prisoners are doing, which seems backwards to me.

The room is long and narrow, with one row of cells on the right side. There's a wall beyond the table on the left side, blocking off an area about half the length of the room. There's a door with a number pad, but no sign to indicate what's in there.

"Medical supply," says the voice, an older woman with a strong German accent. "They require different drugs for us than for the others, so they keep them in there. I have only seen one man – one Reborn man – open that door."

"You don't seem drugged," I say, turning to locate the speaker. She's in a cell about halfway along, and she's sitting on the floor at the far side of her cell, arm reaching through the bars to clasp hands with the person in the next cell. The child. "Except her," I say. "She doesn't look so good."

"The drugs affect children much more. The rest of us have built up a tolerance but we pretend to be more affected than we are."

"We were going to escape," says another voice, a somewhat younger woman in a cell closer to me. She has curly brown hair and intensely deep green eyes. "We were waiting for someone dumb enough to come in without the headgear, but you spoiled our plan." She smiles, so it's not a rebuke. "Now how about you tell us who you are and why you're here, because I don't really think you came for us, not smelling like vampire and carrying silver and fox magic."

She can tell all that? I'm not sure even I could tell that much from one sniff.

"I came to get a friend of mine, but I couldn't… I can't just leave everyone else here. But I have no idea how to get back out. Maybe I could by myself. Maybe with just Evgeny, but not all of us."

At the mention of Evgeny's name, the curly-haired woman makes an involuntary gesture of disgust. "The abomination is your friend?"

Immediately I'm on the defensive. "He's okay," I say. "He can't help what he was force fed, what he was forced to become. He – "

"That is not what she meant," says the older woman. "It is regrettable that he has been fed our blood, but that is not what makes him… repulsive to us."

I wait for her to go on because I have no idea what to say to that.

"It is that one of his bloodline was made… was reborn a vampire. That is what is abomination."

"I don't understand."

"Did he not tell you? But perhaps he did not know. You know his surname, his family name?"

"Alexeyevich."

"Son of Alexei, using an ending once reserved for nobility."

"So?"

"The last of the Tsars of Russia had a son named Alexei, believed to have been murdered. But he was not. He was hidden. Your Evgeny is his descendant. His only descendant."

It's a bit bizarre to think of Evgeny as the last in a line of Russian royalty, especially *that* family, so steeped in folklore and conspiracy theory and urban legend. But I still don't get her point. "So the descendant of a murdered Russian Tsar is a Reborn. Why is that an abomination?"

"It's not the fact that he's a child of royalty, but what legacy that lineage bears. You have heard of Rasputin?"

"Yeah, of course."

"He was a *koldun*. In Russian, that is a sorcerer."

"I've heard weirder things about him," I say.

She smiles, but grimly. "Not all of it is true. But Rasputin was supposed to be guarding a few very special bearers of witch-blood. The royal family."

I'm starting to see the problem, and also maybe the reason Evgeny can digest witch blood. "But witches are female," I say.

Again, the grim smile. "In Germany, our witch powers only manifest in women, yes, and even then it is often not until we are quite mature. A rare few have the abilities from a young age." She glances at her hand, holding that of the drugged child. "In Russia, it is the same, except in one lineage, in which a few – a very few – of the men were witches also."

"So Evgeny might have manifested witch abilities some day, but the vamps took that from him when they took his human life."

"And they made him into a cannibal," says the curly-haired woman.

"Okay," I say. "Okay, I need to think about this." I look at my clipboard and tap my pen. "But first we need to get you all out of here."

As one, the witches turn to look at the door. "Quickly," says the older woman. "Hide."

I look around. "Where?"

"You are *fuchs*," she says, and I remember, *A fox is unseen when she wishes to be.* I head for the end of the row, to be as far from the door as I can. There's a bit of space between the last cell and the end wall, where someone's left a broom leaning.

"The hat, put it back on the table," says the curly-haired woman. I comply, and see the door handle turning. I sprint for the end cell, squeeze myself into the space, and then, because it makes me feel much more of a fox than I am normally, I put on the fox mask.

I didn't notice it before, too caught up in the relief of having the witch voices blocked, but with the mask on the world is in black and white. It's sharper and more detailed, but all in greys. And my nose is so tingling with smells I want to sneeze like you wouldn't believe. But I don't. I suppress it, because the vamp who's just walked through the door, science-fiction hat on his midnight-brown hair, is the same dark-skinned Reborn from my dream-contact with Evgeny. Samuel Charleston himself. He doesn't look like much, really, not from the glimpse I get, but I'm filled with the deepest terror I can imagine. Maybe the fox mask helps me sense more, but there's something about this guy, something very, very wrong.

He stops just inside the door and I pull my head back behind the wall of the cell. Invisible or not – and I'm not even sure I actually am, because *I* can still see me – I don't want to be noticed. I curl into the smallest ball I can and try not to whimper.

"Well, my lovely, poisonous bitches," he says, in his velvety voice. "Time for some of my special cocktail." I hear him open the door to the medical supply room, move around inside and then come back out. I can't tell exactly what he's doing or how he's administering his drug just by listening, and I sure as hell am not going to look, but he works his way down the line. When he gets to the last cell he sniffs. Once, twice.

"Have you been playing with the wolves, pretty filth?" he asks the witch inside. She doesn't answer. "You smell a little doggy."

Crap. He can probably smell me. But he's just a vamp; how can his nose be so good? I hope more fervently that I'm invisible and try to keep my bladder under control.

I hear a clank of the bars, like he's leaning against them, and then he says, "It's really too bad you're a witch. I like redheads. I'd make you Reborn just so I could fuck you every night."

Her voice is faint and groggy-sounding – maybe put on, or maybe a real effect of the drugs – but she says, "I only fuck women." And I know that voice. It goes along with short, messy red hair and eyes so dark brown they're almost black; with perfect breasts and clever fingers and a soft, sweet mouth. I almost say her name aloud.

"Alex," I finally do say, as soon as Charleston is gone. I can't tear the mask off fast enough, and I knock the broom over with a clatter trying to get out of my hiding spot.

"Hey, Panya," she says, with a lopsided grin. She's limp on her cot, but sounds better than she did when Charleston was here.

"Holy fuck, Alex." I reach through the bars and she climbs off the cot to take my hand.

"I thought you were dead," she says. "I missed you. They never found you, but we all thought you were dead. I thought it was my fault, because I left you where that creep could find you." She's crying, and I touch her face, wipe the tears away.

"I'm here," I say and, "You're a witch."

"I didn't even know until they grabbed me," she says. "I thought I was just unusually empathetic and particularly good with plants."

That makes me laugh. She's still as I remember. But I'm probably nothing like she remembers. I don't even use the same name.

"Why didn't you tell me you were okay?" she says, and there's something hurt behind her happiness.

"I wasn't okay," I say. "I woke up not even remembering who I was." I touch her lips. "I didn't remember anything at all from before… before I was attacked. Not until a few days ago."

"*Fuchs*, child," says the older woman. "Put the hat back on, and then if you are going to free us, do so. We will free the other non-humans while you find your friend."

I don't want to stop touching Alex, but the witch is right, so I stick the stupid hat back on and pretend to take some notes, like I'm observing the results of Charleston's drugs. What I'm really doing is checking out the locks on the cells. Each one has a card scanner, and that's it. I don't know if anyone in security will notice me opening each cell one by one, or if they even have that information in the security stations, but there isn't really any other way to get the prisoners out. So I turn my back to the camera to hide what I'm doing, and pretend to be peering in at each captive and taking more notes.

I slide my card into the slot on Alex's cell and the light goes green almost immediately. I open the door just enough so it won't re-lock, in case there's a timer on it, and say, "Wait until I'm out of here, then all of you come out at once. I'll leave the outer door ajar." I try not to look at Alex again, because I don't want to leave her here with the other witches. I want to take her with me.

"Panya," she says, gently, and touches my fingers where they're wrapped around one of the bars. I glance up. She smiles. "I still want that coffee. We'll meet up when we get out of here."

I don't tell her my name's different, and I don't have a phone anyhow, I just nod and smile back. If she can't find me later, then I'll find her.

"Of course," I say. "Coffee… and dessert."

She chuckles, and I move on to the next cell. I repeat the card inserting and leaving the door ajar over and over until all the cells are open. The witches watch me, most of them still prone on their bunks and pretending to be drugged. No sense in giving away the plan before it goes into effect.

"How will you get the rest out?" I ask, pretending to ignore them as I take notes. "The weres and the vamps and the rest? Most of them really *are* drugged into submission."

The older woman with the German accent answers. "There will be technicians. Outside this room, they do not wear the shielding hats. With all of us together, we can bend them to our will, and make them set the others free and administer antidotes to the drugs, if any exist."

"Don't worry," says the curly-haired woman. "Free your vampire-witch, but remember he is not a healthy thing. He may not be who you think he is."

"Maybe not," I say. "But he is my friend." I can't look at Alex as I say this. The only memories I have of her are the ones the fox women returned to me, but they're good memories. Very good. Beginning-of-a-great-relationship memories.

The curly-haired woman shrugs. "Suit yourself," she says. "I hope you're right about him."

I nod. "Good luck," I say. Then I open the door with my card and my fingerprint. It takes so long for the light to go green I've pretty much decided I'm trapped in here and it's all over, but then it flashes and the lock clicks and I pull open the door and step through. And the door immediately begins to swing shut. I catch it with my foot and try to think of some way to hold it open for the witches.

I've just got my pen held between the door and the jamb when I hear footsteps. I whirl around, bashing the stupid hat on the doorframe as I do.

And there's a vamp technician hurrying towards me.

I snatch the hat off my head and try to look like I belong there. I probably have a higher security clearance that he does. That's got to count for something, right? He's not very tall, so I straighten up to my full height and manage to look down at him as he stops in front of me. Nothing registers on his vamp-still face, but he hesitates when he starts to talk.

"Um. Ma'am, there's –"

I hear the door ease open behind me, and the click of my pen as it hits the floor, so when his gaze fixes over my shoulder and his pupils dilate in surprise, I'm expecting it.

"They're es –" He stops mid-word, suddenly, his breath chopping short in a way that sounds really uncomfortable.

"We've got this," says the curly-haired witch, brushing past me.

I stand perfectly still, as if they've got me enspelled, too, and wait for them to pass by, vacant-eyed vamp in tow. Alex pauses, touches my hand, then slips my pen and a scrap of paper between my fingers. "If I don't see you at the end of this," she says, "call me."

My fingers clench on the paper and I flick my eyes sideways to look at her. She looks so tired, but as strong as ever. "I will," I say. "We'll have coffee." I let a bit of laughter creep into my voice.

"I want the whole story," she says. "About your disappearance."

"It's not a nice story," I say.

"Neither is mine. Do you want to hear it anyway?"

"Yes."

She touches my hand one last time, a barely-perceptible brush of her fingertips, then she runs to catch up with the others.

I wonder how soon until someone notices they've escaped and locks the place down. I should have asked Magne if it's just the exits that are locked, or if all the doors inside are rendered inoperable, too. Either way, I'd better hurry.

I go to the door labelled "High Security" and put my hand on it. What if Evgeny isn't even in there? Then what do I do? If he's not here, where do I look? Then I swipe my card, stare anxiously at the red light until it turns green. And I swipe my fingerprint, slowly and precisely, thinking about how I had to re-scan it when I tried to open the witch door. The red light burns steadily. For minutes it seems, until finally it flicks over to green.

I let myself breathe again, then realize I've been holding my breath. I must be really feeling the anxiety if I'm holding my breath and not noticing. I mean, lots of people do, it's why there's always a collective exhale when something happens that's preceded by a bunch of people waiting for that something to happen. But it's not something I do much. When I studied kung fu, I guess I took the breathing control really seriously, and I almost never stop breathing except on purpose.

Then I take an extra deep breath as I reach for the door handle to push it open. I don't know what I'm going to find in there, and it terrifies me. Even if Evgeny *is* in there, as I hope he is, he's probably not going to recognize me. Hell, he's probably not going to be *capable* of recognizing me. If the dream-contact is anything to go by, he'll be scared and sick and hungry and the symbiont will be in full control.

If I can't get him to recognize me, how do I get him out without ending up as his lunch?

I push on the door and it sticks. So I push harder. Nothing. I look at the card slot and the print scanner. Both are red again. I've hesitated so long that the door lock has reset.

I make myself take several long, deep breaths, real lung-fillers, to steady myself, and I cocoon myself in calm inside my head. There's nothing I can do about whatever state Evgeny's in unless I go in there and try. Worrying will get me nothing but caught.

I still hesitate. It's not that I'm having second thoughts about rescuing Evgeny. I still intend to do that, but seeing Alex has raised all kinds of strange emotions and questions I never thought I'd have to ask.

I gently deflect those thoughts aside and re-establish my bubble of calm. Anger's not the only emotion that can get you killed.

So I straighten my back, poke my ID card into the slot again and watch the light turn green. Then I run my fingertip over the scanner and wait. It takes its time, but then it, too goes, green. And just as I'm about to push the door open both lights flash yellow, then go back to red.

I try again. Now the lock won't even recognize my card. Nothing I do works, not even the little tricks cashiers use to get debit cards working.

The lights stay red and the door won't open. I can't get to Evgeny.

Chapter Nineteen

I LOOK AROUND and the witches are nowhere to be seen. I listen carefully, and I can just hear the sounds of cell doors creaking open and voices murmuring. Whatever they're doing, they're doing it quietly, and I don't think security has noticed yet. At least, there's no alarm or technicians running around with tranquilizer guns.

If the witches haven't drawn any attention yet, then it must be me. Maybe someone noticed I wasn't who I said I was, or maybe they found Boss Lady dead behind her desk. Or maybe I was wrong and the *huli jing's* hair pin only disabled her temporarily and she wasn't dead after all. Either way, I'm not going through any more doors with *my* ID, I don't think.

So I'll use hers. I almost forgot about the grisly envelope in my pocket, but now I notice that Boss Lady's blood, little of it though there is, has seeped through the heavy paper and stained my lab coat with rusty red-brown.

Gingerly, I open the envelope. I want to touch the finger even less than I did when I cut it off, but I'm out of choices. So I stick Boss Lady's ID card in the reader and swipe her finger and watch the lights click over to green. Maybe it's just my imagination, but they seem to change much faster that they did with my info, like somehow it could know I was a fraud all along.

I push the door open immediately, stick the card and appendage back in my pocket, and step through. It's exactly like in the dream-contact. The only light comes from two red exit signs, one over the door I've just come in, and one farther along. From its placement, it looks like maybe that door leads into the same medical supply room as in the witch area.

The row of cells, leading back into the gloom, seem to be empty. I walk all the way down, just in case. Each one holds a bare metal table and has a drain in the floor. Otherwise, they're vacant. I stop at the other door and it's labelled "Medical Supply," so probably it does lead to the same room. The rest of the wall is a blank, featureless grey. I wonder if I should try the door in case there's an antidote to whatever they've given Evgeny. But what's the likelihood of it being labelled "antidote for super-vampire drugs"? I wouldn't know what else to look for. Even the names of painkillers like acetaminophen and ibuprofen confuse me.

There's a second row of cells back-to-back with the first, and the featureless wall they look out on doesn't even have an exit sign with a door to break the monotony. I hesitate. While this is definitely the location they were keeping Evgeny in the dream-contact, I distinctly remember two exit signs, one at each end of the hall, and that only fits the first row of cells. This row has only the dimmest glow from the sign over the entry door.

But I hear faint, ragged breathing. It's not as slow as it should be, for a vamp, but who knows how the drugs might have affected him? Speeding up his breathing is probably the least of the changes.

I inhale deeply, sorting the scents I catch. Lots of disinfectant, vampires, fear, confusion, vomit, other bodily fluids. And, faintly, the spicy-vamp scent I recognize as Evgeny. It's so faint I can barely sense it. It could mean he's not here any more, or it could just be that it's overwhelmed by all the really unpleasant smells.

I step forward slowly, taking care to place each foot precisely and silently. I regulate my breathing so it's slow and even and inaudible even to me. And I try to be invisible. If it worked for the fox women, maybe it will work for me, even without the fox mask. Then I realize I'm still holding the anti-witch hat in one hand and I almost laugh out loud. How did I manage to get through the door without noticing? I set it carefully on the floor and continue.

The breathing seems to be coming from the very end of the row, where it's darkest. I pass one cell – empty but for a metal table like the others – then another.

Then the breathing becomes a long hiss, full of pain and hate, and I nearly turn around and tiptoe back the other way. Whatever is making that noise is not the Evgeny I know. But he wouldn't be, after what they've been doing to him.

Finally I reach the last cell. There's a body strapped to the table, arms manacled above his head, ankles locked too. He smells of piss and shit and there's who knows what smeared on his skin. Vomit dribbles from the corner of his mouth and I wonder that he didn't choke on it, because his head is immobilized.

It's Evgeny but not Evgeny. The beautiful tattoo shows under filth and bruises, and his piercings catch the faint light. But his face is vamp-deformed, jaws unhinged, teeth protruding, fangs straining forward. His breathing gets louder, like harsh animal panting.

"Hungry," he says.

Great. He's not himself and he's hungry. I will no doubt seem like a fine snack. I should try the store room, see if there's anything in there besides drugs. But I can't stop staring. Like this, he really does look like an abomination, though it wasn't vampirism *per se* that the witches condemned.

"Evgeny," I whisper and he goes still, even his breathing abruptly silent.

Then he sniffs, loudly, several times. "You smell good," he says.

"Yeah, that's what you always say."

I pull out my biggest stake and hold it left-handed while I get out Boss Lady's card to open the cell door. But this cell doesn't have a card slot. Instead, it has a keypad. For a long, horrifying moment I can't remember the master override code Magne gave me. I've only had to use it once so far, on the door to the top of the elevator.

But I push back panic and punch it in, one deliberate number at a time. There's a pause, then the door swings open with a clang. I step through slowly, hesitantly, and walk to Evgeny's side. He hisses and strains against his bonds and I understand why Boss Lady stepped back in the dream-contact. He seems superhuman, super-vampire. Super-everything. Like he could pull those straps apart like overcooked fettuccine. But they hold and he relaxes.

"Evgeny," I say, in my best small-scared-animal-soothing voice. "It's me. Su. I've come to get you out of here."

I think he tries to cock his head, but he can't move it. So he strains his eyes sideways to look at me. I step closer. Even in the dim light, his eyes are inhumanly blue. Luminous, almost.

He inhales through his nose, then smiles and his face, his jaws, reassemble and he looks like an angel instead of a demon. "You smell good," he says, and I remember the beautiful young man in the bar I felt so sorry for. It seems like years ago – can it only have been a few days? A week, maybe?

I feel my heart go soft and remind myself that he's not a neglected puppy. Now, more than he ever has been before, he's a dangerous killing machine.

"I'm going to let you go," I say. "But you can't feed on me." I reach for the straps holding his head first. He keeps his gaze fixed on mine, something adoring in his eyes. But if the symbiont is in charge, I must be imagining it. "You wouldn't like how I taste, anyway. And I'll stake you if you try anything." And I remember Evgeny saying he'd let me kill him, because if I decided he needed killing, I'd probably be right. I wonder if he'd agree now. But then, he's not capable of agreeing or disagreeing with anything.

When his head is free he turns it so he can look at me better. "I like you," he says. "You smell good." This sweet, stupid boy is so unlike the hate-filled monster I found when I first stepped in here that I'm not sure he's real. But he *is* exactly how he was when we first met.

"Don't get any ideas," I say. "I'm not food." I undo the strap across his chest and the one over his hips and he wriggles and stretches as far as the manacles will let him. I try not to look too closely at the blobs of white on his belly. "You need a bath in the worst way," I say. "Jesus."

Now he's only held down at the wrists and ankles, and I don't know which to tackle first. I decide ankles would be safer, so I turn to his feet. There are locks on the manacles, like handcuffs, almost. I'm no expert at lock-picking, just pocket-picking, but I've done a few and my hair is held up with bobby pins. It takes three of them, and leaves me with my braid hanging down my back, but I get the manacles undone.

The whole time I'm working, Evgeny watches me. It's unnerving. I pick up my stake from where I put it on the table while I picked the locks, and tuck it back in its holster. It won't be as quick to get at that way, but I'd rather not have Evgeny grab it as soon as he's free.

When I move above his head to unlock his wrists, he strains his neck to follow me. But then he relaxes and closes his eyes.

"Hungry," he says, but it's more like a sleepy child than a ravening beast.

The wrist manacles are narrower than the ones on his ankles were, and the locks are smaller. I'm starting to think about looking for something to break them with when the first one finally gives a "click" and opens. I take it off his wrist, but he doesn't move. He just lays there, barely breathing at all. Though he's quiet, it's almost worse than him hostile and hungry. Now he seems barely alive. But that's normal for a vamp, right? I have to remember that Evgeny's not a normal vampire.

The second manacle gives me more trouble that the first and I'm wondering about breaking it again. But then I remember how Evgeny broke free in Papa Vamp's lair and he was not as strong then as he is now. Though of course, he's probably got a lot more sedatives in him now. So I keep poking at the lock and trying not to curse too loud, and hoping it's too dark in here for security cameras to make us out – if there even *are* any cameras in here. I wasn't really looking for them, but I don't remember seeing any.

Then, finally, the lock gives and I pull it away from Evgeny's arm. His wrists are bloody from straining against his bonds and his arms have got to be asleep from being held above his head.

I reach out to stroke his hair, though it doesn't look like it's been washed in far longer than he's even been in here. My hand never makes contact. Before I even see him move he's off the table and out of the cell.

"Evgeny," I call, but quietly, and hurry after him. He's waiting at the door, fists clenched, jaw unhinged.

"It's locked," he says. "Unlock it."

"Wait," I say. "I have to explain –" Again he moves so fast I don't have time to react, though this time I at least *see* him moving, so either he's slower or I'm getting faster. But being faster doesn't help me avoid being pinned to the wall, Evgeny's vamp face in mine, breath hot in my nose. He smells of sick and of blood, but most strongly of just him.

"Unlock it," he says. His voice isn't sweet-stupid-Evgeny any more, it's full-on monster symbiont. He probably doesn't know me, and it's probably only because his drive to escape is stronger than his drive to feed that he hasn't killed me yet.

Every now and then I've wished I could be the damsel in distress, that someone else would come and save me, because I'm just too terrified to save myself. Now is one of those times, though mercifully, the feeling is fleeting. There is no one else to save me. I can't even get mad that he's made me feel weak, because I know it's the symbiont and not Evgeny.

So try not to recoil from the snake-like fangs, the utter wrongness of his unhinged face, and I say – so calmly I surprise even myself – "I'm your friend, Evgeny. I'm here to take you home."

That seems to surprise him, too. He shakes his head. "I don't remember."

"No," I say. "They keep you drugged so you won't remember."

"You don't want to drug me?"

"No."

"How do I know you're not lying? The others were always lying. They said they were helping me, healing me, making me better, but they just hurt me."

"Do I smell like I'm lying?"

"Can I tell that?"

I consider. I can't always tell for sure when someone's lying – not when they're really good at it – and my nose is better. "I don't know," I finally say.

"Me neither," he says. Then he smells deeply of my neck. "You smell delicious."

"I don't taste very good," I say. Then I surprise myself again. I pull out a small knife from my pocket and make a nick on my wrist. A thin trickle of blood starts and I hold it out to him. "Try," I say.

"It's a trick," he says. He tilts his head and frowns – he may be all vamp, but that's a gesture I remember from Evgeny in his right mind, too. "I think… I think they tricked me like that once."

"They did," I say. "They sent drugged minions against you and you fed on them. That's how they were able to catch you."

"You were there." He looks at me closely, his eyes shining. "Why didn't you stop them?"

"I didn't know until too late."

He looks at the blood on my wrist. "You don't seem drugged. Why do I trust you?"

"I'm your friend," I say. "Taste my blood, but you won't like it. We'll find you a nice minion – a non-drugged one – once we get out of this room."

He takes my wrist in his hand, which is good because his pressure on my shoulder was making the fox mask dig into my back and my arm is falling asleep. He looks at it, then back at my face. "I believe you," he says. Then he lifts my wrist to his mouth and touches the blood with the tip of his tongue. He grimaces, but doesn't spit like Magne did. "It does taste bad," he says. "But not as bad as witch."

"You know what they fed you?"

"They told me. The tall skinny one. He told me everything. I think he was pretending to be honest but really he wanted to torment me."

"I'm sorry," I say. "I'm sorry I couldn't get to you sooner."

He shakes his head, touches my face, and then kisses me. I try not to cringe away, because he's still vamped out and it's like he's going to eat my whole face. But then he seems to realize, and his jaws reassemble before his mouth touches mine.

He tastes like puke and blood – some of it mine, but all of it just tasting like more-or-less human blood to me – but beneath that he tastes like himself and I realize how much I've missed him. He can't seem to get enough of kissing me. His mouth pushes against mine insistently and I part my lips, let his tongue in, and all the flavors, good and bad, flood in too. And I don't even care because the strongest taste is Evgeny.

Then I feel his erection pressing against me. And despite all the danger, despite the witches escaping just beyond the door, despite the fact that he's filthy and stinking and completely unsanitary, all I want to do is fuck him, right here against the wall. It's probably a good thing he pulls away finally.

"Why do I feel so strongly about you?" he asks.

At least he remembers that much. Hopefully it will be enough to keep me alive. Maybe it will even be enough to let me keep him from killing the witches and the other captives,

"It's a long story," I say. "But you'll remember when the drugs wear off."

"What do I call you?" he says. Not, "What's your name?" I wonder why.

And I almost answer, "Panya." But I don't. "Su," I say, and he smiles his angel smile.

"I like it," he says. "And you call me… You called me Evgeny?"

"Yes."

He nods. Then as he's turning away, he finally seems to notice the state he's in. "Oh," he says. Then he sniffs. "I stink."

It makes me smile. He does like to be clean, which I have to say is a nice change. Boys who don't wash that often… well, there's lint and worse things that get stuck in awkward places, and giving head is just not pleasant when a guy hasn't washed recently.

"Also, I'm naked." He says it so seriously that I laugh out loud.

"We'll steal you some clothes when we get you a snack. There must be a minion about who's close to your size."

He nods, and runs his hands down his body. "Yuck," he says. "I think I'm glad I can't remember where most of this came from." He scratches at the white on his belly and I look away. "There was a woman," he says. "Cold, mean. She… kept wanting to touch me. Most of the time I blacked out."

"I killed her," I say. "I think."

"Thank you," he says.

I don't explain that I killed her to keep her from putting her mouth on my girl parts, but that's only mostly true. I already hated her for touching Evgeny.

"We need to get out of here," I say. "Fast. But I freed the witches –"

"They're dangerous," he says, staring at me. "Even to me. And they must hate me."

"Maybe," I say. "But one of them's a friend. My friend. And I freed them. They're getting the weres and other vamps and all out. I don't know how, but I think they have a plan."

"Will we go with them?"

I think of Alex. "Maybe," I say. "If they're leaving when we are."

He looks at the door and I see apprehension on his face. "They must all hate me," he says.

I shake my head. "Most of them were here before you, and they're not likely to know their blood was fed to you."

"Okay," he says. "I trust you."

Then I hear a sound that chills me to the core. It's the door unlocking, and there's nowhere to hide.

"Evgeny," I say, but before I can say anything else a figure steps through the door and chuckles.

"Well, well," he says. "A hot Asian chick and my prize pet, trying to escape. We can't have that, now can we?" It's Charleston, and he seems only amused to find us wandering loose. He doesn't seem the least bit worried, which worries *me*.

Chapter Twenty

IGET THAT FEELING of abject terror again, like I felt when Charleston made his drug rounds with the witches, and the same fear I felt from Evgeny during the dream contact except now it's not me feeling Evgeny's terror, it's my own. There's just something so deeply *wrong* with Charleston. I don't like to use the word "evil" because I don't really believe in the concept, not in the pure sense, the religious sense. But it's the only word that fits. Even "sinister" is too nice for Charleston.

Now that I can actually see him in person, instead of through a dream or glimpsed while I'm cowering in a corner, I see that he's tall and thin, fit-looking, dressed in perfectly-tailored, extremely expensive-looking business casual. His face is vamp-blank except for the tooth-revealing smile, and he was probably really good-looking when he was human. But vamp stillness makes him too perfect, like he's not real. Plastic. And maybe it's just the context and he's not always this way, but he doesn't even try to mimic human expressions. If I had to guess, I'd say he's probably one of those vamps who sees the Reborn as the true and proper successor to the human species. Never mind that they can't even reproduce without humans.

Charleston's smile grows when he sees my apprehension. "I just had to get a look at this new employee my dear Cecilia was so enamored of. You must taste awfully sweet to convince her to give you so much security clearance without asking me." I get the idea that when he says "sweet" he's not talking about my blood.

I can't think of anything to say in reply. I can't really think at all.

"I'd like to have a lick or two myself," he says, and smiles even wider. I'm pretty sure he's smiling at all only to show me his fangs. "Before I kill you."

Finally I can move as the terror pushes me beyond fear to the pissed-off stage. But unlike the other times I've faced vamps, the terror isn't *replaced* by anger. It lingers and I can tell it's going to slow me down. I pull out one of the *huli jing*'s hair pins and throw it in one quick motion, then follow it with the second and the third.

He hardly blinks, but bats at them like swatting insects. He at least looks surprised when he can't evade them entirely. The first one takes him in the shoulder instead of the heart, the second in the hip instead of the crotch (yeah, I fight dirty when my life is at stake), and the third in the cheek instead of the eye. He's moved so fast his limbs were a blur. He's faster than Evgeny.

I'm so stunned it makes me stupid and I don't move when he plucks each pin out of his flesh and throws them neatly back at me. But I guess fox weapons don't work against other foxes. Or maybe they don't work in the hands of non-foxes, because they land in a row at my feet and not in my body.

"Interesting," says Charleston. "You are obviously not what you appear to be. I would love to add you to my menagerie, once I round them all up again." He smiles an oily, utterly fake, smile, then lets his face lapse back to vacancy. "I'm impressed you got so far," he says. "And I really must have a talk with Cecilia about whom she chooses to share company information with." So he doesn't know she's dead. Unless she isn't dead.

I manage to stave off the fear again and have a stake out and ready when he comes at me. All I can do is get it between us before I find myself held, back to the wall again, fox mask jabbing me between the shoulder blades. I haven't got the room or the leverage to actually do anything with the stake, and he takes it away from me. He's too strong. Even really old vamps who feed on other vamps aren't so strong. Only Evgeny, force fed on *hexen* blood, comes close.

I let my martial arts training take over and get in a short, sharp jab to his solar plexus that gives me enough room to slip along the wall away from him, until I feel my head yanked back. He's grabbed my braid. He jerks me towards him, wraps the braid around his fist and is about to sink his teeth into me when Evgeny hits him from behind. *Finally.*

Charleston's forehead hits mine with an audible "crack" and I see stars. That's not a metaphor, in case you were wondering. I really do see bright points of light dancing in front of my eyes. When my vision clears, Evgeny's looking at me over Charleston's shoulder.

"Can I eat him?" Evgeny asks.

"Please do," I say.

But just as Evgeny's about to rip the other vamp's neck open, Charleston says, "Kneel, progeny," and Evgeny's on his knees, confusion and fear on his face.

Charleston turns, still holding me by the hair. He twists my braid until I'm kneeling beside Evgeny.

"You're not his parent," I say.

"I am now," says Charleston. "After I killed him again and infected him with my own symbiont."

He's got to be lying, because that doesn't make any sense. Wouldn't Evgeny's existing symbiont fight off Charleston's? I mean, if a person could host two symbionts, then someone could even be both a vampire *and* a werewolf, and that's never happened that I heard of. But does that mean it *can't* happen, or just that no one's ever done it?

"That's impossible," I say.

Charleston laughs. "Maybe," he says. "But nonetheless, you can see he must obey me."

"He can fight it off," I say, and he twists my braid so hard tears come to my eyes. I *hope* Evgeny can fight it off, or that his symbiont can. If not, I'll be battling two super-vamps, and it's pretty obvious how dismally I'm doing against just one.

Charleston laughs again, a hollow, soulless sound. "Now which of you wants to suck me off first? I really do need some action if I want to avoid looking shrunken."

"Fuck yourself," I say.

Charleston shrugs, and it's so carefully and precisely choreographed that it's obviously not a natural gesture for him. "Fine," he says. "My pretty pet can fill my sexual needs while you fill my belly." He jerks my hair so I have to stand up. I'm desperately trying to think of some way out of this and the only thing I can come up with is waiting until he's distracted with surprise at the unpleasant taste of my blood and then stake him.

But then he tells Evgeny to start sucking and I just can't let Charleston do that to my friend. My boyfriend. Dammit, do I really love a vampire? A crazy Russian-royalty-descended witch-vampire?

So I throw all my weight backwards, away from Charleston, pulling him off balance, just enough that he knocks into Evgeny and sends him sprawling, then Charleston's hand pulls free of my hair. I expect a good chunk of strands to yank out of my head, maybe taking some scalp with it, but instead his fingers pull the last elastics and pins out and my hair slips out of the braid to flow free around my shoulders, down my back. It seems longer than when I put it up earlier.

And somehow the world seems to slow down. Charleston comes after me, but he's no longer astoundingly quick. Instead, he seems to be pushing through gelatin, while I'm slipping through a frictionless vacuum.

The *kitsune*'s mask swings around my shoulder and I fit it to my face. The *kumiho*'s scarf has partly unwound from my neck and flows with my movements, a red silk ribbon against the black silk of my hair. And somehow, the *huli jing*'s hair pins are in my hand again. Instead of throwing them, I wield them like blades and swirl through a dance of kung fu moves and Charleston cannot evade me.

I am merciless as I cut him open, face and chest, leg and arm. Tiny cuts all over until his black skin turns red and he begs for mercy. I have no mercy. I am vengeance. When I am finally still, he cringes at my feet. I no longer fear him. He fears me.

"What are you?" he says.

And I remember the fox women. *You are vengeance*, they told me. I shake my head. I want it. I really do. I want to dismember him so he can never violate anyone again, never make another person service him. And I want to kill him. But that step isn't mine to take. Not with Charleston. I pull the mask off, wind the scarf back into place around my neck, and coil my hair up on my head and hold it with the hair pins. I shake my head again.

"I'm someone you don't fuck with," I say.

Then I look at Evgeny. He's staring at me, face filled with awe and something fiercer – joy? He's got a huge hard-on, too, but somehow it doesn't seem obscene. "You *are* glorious," he says.

"Are you okay?" I ask.

He cocks his head, that familiar thinking gesture. Then he shakes it. "I'm still not remembering," he says. "But I feel okay. Better than before." Then he smiles a tiny smile. "But I'm hungry."

I gesture at Charleston with my chin. "He's all yours. You can take his clothes, too." Charleston's garments are covered in blood and full of holes from my cuts. "Sorry about the damage." Then I walk away to let Evgeny feed and dress.

I pause when Charleston says, "You will not harm me, progeny."

But then Evgeny replies, "I'm not your progeny." And I keep heading for the door. I'm not really surprised when even Boss Lady's card and print won't open it. Charleston probably had some way of locking it before he got here, so it would only open for him. Once he realized he had a problem. So I head for the other door, the one that leads to the medical supply room. It's got a keypad and the master override code works.

I try to decipher the labels on the drugs, to see if there's anything that might be useful, and I notice that many of the labels are written in what looks a lot like Liam's handwriting. I'm puzzling over whether that means anything significant when Evgeny joins me. Charleston's clothes are too tight, the sleeves and legs too long. But at least Evgeny's covered. His feet are still bare and for a moment I stare at them. They're shapely. I've never seen beautiful feet before and wonder how I could have not noticed. I wonder why I'm noticing now.

"I didn't kill him," Evgeny says. "Why didn't I kill him?"

"Maybe some remnant of that progeny trick he pulled?"

He shakes his head. "I just didn't *want* to kill him."

So maybe Evgeny's not a killing machine after all. I can't think. I'm not even sure I can plan our way out of here. Now that I'm not in slow motion, fox-time, or whatever that was when I was fighting Charleston, I feel sluggish. Drained. Like all I want to do is curl up in a corner and sleep. I wonder if that glorious feeling of dancing in a void is what it's like all the time, to be a fox woman. I wonder if that's what I could be, if I became a creature of vengeance, as the *kumiho* suggested. I want it. I want that effortless power all the time. I don't want to be helpless any more. I don't want to be weak. The two people I love, with whom I could even imagine spending my life, are both strong and powerful *others* and I don't want to be less than they are. I want to be an equal in any relationship I'm in.

I look at Evgeny. He's so strong it's frightening. But Alex is only just discovering her witch heritage – we'd be more alike. Then Evgeny touches my face.

"You look sad," he says.

I shake my head. "I'm tired." It's completely true, but it's also a lie. Well, a diversion, anyway. I *am* sad. Eventually, I might have to choose whether to be with Evgeny or with Alex. Unless the choice is made for me. But right now, I just have to get Evgeny out of here and trust the witches will take care of Alex.

"Let's go," I say.

We pass through the medical storage and into the witch room. The door's wedged open with the table, and we climb over it and out. It's like the witches knew we'd need to get out again. And maybe they did. Who can say what witches know?

On the other side of the door is…. Well, it's too organized for chaos, but there are weres and vamps and others wandering about. It looks random, but then I realize many of them are pacing and shaking their heads, like they can somehow wear off the drugs faster by exercising. And maybe they can. The one time I avoided a deathwish-inducing hangover after an ill-advised night of drinking, I did it by jogging around my block until I couldn't move another step, and by the time I collapsed I wasn't drunk anymore, just really, really tired. And I didn't get a hangover.

We only get to the next row of cages before one of the witches meets us. It's the older woman, and I'm glad, because the curly-haired one was so disgusted by the very idea of Evgeny. Even the older witch looks uncomfortable at seeing him, but she hides it well and avoids looking at him. The striking-looking dark-skinned woman who follows her, carrying the poor witch-child, isn't so tactful and she stares openly at Evgeny, nostrils flared in fear or disgust.

"Where is the tall Reborn who is responsible for this?" the older witch asks. "Did you kill him?"

"He's alive," I say. "We left him in the high security area."

"A pity," she says, but she actually looks at Evgeny directly and there is curiosity and maybe even hope in her eyes. "No matter. We will deal with him."

I'm about to tell her the master override code, so she can get everyone out, but she holds up her hand. "We will have the tall one's codes," she says and taps the side of her head. "He cannot hide from us now." Then she walks away and the woman carrying the child follows.

Evgeny touches my hand. "I will have to feed again soon," he says. "But I do not think you would want me to harm any of these people." Of course, metabolizing the witch blood he's been fed would make him extra-hungry.

"No," I say. "Don't feed on them." I try to force my brain to think. It's like wading through thick mud. Each concept sticks and has to be dragged through to the front of my thoughts. I feel like I haven't slept for days, and like I could stay asleep for weeks if I could only lie down. "If we can get up to floor X, there's a cafeteria," I finally say. "They have bottled blood."

"Is it safe?"

I picture the employees on those floors, the lab technicians, fangs out because their work smells so delicious. "I think so," I say. "The regular vamp workers didn't seem drugged."

He nods and we head for the elevator. I don't know if we'll make it very far. I don't know if security is asleep at their posts or if the witches have somehow kept them from seeing what's going on down here, but sooner or later someone's going to notice something and then we'll all be in trouble.

But nothing happens. We take the elevator to floor X, borrow some clothes from a startled technician we leave tied up in the Boss Lady's office – really well tied up, because we can't afford to have him get out, especially now that he's not only had his clothes stolen by an escapee, but also knows that Boss Lady is dead. I'm very glad to discover that she's really dead. Her corpse is still where I left it behind her desk.

"Why's she missing a finger?" asks Evgeny.

I pull her tenth digit from my pocket. "In case I needed her fingerprint," I say. "Which I did."

Evgeny looks impressed, but doesn't comment.

"Oh God," says the poor lab tech. "Please don't cut off my finger." He's gagged, but still manages to make himself understood, so I obviously didn't do a very good job. I let Evgeny re-do the gag and when he's done the young man can't even make a squeak. Then I wave the *kumiho's* scarf under his nose. "Be a good boy," I say. "Just sit here quietly and don't try to go anywhere."

He nods vigorously.

"Do that, and you can keep all your fingers, my cuddle-bunny."

He nods again, and sits behind Boss Lady's desk where I tell him to, next to her body.

As I'm about to head back out the door, Evgeny stops me with a hand on my arm. "Cuddle-bunny?" he says, quirking one eyebrow.

"Oh, did you want that to be *your* pet name?" I grin at him.

"Fuck, no," he says. And he sounds so much like himself, like his life-remembering, sweet, maybe-my-boyfriend self that I kiss him. He still smells terrible, despite the almost-clean clothes, but I don't care. Just for a few minutes, I linger and revel in the feel of his lips on mine, of his teeth against my tongue, his tongue in my mouth, his hands on my face, on my neck, the press of his body against mine.

When we finally pull apart he says, "I love that." He traces my lips with his finger. "Su. Are we… Are we together?" I rest my head on his shoulder.

"Sort of, I think." Then I remember Alex. "It's a bit complicated."

"Ah," he says. "I wish I could remember. At least I *think* I wish. It's not something I'd be happier not knowing, is it? The complication?"

I picture Alex's dark eyes, her rumpled bright hair, her engaging smile. "I don't know," I say. "I don't think so."

"Well, I hope I remember soon, then," he says.

I pause a moment longer, savoring the quiet. But we still have to get out of here. "We'd better get you fed," I say.

So we head for the cafeteria – Evgeny's got the tech's ID as well as his clothes, and though they look nothing alike, except they both have prominent cheekbones and dark hair, if no one looks too close it'll be okay. In the cafeteria, they barely glance at our ID and hand over the standard vamp lunch of a bottle of "sustenance" – I guess that's the new PC term for blood. It surprises me that it's only mid-way through the work day. Or work night, I guess. It feels like days have passed underground. Or only minutes. It's surreal and I can't imagine working where I never see the sky and have no external frame of reference for the passing of time.

Evgeny drinks his blood as fast as he can without drawing attention. We're sitting in the cafeteria with vamps here and there at the other tables – we must have missed the main rush – and it feels like we're in disguise in the enemy camp, which I guess we are. When he finishes, I switch his bottle with mine and he drinks the second one more slowly.

"That feels better," he says, when he finally sets it down.

"Good," I say. "Now we have to get the fuck out of here."

The ease with which we left floor Z, stopped off on Y, and came to floor X, stole clothes, and got food is making me nervous. Surely getting out can't be as simple as taking the elevator to floor C, going through security (not that *that* would be simple), and taking the other elevator right up to the surface? But there's nothing else to do but try. So back to the elevator we go and we get on and I hit the button for C.

"I can't wait to take a really long shower," Evgeny says.

"Need help scrubbing your back?" I say.

He gives me a mischievous and charmingly shy smile, but whatever answer he's got never comes because that's when the elevator stops, half-way between floor X and floor C, and all the buttons start to blink yellow.

Chapter Twenty-One

"FUCK," I SAY.

"What's happening?"

"Someone must have noticed the witches, or us, and tripped the alarm."

Evgeny looks chagrined. "Do you think it was the tall one? Charleston? Because I left him alive?"

"Maybe," I say. "But don't be upset about that. Showing mercy isn't a bad thing."

"It is when it puts people you care about in danger."

He has a point, but I cling to the idea that Evgeny deciding *not* to kill Charleston is a *good* thing.

"What do we do?" he asks. He's looking to me like I actually know what I'm doing, and I guess that's reasonable to expect, since I'm supposed to be the one doing the rescuing.

I stare up at the ceiling, like there might be some answer there. I'm actually running through the plans of the Standard Comm Tower that Magne gave me. "If someone noticed us here and stopped the elevator, then we just need to get out and continue on our way." I point to the service hatch in the ceiling. "We might be close enough to reach the doors for floor C. Then we just have to get past the security station to the other elevators." *Just* get past security. But I'm hoping Evgeny is fast enough to disable the two guards before they can alert anyone else. It could work.

"But," I continue. "If it's a general security alert, if they've hit the panic button" – I wonder if there actually *is* a button, or if Magne was just using a familiar expression – "then we're locked in until it's reset."

"So we have to figure out how to reset it."

"Yeah." My mind began to clear while we were on floor X, while Evgeny ate, but it's fogging up again. I'm so tired.

Then Evgeny takes my chin in his hand and turns my face to his. He looks closely into my eyes and I try to look away. I don't want him to see how helpless I feel.

"Look at me, Su," he says. So I do. I'm too tired to fight. My vision is filled with the impossible blue of his eyes and I notice that they're not a uniform color, but have flecks of bright yellow-gold like a mosaic of irregular glass pieces. "Would the witches have reason to mess with your head?" he asks.

"I don't think so," I say. "They know I want to help. I let them out. And Alex… One of them's my friend."

He tilts my face this way and that, like he'll be able to see into my mind if he can just get the right angle. And I remember that he's a descendant of witches, so maybe he can. "Maybe they're trying to confuse the Reborn," he says. "And they can't help but affect you, too."

"Is that why I can't think?" I ask. "How can you tell?" But I know. Because he's a witch as well as a vamp. Maybe being Reborn *hasn't* prevented him from developing witch powers. Or maybe it's because he's been drinking *hexen* blood, and like Boss Lady said, it's given him some of their powers.

He just shrugs. Maybe he doesn't care how. Or maybe it's not important to figure out why when there are more urgent matters at hand. "I will try to block them, but I don't know if I can do it," he says. He frowns, tilts his head, and suddenly my mind clears.

"Shit," I say. "You were right."

"Better?"

"Miles better." I look at the hatch in the elevator again, and now I can remember the plans a bit more clearly. I still should have studied them better. The Standard Comm Tower blueprints were more detailed in the above-ground parts and the parking levels, but some basics of the lower levels – or the first three floors of the lower levels – were included, too. Things that wouldn't change too much no matter how you reconfigured the inside. Elevator shafts, service ducts, plumbing, that kind of thing. I really didn't look at them as closely as I should have.

I point up again. "Whatever we do, we have to get out of this elevator first." So he boosts me up and I climb through the hatch to the roof of the elevator. It's so much like in the movies I'm surprised – except for the shaft being far wider than I'd have thought it needs to be, the whole thing is like a scene from a spy film. And there is the closed door of floor C, just above my head.

Evgeny climbs up beside me and together we pry at the doors. This part *isn't* like in the movies. Nothing we do will get the doors to move. I sit down on the roof of the elevator, feet dangling through the hatch, and watch Evgeny clamber up some pipes on the wall of the shaft to poke at something electrical-looking, to see if he can somehow open the doors that way.

There's something about the elevators in this place that just doesn't fit. I was surprised that there was a second elevator at all because I do remember on the tower plans that there was only one shaft that went below the parking levels. Then again, the three lowest floors weren't shown at all. I try to retrace in my head the path that Boss Lady led me on from the first elevator door on floor C to the security station and the elevator to the lower floors. It was such a maze, and we seemed to be going in circles. And then it hits me. The extra-wide shaft, the blocked-off set of doors opposite the Administration office. The elevator installers *had* got things wrong, but not quite in the way Boss Lady thought. I look up, and where I should see this shaft end not too far overhead if there were separate shafts, it instead continues, widens even, into darkness so deep even my eyes can't penetrate it.

Evgeny climbs back down and sits beside me. "We're stuck," he says.
"Maybe," I say. "Maybe not."

I drop back into the elevator and he follows, not asking, just watching. I ignore the blinking buttons and fit Boss Lady's ID card into the card slot below them. With any luck, if it's Charleston who's tripped the alarm, he didn't think to disable this, too. And if he didn't know she was dead, he probably wouldn't think of it. I hope.

A green light comes on, so I swipe Boss Lady's finger slowly across the print scanner. There's a longer pause, then another green light. I hold my breath and hope as I punch in the master override code on the tiny number pad. If the code is going to fail at all, *this* is where it will fail. But it trips a green light too, then the pad slides back into the wall to be replaced by a touchscreen with up and down arrows.

"Up or down?" I ask Evgeny.

"Which way is out?"

"Up, I guess." I tap the arrow and the elevator comes to life. The arrows are replaced by changing floor numbers and a red hexagon, presumably to stop the car when one arrives at the desired floor.

Evgeny moves close beside me, maybe for comfort, or maybe just to see the display better, and together we watch the floors tick by. C is replaced by B, then A, then the parking garage levels count up from 6 to 1 and then we reach M. I tap the hexagon, even though it's probably unnecessary, since it's the last floor. But if the elevator does go all the way up into the Standard Comm Tower, I don't really want to find out by staying on accidentally.

I expect to see the little anteroom I first got on the elevator in when the doors slide open. It's silly of course, because even though it uses the same shaft, this isn't the same elevator. It's next door, so to speak, or back-to-back, rather.

So really I shouldn't be surprised to see a plushly carpeted, wood-paneled room instead. At least seeing Charleston standing in it isn't something I could have predicted, unless I remembered that movie villains always come back at least once before the credits. But there he is, dressed in a suit as stylish as the outfit I sliced up, and looking perfectly composed and well-rested. All the little cuts I made are gone, and he's washed away the blood so his skin is smooth and perfect. And after defeating him once, I shouldn't feel that deep terror again, but I do, just as strong as last time.

Charleston shows no trace of the fear he displayed when I beat him and he cowered at my feet.

Evgeny steps in front of me and so Charleston hits him first. It's almost beautiful, seeing them fight, they move so quickly and fluidly. But if I'd had anything to drink all day, I'd probably be pissing myself in fear, too. They're fast, and beyond brutal. Evgeny is magnificent, rushing, dodging, striking, but Charleston evades him over and over and only Evgeny seems to be bleeding. And then it ends. Charleston strikes one-handed, knocking Evgeny into a wall, and follows with the other hand to stick him with a syringe.

"You are my progeny now," Charleston says. So it's not another re-birth, another dose of symbiont. It's another drug.

"Yes, Father," says Evgeny, and it sounds like the words are dragged from his throat with physical force.

"Hold her still," Charleston says, and I'm too stunned to move away before Evgeny's holding my arms from behind. Then Charleston saunters up to me – *swaggers*, even – and plucks the pins from my hair. He bends each one double before tossing it aside. Then he takes the fox mask, throws it to the floor and stomps on it. It shatters beneath his heel. And finally he takes the scarf, pulls a shiny gold lighter from his pocket, and lights the red silk on fire.

All I can think is that the fox women will be angry with me when I don't return their gifts. Not that, you know, I'm about to die for real.

Then Charleston grabs me by the throat with one hand. I feel his fingers digging into my neck, cutting off air, and my vision goes grey. Grey like when the fox women gave me a piece of my memory back. And I hear their voices. *You are of us*, they say. *Kitsune, huli jing, kumiho.* The grey deepens to black. *And you are fuchs, child. Fox. You are yourself.* And the black flares red and I open my eyes.

Nothing has changed – Charleston still has me by the throat, Evgeny still pins my arms. And everything has changed.

I jerk my head back, feel it contact Evgeny's nose, and I hear his head hit the closed elevator door behind him, and he collapses. And I bring my hands around and neatly clap Charleston on both ears at once – boxing someone's ears, I think they used to call it – and he reels away from me, his hand dropping away from my throat.

With Evgeny unconscious, I feel pressure return to my thoughts as whatever he was blocking floods in. And I realize it's not the witches. It's Charleston.

"You," I say.

He grabs for me and I step aside. This is not the effortless dance like when I used all the fox women's items together. It's cruder, more earthy. Less ethereal, but still powerful.

"You've been feeding on Evgeny," I say. "You told your associates his blood wasn't digestible yet, but you lied."

He makes his lips into a shape that's probably supposed to be a smile. "Of course," he says. "I have no intention of sharing this."

"How long?" I say, sidestepping his attack again. I'm not dancing in a void now, I'm flickering through forest shadows, a fox evading the hounds.

His smile widens, looks more like a grimace. "Since before his own sire knew what he had discovered." He attacks again, manages to catch a handful of my hair, and I use it to pull him towards me and right into my fist. His nose breaks under my hand, bone breaking the skin to gash my knuckles. It hurts like hell, but he lets go of my hair.

"You're a slimy bastard," I say, watching him clutch his nose.

"Bitch," he says, in a vicious tone.

"No," I say, and I kick him in the gut as he lunges for me. "Vixen."

He looks momentarily confused, the fake smile freezing in place like he's forgotten it's there. "I will kill you," he says. "And I will take this pretty boy back to his cage and feed off of him until he shrivels into nothing, and it will take many, many years and I will make sure he suffers."

This time, his attack connects and he catches my wrist, spins me around and hurls me into a wall. I don't think about pain, I just think, *I need to be faster*. And suddenly the world is a different color – or no color – and everything looks bigger. Charleston towers over me, but I can move like quicksilver and my teeth are sharp and the vamp's Achilles tendons are no match for them.

Then I'm standing over Charleston and my boot's on his throat and I glance over at Evgeny who is awake and staring at me, eyes wider than I've ever seen them. He's looking at me the way he did when I borrowed the fox women's power to defeat Charleston the first time, his face filled with awe and joy and maybe even a little fear.

"Impossible," Charleston gurgles, "That's impossible. You cannot be. You cannot."

I keep looking at Evgeny. "I don't want to kill him," I say. I've never regretted killing the few vamps I have killed. It was the only way to avoid being killed myself, and I refuse to regret surviving. But now, I don't need to kill him in order to get both me and Evgeny out of here, and I don't want vengeance. It's not mine to take. Not from Charleston.

I do step on his throat a bit more, though.

Evgeny nods at me. "Give him to the witches," he suggests.

So he helps me tie and gag someone for the second time that day. And when we're done, we look around the room and discover the only exit is blocked by a solid science-fiction-looking metal door with no handle, no card readers or key-pads.

"Open it," I say to Charleston, though of course he can barely move, let alone open doors. He shakes his head.

Evgeny pulls off the gag and says, "Tell us how to open it."

Charleston laughs. "I can't," he says. "The only way to do it is to call in a code to security, and there's no phone up here."

I rifle his pockets for a cell phone. It's hard with him being all tied up, but soon I find the slick smartphone in his inside breast pocket. I also find a gold pocketwatch in his front trouser pocket. One of my kicks, it seems, has smashed the phone and it won't even turn on. Charleston laughs again.

I want to punch him, but I don't. Instead, I just watch Evgeny tie the gag back in place.

I wonder how the witches are doing. They must be locked in, too, down on the lower floors. Unless they found a hidden staircase. Then the image of the older witch tapping the side of her head pops into my mind and I smile.

"The witches can take his codes right out of his head," I tell Evgeny.

"How about we deliver them his ID and fingerprints, too?" He leans over Charleston to kiss me, then he sits back and looks at me. "I think I remember that I love you," he says.

I look away, then stand up and drag Charleston towards the elevator by the back of his fancy suit jacket. I punch the button on the wall to open the doors, and Evgeny helps me pull the trussed-up vamp inside.

"And you ran away when I told you," he says, as the doors slide closed on us.

"I didn't run away," I say. I poke the floor display and it slides back into the wall and the number pad pops back out. Nothing happens until I scan Boss Lady's card and finger and punch in my override code again. Then I tap the down arrow and stare at the floors flicking by on the display.

Evgeny touches my hair, gently, like he's afraid to startle me. "I know," he says. "I'm teasing."

I look up at him and he's smiling, but there's something in his look – the shy boy afraid the popular girl is going to turn him down flat. But I've never been the popular girl. At least I don't think I have. I can't imagine being her.

"Evgeny," I say.

"I know," he says. "It's complicated. We haven't known each other long enough for confessions of love. And… I think maybe there's someone else you have feelings for?"

"Maybe," I say. "Something like that. But –"

"You don't have to say anything you don't mean." But he looks hopeful.

"I do have feelings for you," I say, though I hate the term "have feelings." It makes something gut-wrenching sound so trivial. "Strong feelings. But I don't even know what I am. Not really."

"Well," he says. "You can turn into a fox."

I stare at him. "What?"

"Back then. Just for a minute or two, you were a fox. And not like a were-fox, but like a real red fox, small and quick. And then you were you again. Except you have a tail."

I actually look, twisting around to see my ass, which suddenly feels all wrong. But he's teasing again. Of course he's teasing.

I pull my torn and bloody lab coat aside. And he's not teasing. There's a tear in the backside of my trousers and sticking out of it is a full fluffy red fox tail.

I think I might almost faint, but I let the lab coat fall back into place and lean against the elevator wall. "Evgeny?"

"Mmm?" He looks amused.

"What the fuck?"

He laughs. "I like it," he says.

"How the fuck can I go around with a tail? A big, fluffy, bright red fucking fox tail?" I reach back and tug on it, and it's definitely attached to the end of my spine. I thrash it like an angry cat and it feels good. "What the fuck am I?"

His face becomes more serious, and he touches my cheek. "You are magnificent," he says in a voice barely above a whisper.

"I don't know how I did what I did up there, or even *what* I did, and I don't know how to make this go away." I feel tears prickling in my eyes and blink fiercely. I will *not* cry, especially not in front of Charleston, who's huddled in the corner of the elevator.

I look back at the display screen so I don't have to look at Evgeny. I watch it change to Z and poke the red hexagon and the elevator slows and stops.

"We'll figure it out," he says.

We. I'd forgotten he'd started to talk about "we," that I'd started to think as "we" instead of "me."

I nod. "I'll talk to the fox women again." Then I realize I've left their ruined gifts in the room above. But they're bent, broken, and burned anyway.

"You'll have to refresh my memory about that," Evgeny says.

"It was after you were captured," I say. "But I'll tell you all about it once we get out of here."

The door slides open and the witches are there, all of them, and I can't meet Alex's eyes. I know, now, that if I have to choose between them, I'll choose Evgeny, and I don't even have a good reason why.

We hand Charleston over to the witches, who stare at him – pulling his security codes out of his brain, maybe – then give him to the weres, who pass him on to the freed vamps. They crowd around him and there are wet sounds and when they move away he lies limp and shriveled on the floor. The vamps look stronger.

Evgeny leans over and says quietly in my ear, "The *hexen* blood should be dilute enough to do no worse than cause them a bit of bellyache, and it will give them the strength to get out of here and find a safe place to spend the day."

"When is sunrise?" I've lost sense of time again. It would be a bad thing to rescue all these vamps only to send them out into the full light of the sun.

He shrugs. "Soon."

After that, it's just a matter of letting the witches go up first, to deal with security and secret codes, and then watching elevator load after slow elevator load disappear behind the door and up to ground level. Alex stays behind and helps me and Evgeny and a few of the more recovered weres round up the stragglers and find the last few test subjects on floor Y. And then we're on the last elevator up. I stand at the back with Evgeny on one side and Alex on the other. They both take my hand, and for the duration of the elevator ride I can be at peace, loving both of them equally.

Then we get to the top, walk out of Charleston's wood-paneled room – the fox women's gifts have vanished, and I don't have the energy to wonder why – and then out an unmarked door onto the street. Alex releases my hand and kisses my cheek.

"I love you, Panya," she says. Then she glances at Evgeny. "Be happy. And if you change your mind, you have my number." I had forgotten about the scrap of paper she pressed into my hand earlier. I can't remember what I did with it.

Then she walks away, toward the ragged group of witches who are waiting for her. The weres and vamps and others have already dispersed into the night and soon the witches are gone, too, Alex with them.

"That was your other lover?" Evgeny says gently.

I nod. I can't make words just yet.

"Do you want to go with her?"

I meet his eyes and still I can't speak. So instead, I pull him to me and kiss him.

Chapter Twenty-Two

WHEN WE REACH THE LOFT, we're both so exhausted we can hardly stand, but neither of us wants to touch the soft blankets with our uncleanness, so we stand under the shower together, then fill the tub with water as hot as we can stand it and lie drowsing in it. As the sky turns orange and pale blue with sunrise we climb out, dry off, and crawl behind the bed curtains. We lie together, naked skin touching, but without the energy to make love. I have no idea when sleep finally comes, but when I wake it's after dark and Evgeny is stretched beside me, eyes bruised-looking, but at peace. He smiles in his sleep.

Then he stretches and the sheet pulls away from his nether region and he's half-hard. I can't resist turning around on the bed to take him in my mouth. His spicy scent intensifies and he moans. I can feel the exact moment he wakes up.

"Oh, fuck," he says, his voice breathy. "Su." My name sounds like angels in his voice.

I know he can't see me in the dark, but he reaches out, finds my hair, my shoulder. He shifts and twists to reach my thigh with his mouth and he pops out from between my lips.

"Hey," I say. "I was enjoying that."

He laughs, sounding like he's having difficulty catching his breath.

"Me too," he says. He rolls on his side, bringing himself back within reach so I grasp him in my hand, touch the tip of my tongue to the tip of him and taste his saltiness.

He slides his hand over my skin, touching me like he's forgotten what I feel like, and maybe he has. When he reaches my thighs he pulls them gently apart, rests his head on one, and buries his nose in my crotch and inhales.

"I love how you smell," he says, and his breath stirs my pubic hair. It tickles.

"Mmm…" I say, and slide my mouth back over his hardness, pulling him in so far I nearly gag, then slowly sucking and sliding until he's almost out of my mouth again. I keep just the head of him in my mouth, tease it with my tongue, until I feel his hips strain towards me and I relent and slide my mouth over his length again.

Then his fingers slide into my pubic hair, part my folds and open them to his tongue and I feel like I'm dissolving. I let myself sink into the feel of his mouth on me, the taste of him on my tongue, and when I can think properly again my whole lower region is throbbing in the aftermath of orgasm and my mouth is full of the salty-bitter taste of him. I swallow and smile, and rest my cheek on his leg.

When I wake again, he's gone but I smell coffee and curry. Curry? He's not in the loft when I crawl out of bed so I get cleaned up and put on a bathrobe and find a note on the counter.

Your neighbor the wolf came by and asked for my help. Back soon, Ev.

Below that, he's drawn a little happy face with fangs and a heart floating over its head. I smile. I'm still smiling after I drink some coffee and eat some of the take-away vindaloo I find next to the coffee pot. When did he go out and get take-away? And why didn't I wake up?

I'm giddy and full of joy. There's sadness, too. I only just found Alex and had to lose her again. And there's frustration that while I know a little more about what I am, I'm still not awakened fully, or whatever. I've tasted what I can be, maybe, but I haven't been able to hold onto it. Except for the ridiculous tail making an awkward lump under my robe.

I guess I'll have to switch to wearing longer coats instead of short jackets. And what'll I do when summer arrives and it's too hot for a coat?

But I have months of icy weather to come up with a solution. For now, I guess I'll be cutting holes in the backs of all my jeans.

For today, I pick open part of the back seam of a pair of grey yoga pants and put on a tunic-style t-shirt over it. It doesn't hide the tail – my tail – but it makes it less obvious, and I'm not going out today, anyway.

Then I look around the loft and realize what a mess it is, even though I have hardly any stuff, so I start cleaning.

I've just about got the place returned to its usual more-or-less-tidiness by the time Evgeny gets back. I smile when he walks in and it's the first time in what seems like forever that it feels like a real, honest, all-out-joyful smile. The one he gives me in return is equally delighted.

"Hey," he says, traces of the shy boy still in his voice.

"Hey," I say, and set aside the broom to hug him. It feels unbelievably good to be able to do something as simple as hug your boyfriend, and not have to worry about anything else.

"Magne's organizing help and rehab and medical stuff for the weres that escaped from Charleston," he says. "He apologizes for not sending an army with you." Then he kisses me, long and sweet, and I want it to last forever. I'm about to tell him just that when he speaks again. "He also asks you to go see him. He has someone… he'd like you to meet."

I look at him, but he won't say more, so I follow him to the elevator and down to Magne's place. As soon as I walk in, every fear and terror I've ever felt seems to hit me all at once.

There, crouched on the floor with Magne standing over him, is the werewolf who raped me.

I fight back the fear, the shame, the humiliation. I'm stronger than this. I can feel Evgeny nearby, standing close to lend support, but not touching me. I'm glad he's not touching me. Right now I don't want anyone to ever touch me again.

The werewolf looks up and stares for a moment. Then he seems to realize who I am and he smiles. It's not a leer or a mocking smile. He's relieved. "Hey babe," he says. "Our friend Magne seems to be a little confused. He thinks –"

"You raped me," I say. I expect my voice to shake, to be strident or overwrought, but it's clear and precise. A simple statement of fact.

"No, baby," he says. "It's a misunderstanding." I hate when lovers call each other "baby." It's creepy and weird. Same with "mama" or "daddy." And yeah, I know, everyone's different and that's a good thing, but it still creeps me out.

I walk up to him, look down at him, and say, "I was with my girlfriend in the garden. You watched us. You watched us make love next to the koi pond." I don't know how, but I say this in the same simple, clear tone, and I don't even blush. "And when she left, you grabbed me, and beat me, and fucked me against my will." I bend over and put my face right up close to his. "You raped me." Then I stand back.

"I couldn't help but get excited," he says. "You and that redhead were so hot. But I know you liked me first. I know you wanted me. You were so wet." He smiles again, hopefully.

"I was wet," I say, "because I had just had sex with my *girlfriend*."

"No," he says. "You wanted me. You still want me. I can see it in your eyes. I can smell your sex."

I know I still smell of making love with Evgeny. I didn't wash *that* thoroughly. I wanted to be able to smell him on me, to smell my reaction to him. I like the way we smell after sex. But I don't explain any of that. This man is obviously deluded and capable of justifying anything to himself.

So I turn to Magne. "He's sick," I say.

Magne nods. "It's your right to take vengeance," he says. "No wolf would dispute that."

"What's the punishment for rape?"

Magne shrugs. "Whatever the offended party wants. But usually the pack... puts him to death after. It one of things we just don't tolerate."

"Death?" That... well it doesn't seem excessive, though maybe it should, but it surprises me.

"It would be considered your right to kill him yourself."

I look at the man – the werewolf – kneeling on the floor. He's dangerous; who knows how many other women he might have violated, believing that they wanted it. And part of me does want revenge. A big part of me would enjoy making him suffer, and then killing him.

But that part of me that didn't want to kill Charleston doesn't want to kill this were, either, even though this time, the vengeance is mine by right.

And I think about what the *kumiho* said to me, just before the fox women gave me part of my memory back. She said vengeance would awaken my latent otherness, would make me fully whatever it is I am. *Fuchs.* Fox woman. And I want that. Man, how I want that. I don't think I've ever wanted anything more.

I look at Evgeny. He smiles. "I won't think any less of you," he says, and I don't know if he means he won't think any less of me if I kill the were or if I don't. And it doesn't matter.

"I'm content to let the werewolves deal with him," I say to Magne. "As long as the result is that he can never harm anyone again."

Magne nods. "The pack will be… brutal," he says. "I told you we don't tolerate rapists."

It might be kinder, he's telling me, if I put the were out of his misery myself. But I'm not forgiving, I just don't want vengeance. I still want him punished.

"I'm content with what the werewolves choose," I say again.

Magne smiles a grim, tooth-baring smile. "I'll see to it personally," he says, and his voice chills me. I'm suddenly very glad I never became lovers with him. I'm tired of violence, tired of struggling to stay alive, and of killing so I don't get killed.

I nod. I should thank him, but I can't quite thank someone for brutalizing another living, thinking being on my behalf. No matter how deserved it is. But neither will I forgive the were and ask for him to be spared. I guess I'm not *that* good a person.

Then I take Evgeny's hand and we go back upstairs and I tell him everything I remember from the memory of Alex and that terrible day until now, only skipping the parts he says he remembers. When I'm done we sit curled on the couch together, quiet and oddly at peace.

Then he starts to tell me about his past. Not everything, of course, because he remembers his whole life and that's too much to tell at once. But he tells me about his ex-boyfriend David, beautiful and vain, who liked to mix pleasure and pain. And Evgeny was so in love that he pretended to like it, too.

He pauses a lot as he tells me this. Sometimes he blushes fiercely over details, like letting David bite his nipples until they were swollen for a week after. It was when they broke up, he says, that he got his nipples pierced. One final pain to remind him that even love isn't worth lying to yourself for.

I hesitate, but finally I ask why they broke up.

"He went too far," he says. "And I guess I finally realized I was miserable. He… We were camping."

I remember the dream we shared. David giving Evgeny a blowjob and drawing blood, then throwing him down on the rock. I say, "You don't have to tell me."

Evgeny shakes his head. "I've never told anyone," he says. "I was ashamed. He… I didn't want to, but he thought I…" He stops and shifts position, so I start to sit up, thinking maybe he doesn't want to be touched as he remembers, but he pulls me back and holds me close.

"Once, we were joking around, saying what crazy stuff we'd done… sexually. I didn't want him to know I hadn't had very many lovers yet." He laughs softly. "How vain. But when you're a man talking to other men, you're supposed to talk like you've either fucked everyone on the planet or just haven't got to them all yet. So I made up lovers. And one of the things I told him was that I'd let a boyfriend tie me up for three days and pretend to rape me."

He buries his face in my hair and when he speaks again, his voice is muffled. "I don't know why I said it. It was a horrible thing to even think up. But I knew he liked to inflict pain a bit, and I thought he'd find it sexy. I wanted him to be as crazy about me as I was about him."

This time his pause goes on for a long time, so I twist around in his arms to look at him. He's crying, silently, just a few tears trickling from the corners of his eyes. And that's something I really like about Evgeny, that he doesn't feel the need to show off and be macho. That he can cry in front of me. He's ashamed, I can see, but not from the tears. I wipe them away gently. "You don't have to tell me," I say again.

The corner of his mouth quirks, just a little. "I want you to know me," he says. "Even the bad things." Then he kisses my forehead. "He took me camping and on the second to last day I was looking at the view from a cliff and he threw me down on the bare rock – he wasn't much bigger than me, but he was strong. He grabbed my hair and he fucked me. And I asked him to stop and he didn't. And then I let him tie me to a tree and all day, every few hours, he'd do it again. By the end I was bleeding so much I thought I might bleed to death. Or be eaten by a bear. By the end, I'd have been glad to be eaten by a bear. And then he untied me and we went back to the city and it was like it never happened."

He sighs, a long, deep sigh like he's glad to get it all out. "I don't think he thought of it as rape. As far as he knew, I consented. And I guess I *did* consent, but I felt violated just the same. As soon as I could, I applied for a job in Riverbend, and I got it, and I came here."

"I'm sorry," I say.

"Mmm," he murmurs into my hair.

"No one should ever have to be violated."

"I let him think it's what I wanted, what I liked."

I shake my head, suddenly angry. "If he was your boyfriend, he should have known you well enough to know you were making it up to please him. He should have been able to tell you didn't like it. And he should have stopped as soon as you said 'stop' the first time, even if you never said it a second time."

He smiles and smooths my hair. "You know your tail thrashes when you're angry?"

I twist around to look at my new appendage. "I will never get used to that," I say.

"Maybe you can learn how to make it go away," he says. He grabs the white fur at the tip of my tail and tweaks it gently.

"I thought you liked it?"

"I do." He laughs, not laughing at me, just expressing happiness. "It suits you, Foxy Su."

Foxy Su. Not Angry Su anymore. I don't feel much anger, and what's there fades quickly. I remember, just a fuzzy, half-formed memory, that I was always angry when I was young. But that's gone. There are still things to figure out in my life, starting with the fox tail, and continuing with getting my memories back, but for now I'm content. More than content.

I'm full of joy.

"You're smiling," Evgeny says.

"I'm happy," I say.

"Me too." Then he tugs off my shirt in one neat motion, pulls my bra out of the way, and fastens his lips on my nipple. He pulls away long enough to say, "Especially when I have some delicious part of you in my mouth," and then he nibbles and sucks until I'm sure I must be wet right through my yoga pants, and the smell of my own desire fills my nose. It's hard to get his clothes off while still keeping some part of me in contact with his mouth, but I do it, and I get the rest of my clothes off, too.

And then there's the problem of a condom. I want him inside me, but I'm determined to be responsible. I settle for rubbing my slickness up and down the length of him, but then he takes his mouth away from my skin to say, "Here," and he's dug a condom out from somewhere and presses it into my hand. I'm afraid I might finish before I can get the thing unwrapped, but I manage and I unroll it onto him and then he's in me and I climax while he moves inside me, and I think I yell louder than I ever have – and our sex has already been pretty loud. For a moment I hope Magne can't hear us, but then I decide I don't care if he does, and I'm still gasping and panting when Evgeny moans long and loud and thrusts into me harder and harder. Then he strains and goes still and collapses back on the couch.

"Holy fuck," he says, when he catches his breath. "Holy fuckity fuck."

"You are eloquent," I say. "Now I can see why I fell in love with you." I relax against him until I feel him go soft inside me and then I slide off. We lounge naked on the couch until the night ends and then we curl up in bed, safe behind the heavy curtain.

We spend a long time kissing, slowly, gently, lingeringly. Then, just as I'm about to drift into sleep Evgeny says, "What was that you said?"

"I didn't say anything."

"Not now. Earlier."

I snuggle closer to him. "All I remember was moaning and not being able to make actual words."

He snorts. "Mm. There was a lot of that from both of us. But after than, you said something about my eloquence."

I remember and laugh. "Did you want me to praise your poetic diction, Mr Fuckity-Fuck?"

He nips my earlobe. "No," he says. "I just want you to repeat what you said after that. I want to know if you meant it."

I frown, trying to remember exactly what I said, and then I realize what he's getting at.

"Oh, well," I say. "You didn't think I'd stage a daring rescue against an army of evil vampires for just anyone, did you?"

"I don't know," he says, "You're a pretty decent person. You know, the sort who'd take in a stray newborn."

"Only if he's hot," I say.

"Liar."

I laugh and I'm suddenly overwhelmed with giggles. And it's infectious, because soon we're both laughing hysterically. Finally, ribs aching, we lie side by side in the dark, just barely touching. I can feel my skin tingling and I want him again already, even though I'm also so sleepy I could nod off at any moment.

"Evgeny," I say.

"Mm-hmm?"

"I know what you want me to say."

"I don't want you to say it if you don't mean it."

"I know," I say. "But I do mean it."

"You do?"

"Yeah."

Then he starts laughing again. When he stops I say, "What?"

"You haven't said anything yet."

I smile, roll over on top of him and kiss the end of his nose.

"Evgeny Kostas Alexeyevich?"

"Panya Su Fuchs," he says, all serious now. "I love you. I don't care if you love me or not –" I put a finger on his lips and he stops.

I lean close to his ear and say, softly, "I do love you Evgeny. It terrifies me, but I do love you." And then there's sex, and sleep, and joy, and all is right with the world, at least for a little while.

BORN of GHOSTS

read on for a preview of book two of the *Fictive Kin* series

Chapter One

I'VE NEVER BEEN addicted to anything stronger than caffeine – not that I remember, anyway, and since my memory's not much longer than a year past, I guess that doesn't count for much. But *that I recall*, I've never been addicted to anything stronger than caffeine, and I've never tried to kick that habit, so I have no idea what withdrawal is like.

I suspect, though, that the kind of withdrawal most people go through when they clean up from booze or heroin or whatever their self-destructive substance of choice was, is nowhere near what Evgeny felt when he stopped drinking *hexen*.

Hexen's not a drug, though, it's a kind of person, a witch. And Evgeny's a vampire.

Yeah, I'm Su, and my boyfriend's a vampire. And let me tell you, before you decide to go looking for a pretty vampire lover of your own, you don't want one.

Not all vamps are gorgeous, like Evgeny – I got lucky there – though most of them are in pretty good health. Except the ones that aren't. Because vamps – they call themselves "Reborn," by the way – are pretty much like humans. They come in a variety of shapes and sizes (though the vamp symbiont keeps them on the lean side), colors and temperaments. Except they're stronger and faster, they hear and see better, and in general they're more *powerful* than the humans from which they're made. And that makes a lot of them much bigger pricks.

You know that saying about power and corruption, absolute power and absolute corruption? Yeah, that's vamps. Well, a lot of them. To be fair, aside from Evgeny, who's not exactly a normal bloodsucker, I met a bad crowd. It *is* possible for someone who's a decent human to remain decent on becoming a vamp. It's just really, really unlikely. First thing, vamps don't tend to choose decent people when they select their offspring. Second, if they *did* choose someone nice, that person isn't likely to survive very long, because vamps are not at all against cannibalism, so it takes a distinct lack of niceness to make it through the re-birth process. And third, give a hundred nice young men (or nice young women, though female vamps are rarer for some reason I never discovered) a taste of super-strength, and how many nice young men do you suppose you'd have left? Probably not many.

But like I said, Evgeny's different from other vamps. Hell, he was different from other humans. But I'm biased, 'cause he's mine.

Right now, I'm wishing he was someone else's problem. And how's that for being a great girlfriend? But as soon as he started showing signs of the DTs (that stands for detox, right, because if not, I have no idea what it means), he decided to stay at my place until it passed. Because I live on the top floor of a converted warehouse, and my only close neighbors are the werewolf downstairs and a guy on the first floor who's so seldom home I can't even remember what he looks like.

Yeah, weres are real, too. And good thing, because when things started getting real bad, I thought Evgeny might try to drink *my* blood, and that's one place I will not go, no matter how pretty the bloodsucker. So Magne – he's the werewolf neighbor – helped me tie Evgeny to a metal roof-support pillar in my loft.

You know how a shark's jaws kind of unhinge when it chomps on something? Or a snake's? Well, a vamp's jaws can do that, too. Both upper and lower, till their mouth is like a gaping red hole in their face. And their fangs are like a snake's, too. A cobra's maybe, or a cottonmouth. They fold out of the way when they're not needed, with only little gaps between the other teeth to show where they fit. But they can fold down like a venomous serpent's, and they're curved and needle-sharp like that, too. And when the symbiont's foremost, a vamp's eyes catch the light and appear to glow — blue-orange in incandescent light, purple in fluorescent.

It's pants-pissing scary, even when you know the vamp, when he shares your bed and brings you flowers (night-blooming jasmine), and helps you build the stupid cheap bookcase you bought at the discount department store so you'll have somewhere to keep the boxes of books he helped you carry home. Even when he starts building you a real bookcase out of real wood the next day, and then cooks spicy noodles for supper and gives you a backrub and…

Well, I'm looking at this vamped-out *beast* tied to a pole in my loft and it's only because I'm stubborn and it's my damned apartment that I don't turn and walk out. And also because, fucking bloody hell, I fell in love with him, hard and completely. I'm pretty sure Evgeny wouldn't hurt me, even like he is now, but I'm not *certain*.

I crouch down on the floor in front of him, talking quiet, like you do to a frightened animal, but making sure I'm out of his reach. His mouth's reach, that is.

"Evgeny," I say, and I try to put all my feelings for him into his name, though it's hard to bring those feelings to mind looking at him, jaws gaping and fangs straining like they could almost shoot out of his mouth and fasten onto my neck like the proboscis of some huge, horror-movie insect.

"I know you feel like shit," I say. "But you're stronger than this." I say a bunch of other stuff that doesn't really make sense, but that sounds nice, and somewhere in the middle of it, he actually starts to listen.

I shift my weight a little, to reach behind me for the bloodbag I've warmed up in a pot of hot water on the hotplate — I bought a microwave specifically so Ev could heat up blood without having to use the hot-plate, but you can't microwave blood in a bag unless you want an explosion, and he can't deal with a cup right now. A little drool escapes the corner of Evgeny's mouth and splats onto the floor. His hands are tied behind his back, secured to the pole, and he sits with his legs tucked under him, leaning forward, straining his shoulders.

"Hungry," he says.

"I know," I say. "This'll help." I had to buy the blood from Liam, who runs a vamp market not far away. I don't trust Liam — I trust him even less now that I know some of the things he's involved in – but since I sort of… disrupted the running of a big vamp corporation that supplied a lot of "sustenance" as the PC term is, there aren't so many choices of vendors around. Though I have noticed a lot more vamps being nice to me.

I don't trust Liam not to try drugging Evgeny, so I asked Magne to test the blood before I gave it to Ev. See, werewolves are created by a close relative of the symbiotic organism that creates vamps, so a lot of the things that affect vamps will affect weres, too. Of course, Magne reminded me that if something's undetectable to vamps, it probably would be to him, too. But at least he could tell me it wasn't *obviously* tainted.

I cut open the sticky-out bit on the bloodbag where the IV attaches – Liam's goods are strictly black market and stolen, or so he'd have us believe, but the IV thing makes a handy straw – and edge closer to Evgeny.

His nostrils flare and he says, "You smell good."

"So you always say," I tell him. It was the first thing he ever said to me, when he was a newborn vamp and I saved him from becoming a snack for his own kind. All vamps like the way I smell. To them, I smell delicious, but the joke's on them, because my blood tastes foul, and it's probably toxic for them, too.

Because I'm not human. I'm not exactly *other*, either. Not yet. I'm in the process of becoming something, though. I was healed once, and given a sort of gift by three old Asian ladies – fox demons, though realize that I use "demon" metaphorically. A better term might be "spirits" or even "fairies," though the supernatural connotations aren't quite right. But it turns out I already had an inheritance of my own, something that came with the German half of my DNA and my German surname, Fuchs. It means "fox."

And there's a reason a powerful, sexy woman is called "foxy" and "vixen." Whatever it is I'm becoming exudes a strong, you could almost say supernatural, sex appeal. And for vamps, that means I must taste good, because bloodsuckers like to feast and get laid at the same time. "Fuck 'n' feed," they call it. Elegant, no? But sex and blood are the two things that keep them from shriveling up like Count Orlok over their very long lives.

"Hungry," Evgeny says again.

"I know, Ev," I say. "But I have to make sure you drink the bloodbag, and not me." I scoot closer, and get the tube into his mouth, but he's still vamped out and can't suck. I squeeze the bag and a little blood squirts into his mouth and it surprises him.

He jerks his head back and looks at me, eyes flaring in the lamplight. Then he licks his lips and the action makes his jaws fold up into their human configuration. He sucks on the bloodbag until it's flat and empty. Then he sits back, eyes closed, head resting against the pole he's tied to.

For a moment, I think he's fallen asleep, but then he says, "Thank you."

"Sure," I say.

He opens his eyes and there's no vamp glow. Just crazy bright blue that looks even brighter because of the black hair falling over them.

"I'm sorry," he says. "It's getting harder to stay in control."

I relax. The symbiont's dormant, as it should be, and the sweet man I love is back.

"You scared the shit out of me," I say. I crawl the rest of the way to him, and start to untie him.

"Maybe you should leave me tied up," he says. When his hands are free, he looks at the rope burns on his wrists. His fingers tremble and he folds them into fists. "Or find a cell to lock me in. If I get really crazy, these ropes won't hold me."

I lean against him. "It'll be morning soon," I say. "It hasn't been so bad when you're asleep."

He turns his head to kiss my cheek. "It's getting worse."

"I could ask Liam – "

"You know how much I trust Liam," he says. Yeah, no more than I do. Less, probably, because it was Liam's drug cocktail, fed to a handful of minions who Evgeny then fed off after they attacked us, that led us to where we are now, sitting on the floor trying to figure out how to get through the worst withdrawal in the universe.

But that's not quite true. Evgeny's papa vamp, the bloodsucker who made him, had been experimenting on his progeny by feeding them witch blood all along. Evgeny's been fed it since he was a newborn – he was the only vamp ever discovered to be able to consume it without dying. It *had* almost killed him, but he lived and it made him stronger, so strong he broke his chains, fed on the old vamp's other progeny, and wandered out into the street. And then I found him.

If things had stopped there, he might have been free of *hexen* relatively easily. But there were others, including the shadowy Reborn council, who wanted a vamp able to metabolize *hexen*, because they could then feed on *him*, and gain some of the abilities that witches have genetically. And Liam helped the council capture Evgeny. And they force fed him so much *hexen* it really *should* have killed him. But it didn't, and I rescued him. And then we should have had our happily ever after, but things never turn out that way. Not in real life. Not even when your real life is full of fairy-tale creatures.

Evgeny touches my face and I startle out of my thoughts.

"Su?" he says gently, his voice making my name sound so much more beautiful than it is.

"Mm?" I say. I'm tired, but he must be exhausted.

"If it gets too bad, if I try to drink you – "

"It won't," I say. "It's just withdrawal. You'll get over it, and you'll be fine."

His fingers slide over my cheekbone, behind my neck, and he kisses me. He tastes like blood and it makes me hungry. Whatever I am – fox woman, *fuchs*, demon – it doesn't drink blood, but it sure doesn't mind the taste. I open my mouth to his tongue, ready to start shedding clothes.

Because not only does this fox attract anyone who likes sex with women, but she also likes to *have* sex. Lots of it.

Evgeny pulls away, tilts his head so our foreheads rest together. "If I try to feed on you," he says. "Kill me. I don't want to live if I become that kind of monster."

"It won't come to that," I say. I *hope*.

Late in the day, I wake up next to him and lie in the darkness of the heavily-curtained bed, trying to figure out why I woke. I listen, I breathe in the loft's smells. Nothing's out of the ordinary, but there's a nagging feeling of not-quite-rightness.

I roll over and look at Evgeny. Unlike a vampire, who actually needs a fair bit of light to see, I can see in almost total black. Just a little faint light and my vision's good, if only in black and white. Foxes have eyes like cats, slit pupils and reflective retinas and all.

His breathing is rough and he's shaking, even in sleep. No doubt I'll be tying him to the pole again when he wakes, but for now he doesn't seem too bad. No worse than yesterday, anyway.

I crawl out of bed, between the curtains, and into the brightness of daylight. I prowl around, but nothing is out of place, so I sit on the couch in a pool of sunlight and brood. Whatever woke me up is in my own head, and it annoys me that I can't figure out what it is. It makes my tail thrash, which feels really odd because I'm sitting on it.

Did I mention I have a tail? A big, red, fluffy, completely ridiculous fox tail? I didn't always have it. In fact, it's so new I'm still surprised every time I feel it twitch or catch sight of it in the mirror.

Something happened when I went to rescue Evgeny. Something I don't understand, and that I only remember in a sort of slideshow of snippets. But Evgeny was watching, and he says that just for a moment I turned into a fox. Not in the way weres seem to become wolves, by reconfiguring the way their joints bend and their bones articulate so they appear to have transformed without actually shapeshifting, but really, actually turned into a fox. And when I turned back, I had a tail stuck to my ass. A for-real, living tail properly connected to the end of my spine, that hurts when you tweak it and goes all pins-and-needles when I sit on it too long.

And while it's pretty cool to have a tail, it pisses me off that I have to cut holes in the seats of all my jeans, and I have to wear long coats when I go out. So much for my favorite motorcycle jacket.

So that's another thing that makes me brood, that I still haven't figured out how to call on my fox-woman powers – or whatever you want to call them – at will. Never mind that it's only been a couple of weeks since I sprouted this furry appendage. I can still only use that extra strength and speed, it seems, whenever I'm about to be killed.

But Evgeny's the bigger problem now. I resisted falling for him because he's a vamp, and even though I've had to kill a few (so I know I *can*), he's more powerful than any of them. Because of what the witch blood did to him. And because he's got witch ancestry himself. It made him scary strong, scary fast. Hell, scary *everything*. Except he's also sweet and gentle and nice. But right now he's really scary again.

When the sun moves away from my spot on the couch, I get up, put the kettle on, and rummage in a drawer in the kitchen. At the very back, under a box of emergency candles, I find it. A tattered slip of paper with a name and phone number on it.

Alex.

It's a name irrevocably associated in my memory with terrible things, and wonderful things.

I lost my memory a little over a year ago when the fox women saved my life. I'd been raped and beaten and left for dead, and they'd healed me, taken the worst of my memories of the attack so I'd be able to function like a normal person, and left me to my own devices. Except they didn't just block the few memories they'd intended to, they erased them all. And later, they had no way to give them back, except for that one night, the night they found me and started to awaken the fox in me. So the only memories I have from before are of being raped by a werewolf – and he's had his punishment, care of Magne – and of falling in love with a red-haired gardener's apprentice named Alex.

I trace the letters of her name with one finger. I've dug this bit of paper out of the drawer so many times, but never called. I made my choice, and I chose Evgeny.

Alex, as it turned out, was a witch – as much a surprise to her as it was to me – and she was one of the ones captured by the council to feed to Evgeny. I'd freed her, and the rest of the witches, along with a bunch of vamps and weres and less identifiable *others* when I broke Ev out.

She remembers all our past together, when we worked at the same tourist-trap formal gardens, and I slowly worked up the courage to ask her out. *I* only remember that one night. The night she sent away a creep who'd been hitting on me, and then we'd walked around the garden when we should've been working, and made love next to the koi pond.

I can feel the damp between my legs, remembering her. The smell of her skin, the feel of her nipple in my mouth, the way she kissed me hard as she slid her fingers through the folds between my legs and made me come, kissed me so no one would hear me cry out in pleasure and find us there.

Evgeny moans and I glance towards the bed. Soon I'll have to tie him up again. And hope he doesn't break the rope. I should ask Magne if he has any chains. If this goes on much longer, I might go mad.

I look back at the paper in my hand. I don't have a phone, never saw the need, but I could borrow Magne's. Alex is a witch. She might not know much about being a witch yet, but she'll be in contact with the other witches. Witches are rare, and it seems to me they'd want to keep in touch. For safety from vamps, if nothing else, in case any of them try to rebuild what Samuel Charleston, self-appointed head of the vamp council, had lost. When I let his imprisoned minions kill him.

I don't know what I think the witches can do. Donate a little blood, maybe, to take the edge off for Evgeny? Does that even work? Taking the edge off? Or is it best to just quit flat?

Even if they *could* help me, it doesn't mean they would. Not even if Alex doesn't hate me for choosing Evgeny. To the *hexen*, Evgeny is an abomination. Not because he's a vampire, but because he's a witch – and male witches are vanishingly rare – who was *made* a vampire. Just a witch is great, just a vampire's okay, too, but both – that's apparently the worst thing anyone can be, to a witch, never mind that he didn't choose to be made a vampire, and didn't know he was a witch.

I stare at Alex's number until the sky starts to dim, and then I put it back in the drawer, under the box of candles, and reach out to shut off the madly boiling kettle.

Not yet. I might call her, if Evgeny gets worse. But not yet.

About the Author

NICO SILVER LIVES like a hermit on the edge of the woods, but haunts used bookstores like a wraith. They fully expected to be found someday as a mummified old corpse crushed under a toppled to-be-read pile, but the rise of e-books has made that somewhat less likely, though the books will always outnumber even the dustbunnies. Nico will read just about anything, including the instructions on the back of medicine bottles, but has a particular fondness for good stories with a hint of magic. They write dark, sexy urban fantasy, and sometimes dream in black and white.